Charlotte's
PROMISE

6/19

Charlotte's PROMISE

a novel

JENNIFER MOORE

Covenant Communications, Inc.

For Wende
You are a creative, joyful, gift-giving ray of sunshine with a laugh
that's the most infectious sound on the planet.
I adore you.

Cover Image: *First Recognition of the Stars and Stripes, 14th February 1778 (oil on canvas)* by Edward Moran ©
Bridgeman Art and *Woman* © Lee Avison, Courtesy Arcangel.

Cover design copyright © 2019 by Covenant Communications, Inc.

Published by Covenant Communications, Inc.
American Fork, Utah

Printed in the United States of America
First Printing: May 2019

25 24 23 22 21 20 19   10 9 8 7 6 5 4 3 2 1

ISBN 978-1-52440-933-3

Chapter 1

CHARLOTTE BOWER JERKED AWAKE AND out of habit forced herself to remain still while her heartbeat settled and her breathing calmed. Motionless, she stared up into the darkness and listened, hoping she hadn't cried out in her sleep and alerted anyone to her hiding place. That reaction had cost her dearly once before, and she wasn't about to let it reveal her again.

The familiar images from her dream were still fresh in her mind: painted Indian braves, frantic soldiers, crying women, and . . . *Will*. She swallowed hard as the images faded into impressions, but as always, the emotions they evoked remained strong, twisting around her heart and choking her throat. Sweat broke out over her skin as she pictured his face, heard his screams and her own as the two were pulled apart. Her precious little brother. He was so young—only seven. *No, not anymore*, Charlotte reminded herself. She hadn't seen her brother for more than a year. Will would turn nine years old in October. Or perhaps he already had. Even though she wasn't certain of the date, she could feel by the cool nights and shorter days that winter was approaching.

How had the past year changed the boy? She pictured his face again—wide hazel eyes she was often told looked exactly like hers and thick blond curls she was just as often informed looked nothing like her own straight mouse-brown hair. Was Will being treated well by his captors? Had he been traded as she had, or was he still with the Red Sticks Indian tribe? Did he have enough to eat? Did he suffer from the same nightmares? Was he even . . . ? She squeezed her eyes shut and pushed the thought away. *Will is alive.* She knew it. And nothing—not hostile Indians, slave-traders, or the hundreds of miles of rivers, mountains, and swamps of the southern United States would keep her from finding him.

Still listening for movement, she focused on her goal. *New Orleans.* When the captives had been split after the raid, she'd heard the other group was headed to the mouth of the Mississippi. With the city's reputation for smuggling, slave-trading, and a turn-a-blind-eye approach to law enforcement, she imagined New Orleans was exactly where the Indians would trade their captives.

If only Charlotte had been able to escape earlier, she could have been there by now. But over the past months, she'd been moved from place to place and eventually taken to work on a remote poultry farm in Georgia. She'd attempted several times to escape, and, in spite of the punishments when she was caught, she'd kept trying. She'd had to. Giving up would mean giving up on Will. And she'd never do that. She'd promised that no matter what happened, she would find him. Finally, three weeks earlier, a fierce thunderstorm had provided the distraction she'd needed, and she'd used a stone to break open the cellar's lock to flee into the thick woods.

After a long moment of listening, she wriggled out from beneath the wooden porch but remained crouched close to the house behind a row of shrubbery. The night was still dark, but she could see the purple of predawn in the eastern sky. That was one benefit to the nightmares. She never overslept—a habit essential for a fugitive.

Charlotte slipped from behind a rhododendron bush and glanced back at the opening she'd come from. A year earlier she'd have been too frightened of possums or snakes to crawl into the small dark space. She'd have worried about dirt on her dress, tearing her petticoats, or getting spiders in her hair. How much difference a year could make.

She fingered the uneven strands at the base of her neck then pulled her knitted hat down tight, feeling a pang as she remembered how her mother had carefully brushed her hair each night before putting it into braids. She would have been saddened to see her only daughter's hair cropped with a pair of old shears found in a barn.

Brushing dirt off her pant legs, Charlotte lifted her chin and pushed away the memories. She was a different person now. A survivor. She'd endured cruelty and horrors previously unimaginable to a young girl, clinging to the vow she'd made. Remembering Will and her promise to find him gave her a purpose and kept despair from taking over during the darkest moments, when it felt like even God had forgotten her. She often thought of the day of the raid, her parents' deaths, her capture, and how entirely her life had transformed in a matter of moments. Her memories of the person she had been seemed distant, almost as if she were thinking of a friend she used to know. Her character and appearance now were nearly unrecognizable from the carefree young woman who'd flirted with the soldiers at Fort Mims.

She hurried across the garden and slipped down an alley on the other side of the road. If she'd had any idea how convenient it was to travel in trousers, she'd have replaced her old dress ages ago. Not only were the clothes more comfortable but the disguise afforded her an anonymity she loved. Nobody questioned or even gave a second look to a young man walking alone.

She tried to imagine the farmer on the other side of town who'd woken one morning and found his shirt and trousers missing from the clothesline. Had he been angry? She wished she'd been able to leave money or something else in exchange. Based on the size of the clothes, she assumed he was small like her, and skinny. Perhaps he was only a boy. She hoped he'd had something else to wear. The clothing was tattered and old, the elbows and knees threadbare, and she had assured herself that it was probably what he wore to do jobs that would get his regular clothes too dirty. Pa had read to the family from the Bible in the evenings, and Charlotte knew stealing was wrong. She wished it hadn't been necessary. But if she was captured again, she might never get to New Orleans, and finding Will was all that mattered. She shivered, wishing she'd managed to find a coat, and set off. She'd warm up once she got moving.

Charlotte walked through the now-familiar streets of Savannah, Georgia. As she drew close to the river, the calls of dockworkers and fishermen sounded. Morning began early on the waterfront, but Charlotte had learned to avoid the area at night, finding other places to hide during the dark hours. Her first night in the city the smell of liquor and men's drunken laughter reminded her that even though she was free, she was not safe. Over the past weeks, she'd come to the riverfront daily, performing small tasks to earn a penny or two. As she worked, she'd listen to conversations and watch the various ships and their sailors. At last she'd overheard a rumor of a ship bound for New Orleans, and it was supposed to depart today. She walked faster now that the sun was up, fearing the *Belladonna* had left without her. The war and the British blockades had almost completely halted trade among the states, and with so few ships traveling up and down the coast, months could pass before another opportunity arose.

Reaching the end of the alleyway, she stepped into the open and when her gaze landed on the figurehead of a woman with dark hair blowing in the wind and the bare masts of the large vessel bobbing in the gray water, she breathed a sigh of relief. It hadn't left yet. She had no way of knowing what time of day a ship would set sail. The schedule had something to do with the tides, she'd heard, but Charlotte was a farm girl from the Mississippi territory and had only ever been in a small rowboat. She'd never even seen the ocean. The idea of sailing on the enormous ship far out to sea was both terrifying and exciting. Thankfully her pa had taught her how to swim, but in the vast ocean, would such a skill even matter?

She purchased a bun from a vendor and sat on a crate, taking small bites to make the scant meal last as she watched the ship. The morning was chilly, and she rubbed her arms, wishing she had something warm to drink.

At last the man she'd been waiting for emerged onto the ship's deck and walked down the gangplank to the dock. He'd taken breakfast every morning at the same riverside public house, and Charlotte was relieved he'd not altered the routine on the day of departure. She'd watched the man ever since learning who he was, studied his interactions. He appeared to be even-tempered, if not particularly friendly. She had considered for days exactly how he might be convinced to allow her aboard, and she was pleased he was alone this morning.

She steeled her nerves and rose as he passed. "Pardon me, sir. You're the first mate of the *Belladonna*?" She took care to lower her voice.

The man stopped and nodded. "Leroy Dobson, quartermaster. On this ship they're one and the same."

Seeing him up close, she realized he was older than she'd thought—past his fortieth year, easily. Strands of gray mixed with the blond hair tied at the base of his neck. He had a broad face and square shoulders. Tanned skin and deep lines around his mouth and eyes told of years squinting against the sun. She hoped some of the lines had been formed by smiling as well.

He scowled. "Who are you?"

Charlotte was ready for the question, and she was determined to be as honest as possible. As long as he didn't directly ask her if she was impersonating a man, she had no reason to lie. "Charlie Bower, sir." She used the nickname her brother called her. She caught herself before curtsying and bowed instead. "Sir, I wish to join your crew."

His gaze moved over her, and his scowl deepened. "Rather small for the job, aren't you, lad? How old are you?"

"Eighteen, sir."

Dobson crossed his arms, studying her. "Do you have experience aboard a ship?"

"No." Inside she winced, but she kept her chin high and shoulders back, wanting to project confidence. "But I am a fast learner and a hard worker."

He lifted one of her hands, turning it over to study her palm.

Charlotte winced but forced herself to relax, reminding herself that as a boy, she had no need to fear a man's touch. Before today, Charlotte had been ashamed of the broken fingernails, scars, and callouses on her once-soft hands, but now she felt proud of them. She *was* a hard worker, and seeing the proof, the quartermaster couldn't refute it.

Dobson dropped her hand and shook his head. "I'm sorry, lad. I can see you're earnest. But it takes strong men to pilot a ship."

He started to turn away, but Charlotte moved in front of him. "It is wartime, Mr. Dobson. With the militia taking so many and the British impressing others, maintaining a complete crew must be difficult."

He opened his mouth to respond, but Charlotte didn't give him the chance.

"I am willing to do any job you need, sir. Without complaint."

He shook his head again and walked around her.

"I am an arbitrator," she called after him in a final effort, embarrassed by the desperation in her voice.

The quartermaster stopped. He cocked his head and turned. "What was that?"

Charlotte swallowed. She felt supremely foolish at her outburst. "An arbitrator." She shrugged and spoke in a quiet voice. "It's something my mother used to say. I don't start arguments, but I am good at diffusing them, coming up with a compromise."

"An arbitrator." Leroy Dobson's scowl softened, the muscles around his mouth jerking as if he was trying to suppress a laugh.

"Yes." Charlotte pressed her lips together tightly so they wouldn't shake. She swallowed the lump in her throat, blinking against tears. He must think her utterly ridiculous. Knowing she needed a new plan and not wanting the man to see her cry, she turned and started away.

"Mr. Bower?"

The sound of Mr. Dobson's voice stopped her. "Yes, sir?"

"Diffusing arguments is a skill I wish more of the crew possessed." His scowl returned, but it didn't seem as harsh. "Captain Thatcher might disagree, and he will, of course, have the final say . . ." He studied her a moment longer and then gave a sharp nod. "Report to the ship right away; we set sail today. Ask for Mr. Ivory, the boatswain."

When she realized he was serious, the tears clogging her throat turned into a nervous laughter. She clasped her hands together and again caught herself before she curtsied. Instead she stood straight and gave what she thought was a serious and masculine-looking nod. "Yes, sir. Thank you, sir. I will. Right away."

He shook his head, a hint of a smile on his lips. "Sailors say, 'Aye aye, sir.'"

Charlotte grinned. "Aye, aye, sir!"

He nodded, clasping his hands behind his back. "And Mr. Bower, if it turns out you are not a quick learner, a hard worker, nor an arbitrator, you'll be put ashore at our first port. No arguments."

"Yes, sir. I mean, aye, aye, sir. I understand. I won't disappoint you."

"See that you don't."

Charlotte ran toward the ship before the quartermaster could change his mind. Behind her, she thought she heard the man mutter the word "arbitrator," but she didn't care at all if he thought her silly. He'd given her a chance, and she'd prove it wasn't misplaced. For Will's sake, she had to.

Chapter 2

"An *ARBITRATOR*?" Captain Alden Thatcher pressed fingertips against his eyelids as the beginnings of a headache threatened. "That is the most . . ." He looked toward the skinny lad dangling from the rigging and then back at the quartermaster, wondering what could possibly have possessed the man. "Dobson, have you lost your mind?"

The quartermaster grimaced, squinting as he watched the boy strain for a foothold. "The crew is diminished ever since Annapolis. We need men."

He spoke the truth. The *Belladonna* required at minimum of eighteen crewmembers, with twenty-five being the optimal amount. Thanks to the war, the crew's numbers had been lacking for years. Alden's men were loyal, but compensating for the deficiency was demanding on all of them.

Shaking his head, Alden held up a finger. "We need *skilled* men. Not just *more* men." He pointed with his chin. "Look at him. Eighteen years old, you said? I would have guessed closer to fourteen, and I'd put his weight at seven stones—with lead in his pockets." It was practically impossible to believe the small lad was only ten years Alden's junior.

He had no time for this kind of delay. They were already well behind schedule. The *Belladonna* had taken a detour to assist Joshua Barney's flotilla in Chesapeake Bay and had been damaged in a skirmish with the English. His adopted brother, Jacob Steele, was a shipbuilder, and of course Alden would trust nobody else to make such a vital repair to his darling. But Jacob had been involved with the war in Washington City and had gotten married, and other obligations—such as delivering crucial information to the capital—had delayed the repairs further.

Alden squinted east, following the river, half-expecting to see a British ship. The blockades and tariffs had made trade nearly impossible for the past two years. English ships had confiscated goods, supplies, and even sailors, and exports were at a standstill.

Alden tapped his foot on the deck, feeling a sense of urgency. The *Belladonna* had hundreds of dollars' worth of Virginia tobacco, coffee, and sugar in her cargo hold, and with the Indian tea he'd purchased in Savannah, Alden's investors in New Orleans would consider this voyage profitable indeed. As long as the ship could avoid the English, which just happened to be a particular talent of Alden's. He'd chosen Savannah specifically because of the city's complicated network of rivers. He knew the waterways well, and the *Belladonna* was small enough to navigate the narrower routes, giving him the advantage over a heavy warship.

Hearing a yell, Alden turned his attention back toward the lad in the rigging. He and Dobson watched as Bert Ivory, the boatswain, waved his arms around and called up direction from the deck beneath the boy. The man's long braid swung back and forth across his back as if it were giving directions as well.

The boy had placed his foot onto a ratline, but it slipped off again. He kicked out, sticking his other leg completely through the ropes of the rigging up to his hip. Pulling with his arms, he struggled for purchase with either foot, but it was no use. Charlie was stuck.

Alden shook his head, muttering a curse.

At Ivory's order, Tom Stafford, an experienced seaman, scampered up the ratlines to help the lad. Wrapping a muscled arm around the thick cable shroud that ran from the mast to the bulwark rail to steady himself, Stafford tugged on Charlie beneath the shoulder, pulling him up until he was untangled and his feet found a hold. Stafford showed the boy how to move up the rigging, holding with hands on the angled shrouds and stepping on the ratlines like one would on ladder rungs.

Charlie followed Stafford's lead, placing a foot and then putting weight on it to take a tentative step upward, but he slipped through the ropes, one hand losing its grip.

Stafford's arm shot out, and he grabbed the boy again, saving him from falling.

Dobson winced at the pitiful demonstration. "He'll learn . . ."

Alden gave the quartermaster a flat stare. Leroy Dobson might appear surly and bad-tempered, which inspired a healthy amount of fear in the crew, but behind the barking voice and scowls, the man's heart was as soft as a goose-down pillow. Alden sighed and started across the deck. Apparently it was up to him to send the lad on his way.

Stafford jumped down from the rigging and stood with Mr. Ivory, watching as Charlie climbed down. His descent was every bit lacking in grace as his climb.

Alden found it painful to watch.

When Alden joined the other men, they nodded a greeting. Stafford's jaw was tight as he glanced back toward the boy, but Alden didn't give it much attention. Frustration was Stafford's typical expression.

The boy had nearly reached the bulwark rail.

Alden stepped up beside the rigging and looked up at where the lad was on the ratlines. "Bower?"

Charlie started and gave a yelp. He twisted around, one foot slipping, and lost his grip, falling to the deck and landing hard on his backside.

Mr. Ivory shook his head, and Stafford's jaw tightened even more.

Alden reached down to help the boy to his feet.

When Charlie took his hand, the boy's cheeks reddened, and he turned his gaze downward. "I beg your pardon, sir. You startled me."

"Charlie." Mr. Ivory's voice was heavy with exasperation. "This is Captain Thatcher."

"Oh." Charlie shuffled his feet, tugging on his trouser leg. He winced and straightened, clasping his hands behind his back, and giving a bow. "How do you do, Captain?"

Alden stared, and for a moment he was speechless. Charlie Bower was not a boy at all, but a young woman. He glanced at the other crewmembers, but they did not appear to notice anything out of the ordinary, aside from Charlie's ineptitude in going aloft. How did they miss the blush? The near-curtsy? The squeal? And those huge eyes? Surely the others weren't fooled, were they?

He released Charlie's hand and pinched the bridge of his nose. A young lady running off to sea for a splendid voyage to divert her from her dull life was the last thing Alden needed. She no doubt imagined a romantic adventure where she'd fall in love with a dashing sailor, and the two would sail away happily to a flower-covered tropical island. Well, in that she was certainly mistaken. Love stories were just that: stories. And they didn't end happily. A fact he knew firsthand.

"Charlie, is it?" Alden studied the young lady. She was certainly small, but he thought her age of eighteen might be accurate. She was slender, but beneath the men's clothing she wore, he could see the curve of a waist, and he imagined she'd likely tied a cloth tightly around her chest to disguise her figure. The cap she wore covered her hair, but some strands still poked out around her ears and neck. Apparently she'd cut it short. She was certainly committed to her adventure, he'd give her that, but she'd regret the hasty barbering soon enough.

"Yes, Captain." She clasped her hands then apparently thought better of it and let them hang at her sides, pushing down her shoulders. "I mean, aye, aye, Captain. Charlie Bower at your service."

"And you think to join the crew of the *Belladonna*?"

"Yes." She nodded. "Mr. Stafford is teaching me how to go aloft to . . . ah . . . tie up the sails."

"*Furl* the sails," Alden said.

"Oh yes, that was the word he used." She gave a thoughtful nod, her brows pulling together in a solemn look that made her eyes enormous.

Alden supposed that expression was exactly what had aroused the tender feelings in the quartermaster.

Charlie glanced toward the other men. "But I shall have to practice, I'm afraid." One side of her mouth pulled into an apologetic smile. "Mr. Ivory said perhaps I would do better as a swabbie." The uncertain smile revealed dimples in her freckled cheeks.

She was attempting to charm him. Alden forcibly restrained his eyes from rolling. This young lady would be bored, tired, and hungry within a day at sea, and whining to return home to her soft bed. Sailing a ship was difficult, not romantic and thrilling like it was portrayed in the novels of which she had undoubtedly read too many. And there was not a member of Alden's crew he would consider dashing. Surly, perhaps. Scarred, smelly, and pockmarked. And in Mr. Gardner's case, bald.

Alden, of course, didn't consider himself to be *un*-dashing. In fact, he took quite a bit of pride in his presentation. He smoothed fingers through his hair, flipping back the curl that fell jauntily over his brow. He was a tradesman who worked with investors, vendors, and salesmen, often sweet-talking and charming them to win their business. Entrusting money and goods to a merchant sailor was, at the best of times, risky. But during wartime the liability was downright hazardous, and he thought it important the owner and captain of the *Belladonna* make a good impression.

The crew of the *Belladonna* were serious sailors, working a difficult job, taking daily risks, and falling exhausted into their berths at the end of their watches. None had the time, energy, or disposition to be smitten and carried away in a silly young girl's pretend world.

His annoyance deepened to anger. She thought this a game, considered the challenging profession of a seaman an amusing way to pass the time, and while she chose to foist her starry-eyed fantasy on him and his crewmembers, he would be the one to manage the inevitable consequences when she grew tired of it. Not to mention dealing with an angry father accusing him of tarnishing the young lady's reputation by taking her out to sea with a ship full of men.

He clasped his hands behind his back and leaned forward. "Mr. Bower, I am very sorry to—"

The sound of raised voices interrupted him.

Charlie's eyes widened. She darted a glance toward the dock, and her face went chalk-white.

Surprised by the reaction, Alden followed her gaze. Two rather seedy-looking men stood at the gangplank, arguing with the quartermaster. They wore dirty boots, wide-brimmed hats, and coats that were much too large, very likely with hidden pockets for stashing valuables they lifted from careless passersby. The sight of such men on the docks of a large city such as Savannah wasn't unusual, and Dobson would deal with them well enough. Alden turned back to finish speaking with Charlie, but the girl had disappeared.

"What the deuce?" Where had she gone? His curiosity piqued, he glanced around the deck as he strode toward the gangplank, slowing his steps to watch the interaction beneath.

The quartermaster stood at the foot of the gangplank, arms folded and legs apart. Dobson could truly look threatening when he wished to. "I told you I've not seen a girl," he said to the men. "And there's certainly not one aboard this ship."

"Perhaps we might come aboard and have a look, sir." One man, the taller of the two, spoke through a tobacco-blackened mouth. "She may be hiding."

His voice made Alden think of oil slipping over water. And the way his companion's eyes darted about made him wary of the men's intentions. They were surely up to something nefarious.

"You'll take my word for it," Dobson said. He made a shooing motion. "Now, off with you."

The suspicious-looking men shared a glance, and the taller held up his hands as if to assure the quartermaster that they meant no harm. "If we—"

The sound of Alden's boot stepping onto the gangplank stopped the man's speech. "What's all this about, Mr. Dobson?" Alden asked.

The quartermaster turned, jabbing a thumb over his shoulder. "These men here are looking for a runaway. A girl. They think she's hiding aboard."

Alden descended partway down the gangplank, his position above the men making them have to crane their necks to see him. "You think a girl boarded this ship without my knowledge?"

"We do, sir," the tobacco-chewing man said.

The shorter man made a very wet sniffing noise.

If one drop of fluid—any fluid—got onto Alden's decks, the men would be sorry they'd gotten out of bed this morning—or out of whatever filthy den such men slept in.

"Could have slipped aboard while everyone was sleeping." The shorter man looked toward the portholes as he spoke, wiping his nose on his sleeve. "She's wearing a blue dress and her hair in long braids." He made a motion down the side of his head and chest to indicate the length of her hair.

Alden took a few steps closer, making certain he was still positioned higher than the men. He didn't feel one bit guilty about using intimidation. "And what is this girl to you?" He looked between them. "Why are you searching for her?"

The taller man's brow furrowed then smoothed. "She's our sister, sir. Our dear sister."

"Our poor ma misses her so." The smaller man looked at the smear on his sleeve then sniffed again.

Alden's lip curled, disgusted at both the leaking sinuses and the obvious lie. "What's her name?"

"Who? Oh. Uh . . ." The taller man's brow furrowed again. "Mary."

"Anna." His companion spoke at the same moment.

The two looked at one another, eyes widening.

One would think men of their low caliber would not be such superbly terrible liars.

"Maryanne," the shorter man said, looking proud of himself for the quick thinking. He tipped his head and gave what he must have thought appeared to be a loving smile, but was exactly the kind of forged innocent expression Alden knew firsthand led to a schoolmaster's paddle.

The taller man nodded. "How we miss our dear Maryanne."

The hairs on the back of Alden's neck prickled. He thought again of the frightened look on Charlie's face. The anger he'd felt toward the young lady found a new recipient in these men. If he had anything to do with it, they would never see her again. He crossed his arms. "I have very little tolerance for liars, gentlemen. This girl, wherever she is, should consider herself lucky not to be in your company. Now, move away from my ship, or we'll see how you like the taste of buckshot for breakfast."

"How dare you?" The tobacco-chewing man spat, narrowly missing Alden's toe. He did, however, make the mistake of dirtying the gangplank. "Give her to us at once."

From behind, Dobson called a command to arms.

The crew of the *Belladonna* appeared at the rails with muskets trained on the men.

Alden held the man's gaze steadily. He stepped over the offensive splash on his polished gangplank and grabbed him by the collar, wary of the brown liquid at the edges of the man's lips. Standing on even ground, Alden was still taller. "Gentlemen"—he kept his voice low, forcing it to remain even—"no girl is aboard my ship. Now, I'll not ask again." He gave a shove, and the man stumbled backward.

The two glared at him. The dripping-nosed man muttered a curse, but they made the first wise decision of the day and scurried away.

Alden shook his head. A sick feeling turned his stomach. Slave traders. He'd been wrong about Charlie. She wasn't a spoiled girl after all. She'd been captured—likely by Indians—and sold to those repulsive men. The nausea moved to constrict his throat as he considered what the young lady had likely endured, and he understood the need for her disguise.

He turned back, climbing the gangplank again and nodding to Dobson as he passed.

The men returned their weapons, save for two who remained as guards at the top of the gangplank, should the slave traders return with reinforcements.

Alden didn't think there was much chance of that. Those men were cowards. While he himself had done his fair share of not entirely legal importation of goods, there was a line he'd never crossed. He had no respect for men who resorted to outright murder or thievery and even less for human traffickers.

Unfortunately, in the merchant and privateering business, it was often necessary to remain on civil terms with the dregs of society. But Alden had vowed never to stoop to their level. He'd witnessed slave auctions, seen frightened babies and children torn from their helpless mothers. And the sight had been heartbreaking. He didn't consider himself an overly sensitive person, but he couldn't understand how anyone could look upon such a thing without feeling compassion—and guilt. No amount of money could make trading human lives into anything but sheer evil.

He stepped down the companionway onto the lower deck and thought again of the terror on Charlie's face when she'd heard the voices and feared she'd been discovered. A surge of defensiveness rose inside him. He had no sisters but had spent his early years in an orphanage in Washington City before being adopted. The younger children had looked up to him as a leader. Well, not a leader, precisely. *Jester* was perhaps a better term. He'd found it much easier to laugh at the difficult situations in life than to face them. His joking helped the other children forget their sorrows. In some cases, laughter worked better than a comforting word. And making a joke seldom involved uncomfortable emotions.

Scowling, he realized how much had changed. Laughter was a rare element in his life these days. He felt like that part of him—the part with jokes and smiles—was a disguise, a wall to protect his feelings. Alden sighed. It appeared he hadn't changed so much after all.

He sent for Charlie, and a few moments later, she stepped into his cabin. The captain's quarters on the *Belladonna* were the most luxurious of all the sleeping spaces by far. That being said, the room was very small, with only space for a wooden berth, a trunk, a chair, and a washstand that doubled as a desk.

"Sit down." He stood aside and motioned toward the chair.

She glanced around the confined space, and her brows pinched together nervously, but she sat straight-backed on the chair, with her knees together and her hands folded. Hardly a masculine posture. Alden's lips twitched as he leaned his shoulder against the doorframe. "Where are you from, Charlie?"

"Bay Minette; it's a small town in the Mississippi Territory."

He nodded. The area was notorious for a violent Creek Indian faction, the Red Sticks. He studied her face for a moment. Charlie held her chin up and her jaw tight. Her muscles were tense, and her gaze scanned her surroundings as she watched him carefully. Hers was not the attitude of a confident young lady but of a survivor, bracing herself. Alden rubbed his chin, feeling a kinship with the girl. It appeared she had walls of her own.

"You were raised on a farm?"

Charlie nodded.

"Then you are not a stranger to physical labor," he said.

"No, sir."

"I require my crew to work hard." He folded his arms. "You won't be cut slack just because you're . . ." He tipped his head, regarding her, and decided for the sake of her pride and the order of his ship to keep the secret of her gender. "Because you're the smallest crewmember."

Her eyes brightened but still held caution. "I understand, sir. I know I need to practice going aloft." She winced, as if remembering her fall from the rigging. "And Mr. Ivory said he will teach me how to maintain the decks."

Alden lifted his chin. "I take pride in the appearance of this ship. I expect the decks to shine." He looked over her thin clothing, wondering where she'd gotten it. Perhaps she'd traded the blue dress for it. Or her hair. The idea of her having to resort to such means to escape her captors made him respect her determination and also gave him a pang of sadness. "Do you have a coat?"

Charlie shook her head. "No."

"Not very prepared, are you?"

"I'm sorry." Her brows pulled together but smoothed when she saw his words weren't a reprimand.

"The sea is very cold this time of year, even in the Caribbean. I'll have Mr. Ivory find you one." A coat would cover her figure even more, ensure her secret remained hidden—and it would keep her warm.

Charlie looked relieved. Dimples appeared with her smile. "Thank you, Captain."

Alden considered again whether to reveal that he knew her secret but decided against it. After what he imagined she'd endured, posing as a man would give her a feeling of safety, especially surrounded by an all-male crew.

"Welcome aboard, Charlie Bower." Alden extended a hand to shake hers. He didn't regret permitting her aboard. He'd never allow any person to be taken by the likes of those men, but an uneasy twist moved through his gut, and he wondered exactly how much disruption the decision would cause.

Chapter 3

CHARLOTTE STOOD ON THE DECK, nerves tingling, both in excitement and trepidation, as the *Belladonna* made ready to set sail. At the captain's command, Mr. Ivory called out orders, which Charlotte tried unsuccessfully to understand. It seemed sailors spoke a unique language. The crew all came together to heave a thick rope the width of a man's leg, haul in the anchor, and secure it to the front end of the ship. The *bow*, she reminded herself.

She gasped and clutched the rail, surprised by the lurch as the ship was freed and the *Belladonna* moved out onto the Savannah River.

From beside her, Mr. Turley, the ship's cook, laughed. "If a bit o' jostling frightens ya, lad, just wait 'til we reach the open sea." He smirked, making his dark whiskers rise above his lip. "Swells the size o' mountains."

She tried to read his expression but found it difficult to determine beneath the thick beard whether he was teasing. He was exaggerating; she was almost certain of it. *Almost.* "I'm not frightened." Charlotte forced her hands to relax their grip. "Just startled." She looked away from the cook, watching the activity on and above the deck.

Captain Thatcher stood beside Mr. Dobson at the wheel. He patted the man on the shoulder then stepped up to the higher deck above the stern for a better view. Hands on his hips, he surveyed the ship and then nodded to Mr. Ivory.

The boatswain called out an order.

At his words, the crew darted around, every man knowing his duty. The sailors moved quickly, some scampering up the rigging to let down the sails, and others tying them into place. The ship had a feeling of orderly chaos, and Charlotte was excited to be part of it, albeit a very small part. Mr. Ivory had indicated a spot by the rail and told her to remain there until he came for her. Apparently a significant part of a swabbie's duties were to stay out of the way.

Charlotte didn't mind. She was glad to watch. The entire process was fascinating. The ship operated like a machine. Ropes adjusted sails, the wheel shifted course, and somehow, from his position on the top deck, Captain Thatcher directed all of it.

The sails filled with air, propelling the ship forward. Charlotte was glad Mr. Turley had moved away so he didn't see her clutch the rail again. She'd seen boats and even the occasional ship sailing on the Tensaw River by her home, but riding upon the water with the wind blowing in her face and the ship moving beneath her was an entirely different experience, one that would require getting used to. The sails rose impossibly high, and the ship creaked, swaying from side to side. The motion made her uneasy. She worried the ship might topple over.

"No time fer daydreamin', Swabbie."

Mr. Ivory's rough voice startled her, and she spun. Out of habit she put up her hands to defend herself then, realizing she wasn't in danger, lowered them. "No, sir. I was just—"

He shook his head, giving what she thought might be his version of a smile, although the expression mainly consisted of squinting and pressing together his lips. "Was wide-eyed as a puffer fish first time I set to sea." He glanced toward the rigging overhead, his long braid swishing across his back, then back to her. "Excitin' time for a lad. Lots to look at." He pointed downward. "But decks don't swab themselves."

The last thing she wanted to do was give the impression she was shirking her task. She intended to work hard on the voyage. She'd recognized the skepticism in the expressions of the other sailors when they looked at her, and she wanted to prove their worries were unfounded and she was capable of the labor required.

Captain Thatcher's wary expression had concerned her more than the others'. When they'd met earlier, his eyes had held a flicker of doubt, and she'd feared for a moment that he saw through her disguise, but after their talk in his cabin, she decided his skepticism was based on her diminutive size and lack of experience. Her secret was safe.

"Where shall I find a mop?" Charlotte asked Mr. Ivory. The idea of swabbing actually sounded rather nice. Mopping a deck of this size would be time-consuming but not difficult.

He squinted again. Yes, it was definitely a smile. But not a kindly one. The expression was rather sardonic. "Get below, and find Mr. Yancey, the carpenter. He'll teach ya about maintainin' the decks." He smirked. "But I doubt you'll need a mop—not for a while."

Charlotte wasn't certain what he meant, and his mocking tone made her apprehensive.

She descended the wooden steps and blinked as her eyes adjusted to the dim of the lower deck. In an alcove near the galley, she saw an area stacked with boards. Tools hung on a wall, dismantled barrels and crates sat on the floor, and a wooden shelf held buckets of nails and other implements. The workshop was very small but seemed well-organized.

A man sat, bent over, on a stool, working with a chisel on a block of wood he held between his knees.

"Mr. Yancey?" Charlotte asked.

The carpenter looked up. In the light of a hanging lantern, she could see his skin was very fair and his blue eyes pale, almost gray. He studied her for a moment. "Yer the new swabbie?"

"Yes, sir. Charlie."

He sniffed. "A small one, aren't ye?"

Charlotte wasn't exactly certain how to answer. "Mr. Ivory told me you'd give directions on swabbing the deck."

Mr. Yancey set aside the block and tool and stood with a grunt. He took a white brick from a shelf and climbed to the upper deck without giving a backward glance.

Charlotte imagined the swabbing equipment must be kept on the top deck, though she hadn't seen any mops or spare buckets lying about. She followed him back to the upper deck and forward, to the very tip of the bow.

Looking even paler now that they were in the bright sun, Mr. Yancey turned and leaned his lower back against the rail. He glanced down at her legs. "Ye'll want to remove yer boots. And roll up yer trousers." He nodded as she did. "That's it, past the knee."

She blushed at the idea of exposing her legs but reminded herself that a boy would have no qualms and did as he said, having no clue as to why. Perhaps he didn't want the mopping water to slosh onto her clothes.

Once Charlotte finished with the second pant leg and placed her boots against the rail, the carpenter set the brick onto the deck. "Well, what are ye waiting for?" He pointed at the brick and crouched down. "On yer knees, then."

Charlotte knelt next to him and picked up the block. It was made of rough stone. She inspected it for a moment, hoping for some clue as to how she was supposed to use it.

Mr. Yancey took it from her hands and set it back onto the deck. "This is a holystone, lad." He pushed it back and forth along the board like he was sanding a piece of furniture.

Charlotte's shoulders sagged in dismay when she realized that was exactly what he was doing. Was she to sand the deck?

He let go of the holystone and motioned with a flick of his finger for her to continue. "Each board needs to be scraped until it's white and smooth."

Charlotte pushed the stone forward then pulled it back, the brick making a harsh sound over the boards. "Like this?"

"Lean into it." He nodded. "There ye are. Ye'll want to use yer legs and arms to move back and forth; keeps the strain from yer back."

He sat against the rail, watching as she pushed forward on the stone and drew it toward her. "Water damages pine, as does sunlight. Out at sea, we've an abundance of both. Mother Nature's a ship's worst enemy." He ran a finger over the board, coming up with a dusting of white powder. He rubbed it between his fingers and nodded, pointing to the next. "Move on, then."

Charlotte scooted to the side and started on the adjacent plank. Her thigh muscles were already starting to ache.

"Holystones scrape the deck every other day. Ye'll do the upper deck one day and the lower the next. Twice a day ye'll sweep up the dust then give a saltwater rinse. The galley and mess area are swabbed after each meal. To keep water from dripping below, the deck needs re-caulking with oakum. That'll be done in sections on the days yer not scrapin'. Every other month, all of the planks are treated with a sealant." He ticked each item off on his fingers. "But we'll wait until the new caulkin's finished." He gave a nod. "Any questions?"

Charlotte stared at the man. Her gaze moved over the deck from bow to stern. The *Belladonna* must be more than a hundred feet long and at least thirty across. How could she possibly scrape, sweep, and mop the entire deck each day? Inside she felt a dropping sensation, and the immensity of the task nearly overwhelmed her. She looked back to Mr. Yancey and saw a hint of a challenge in his eyes. He was waiting for her to complain or object to the enormity of the assignment.

Well, she would not. She sat back on her heels and forced a confident smile. "I've no questions, and if one arises, I know where to find you. Thank you, sir." She leaned forward and returned to the current task, scraping the stone over the board.

"Good lad," Mr. Yancey said, pushing himself to his feet. "Don't forget the edges against the gunwale." With the side of his foot, he tapped the side of the ship above the deck and beneath the rail.

"The gunwale," Charlotte said to herself. *Another word to remember.*

She set to work, pushing and pulling the stone over the wood, making certain not to miss any spots. The sun was warm but not hot, and she removed her coat, setting it beside her boots. Kneeling on the deck was not comfortable. She experimented with various positions, leaning on one knee, sitting and drawing the stone from side to side, even squatting, but in the end, she realized kneeling was the most efficient way to perform the task. As she worked, she reviewed the new terms she'd learned since coming aboard the *Belladonna* this morning. *Bow, stern, starboard, port, bulwark, gunwale, companionway, galley, porthole*... She wondered how many more she would know by the time they reached New Orleans. Would the use of the new words come naturally to her by then?

In the center of the deck were large hatches covered by rectangular grates through which she could see the lower deck. She assumed they provided light and ventilation, and were likely opened to load cargo. But the very best part about the hatches was the amount of deck space they occupied.

Charlotte worked along one side of the hatches and then crossed over to the other, rubbing her back as she went. She had been scraping the deck for hours, and by her estimate, she was just more than halfway done. Scooting backward as she went, she worked along the starboard side of the hatches and came to the area around the ship's wheel.

Seeing Captain Thatcher and Mr. Dobson in conversation, Charlotte stopped, not wanting to crawl beneath their feet and disturb them. She sat up on her knees and rolled her shoulders.

The captain shaded his eyes, looking ahead. "Steady on, Dobson."

"Don't like this narrow river, Captain," Mr. Dobson said. "We could run aground, and then where would we be?"

"The tributary *is* narrow." Captain Thatcher continued to look toward the bow. "But that's the point, isn't it? An English Man-o-War would never dare to venture on this route."

"We've not seen any English ships for months, Captain. Not since Fort McHenry. Maybe they've all left. Retreated back home for tea and crumpets."

Captain Thatcher shook his head. "It's never that easy. Keep yer guard up—" He glanced down and, seeing Charlotte, cut off his words. "Beg yer pardon, Charlie." He stepped back, and Mr. Dobson did the same, holding on to the wheel but giving her room to maneuver around them.

Charlie kept her head down, contemplating as she scraped the planks. She knew of the British blockades in port cities but hadn't heard anything about Fort McHenry. What had happened there? Had the American navy defeated the English ships? Captain Thatcher still seemed concerned. Was the *Belladonna* in danger?

Once she'd moved away a sufficient distance, she glanced up at the men. Captain Thatcher wore his coffee-colored curls tied back at his neck. His eyes were dark and lively, holding a bit of mischief as they scanned the ship. The way he stood, legs wide, shoulders squared, he carried such an air of assurance. She felt comforted by the notion, but not safe. Charlotte had not felt safe in a long time. She'd almost forgotten how it felt to not be constantly on her guard, looking over her shoulder, hiding, and calculating how much she dared to trust.

With the rhythm of the ship, the sound of the water, and the constant back and forth movement of the holystone, Charlotte fell into a sort of stupor, her eyes glazing as she stared for so many hours at the same view of pine planking.

Someone kicked the stone from her hands, and she jolted, fully alert.

The sailor who'd kicked the stone was a man she'd seen but whose name she didn't know, a lanky man with a large nose and a blue kerchief tied around his neck. He picked up the stone and tossed it to another man, who caught it, laughing. "Come and get it, Swabbie!"

Charlotte considered. She couldn't just ignore the teasing. If Mr. Ivory or Mr. Yancey came along, they'd see her shirking her task. Perhaps they'd think she was joining in on the amusement. She couldn't risk giving the wrong impression. Besides, if she was to finish her work, she needed the stone back.

She stood, wincing at the stiffness as she straightened her knees and crossed the deck to retrieve the holystone.

The other man was shorter, with pockmarked cheeks and red hair. He tossed it from hand to hand while she drew closer, and, as she knew he would, tossed it back to his friend.

Charlotte sighed. She turned and started toward the kerchief man. Perhaps if she didn't react, they would get bored with the teasing.

When she reached him, the man with the kerchief held the stone out to her. "Here ya go, Swabbie."

The harassment was over. "Thank you," she said and reached for it.

But at the last second, he swiped it away and tossed it over her head. He gave an ugly laugh. "Gotta be quicker."

Charlotte's cheeks burned as she turned back to the red-haired man. She was sore and tired and humiliated. *Remember Will.* She repeated the mantra that had gotten her through months of abuse and fear. *I can endure this to find Will.*

The sound of the ship's bell ringing caught the men's attention. The man with red hair dropped the stone, and they both hurried to the companionway to go belowdecks.

Charlotte picked up the stone and noticed the other men on deck went below as well. She had deduced the ringing marked time somehow, but didn't know what the different number of bells meant. She'd need to start keeping track.

Mr. Ivory came from below and motioned her toward him. "First watch is over, lad. Time for the midday meal."

Her stomach growled as she noticed the smell of food coming from below. The hour must be past noon.

Not knowing what to do with the stone and not wanting it to get taken again, she wrapped it in her coat, grabbed her boots, and followed, stowing the bundle in her bunk. She rolled down her pant legs, brushing away the dust as best as she could, and tugged down on the edges of her hat. Her mother had instilled in her the need to look one's best at the dining table, but not wanting to make Mr. Ivory wait, she didn't pause to put on her boots. Hardly any of the other sailors wore shoes anyway. She joined the boatswain near the galley on the lower deck.

"These are yer messmates." Mr. Ivory gestured to one of the makeshift tables that was really just a large panel of wood set on two barrels. Three men sat on stools around it. Charlotte only recognized one of them: Mr. Stafford, the man who'd tried to teach her how to climb the rigging.

"I'm Charlie," she said, scooting in to sit on an empty stool.

"That's Marchand's seat." A man on the other side of the table pushed the stool away from her with his toe. "He's gone for our provisions." He glared beneath thick dark brows.

"Oh, I beg your pardon." She glanced around the deck and, seeing a stool, pulled it over, taking care to avoid Marchand's seat. She sat beside Mr. Stafford, facing the other two.

The men ignored her, returning to their conversation.

Charlotte studied her messmates. The man who'd kicked her seat could not be many years older than herself. His hair was dark and grew low over his forehead, side whiskers covering his cheeks. He appeared to be the youngest of the group. Next to him sat a thin man with a red face and a bulging Adam's apple that moved up and down when he spoke, which, if the past few moments were any indication, he did a lot.

Tom Stafford was by far the largest of the messmates. She thought he must be the largest man on the ship or on most ships. His shoulders were broad and his arms thick and muscular, covered with a dusting of light hairs. He listened as the others spoke, occasionally giving a nod or a grunt, but his expression didn't vary far from a frown. Charlotte had hopes he'd be in better spirits once he'd eaten.

A younger Charlotte would have studied the men with thoughts of developing friendships with her new acquaintances. But that Charlotte was a memory left behind at Fort Mims. Experience had taught her that if she intended to survive, a person of her size needed protection. She calculated which of the men would make the best allies and which to avoid.

The sailor she assumed was Marchand returned with a bucket, a stack of wooden bowls, utensils, and a sack under his arm. He hardly gave Charlotte a glance as he scooped pea soup into each bowl and plopped a hunk of pork into the center. The men watched carefully and snatched away their bowls.

Charlotte took the one that remained, assuming it contained the smallest portion. "Thank you."

Marchand glanced at her, blue eyes squinting as he studied her. Finally he must have decided she wasn't speaking sarcastically. He tipped his head in acknowledgement, handing her the sack. "You are ze new swabbie?"

His accent was thick, and she thought it might be French. Perhaps Marchand was Cajun. The way he spoke reminded her of a man her father had known from a village near Baton Rouge. "Yes. I'm Charlie." She reached inside the sack, pulling out a hard biscuit, and then passed the sack on to Mr. Stafford.

Marchand gave a nod and turned his attention to his food.

He may prove a good ally. He appeared confident, and the others seemed to respect him. Charlotte took a bite of the hard biscuit. She ate a bit of the soup and a few bites of the pork but decided if she were to win any of the men to her side, some sacrifices needed to be made. And she was not a stranger to hunger.

She sliced the meat into fourths and pushed forward her bowl.

The motion caught the men's attention. They stopped their conversation and looked at her meal.

"I'm not used to so much meat," Charlotte said. "You gentlemen are welcome to the r—" She didn't even need to finish the sentence before each of the men speared a portion of the pork. They scooped away the soup just as quickly.

Charlotte nibbled on the biscuit. Once they were finished eating, she helped put the table away and clean the dishes then retrieved her stone and started to the top deck but stopped when Mr. Yancey called her over.

She stepped back down the stairs and into the space he used as a workshop.

Mr. Yancey pointed to a bucket. Inside was a broom and mop. "Lower decks need sweeping and swabbing after meals. You'll be able to use saltwater now." He motioned with a raise of his chin toward a porthole.

Charlotte stepped closer and peered through. Outside she saw nothing but open sea. She leaned to the side, looking as far toward the stern as she could, but they were surrounded by blue water. The sensation of being unable to see any land was unnerving. She felt like a kite that had come loose from its string. She pressed her hand to the bulwark, glad to have something solid to touch.

She swept the lower deck and then Mr. Yancey took her above and showed her how to lower the bucket on a rope into the sea to fill it. Charlotte was terrified leaning over the side but after a few times figured how to hold on to a coil of rope with one foot while she used both hands to pull the bucket up. Once the lower deck was swabbed, she returned above to continue scraping with the holystone.

Hardly an hour had passed before the man with the blue kerchief snatched away the holystone again. He tossed it toward his redheaded friend, but before the man caught it, Marchand seized the stone out of the air. "Do not bother ze swabbie." He spoke in a low voice, his tone nonthreatening.

Nevertheless, the men left Charlie and went off to find something else to divert themselves.

The Cajun man dropped the stone beside Charlotte and gave her a nod then left.

She let out a sigh. While Marchand's action hadn't been outright friendly, it was certainly an improvement.

The evening meal passed much the same, and afterward, Charlotte swabbed the lower deck by the light of the lanterns. Finally, decks swabbed, scrubbed, scraped, and swept, Charlotte climbed onto the shelf she'd been assigned as a berth. On one end was a cupboard that held nothing but her boots. Aside from her clothing, she had only one possession. She took the silver ring from inside her trouser pocket and ran her finger over the turquoise stone. Then she opened the cabinet and hid the ring deep inside one of her boots. She didn't imagine anyone would bother to steal the boots or look inside. At least, she prayed they wouldn't. She hoped the ring was valuable enough to purchase her brother's freedom.

Exhausted, she put her coat over the thin wool blanket and used her arm for a pillow. The berth was hard, and the men around her snored, grunted, and sniffed in their sleep. Every muscle ached, her knees were worn raw, and her hands blistered, but for the first time in more than a year, Charlotte dropped into a deep sleep.

Chapter 4

ALDEN STOOD ON THE QUARTERDECK with Dobson and Ivory. The *Belladonna's* size didn't allow for a truly private meeting between the captain, quartermaster, and boatswain, which was perfectly fine with Alden. He had no secrets from the crew, and if any cared to listen in, he'd welcome it. He'd found over the years, however, that many of the sailors were just content to do their jobs and leave the planning, business, and navigation calculations to those in charge.

Clasping his hands behind his back, he swept his eyes up over the sails then down across the deck, confirming that the ship operated smoothly. His gaze took in Mr. Gardner inspecting a sheet of sail, Marchand tending the helm, Mr. Yancey patching a crack in the binnacle box, and Charlie, on her knees, scraping with the holystone.

Alden winced, remembering the discomfort of the task. He and every sailor upon the high seas had put in their share of time on their knees, and it was a duty he hoped to never perform again. The voyage had been underway for nearly a week, and the young lady had kept the decks in excellent condition.

He turned back to the others. "We should arrive in New Orleans in ten days, two weeks at the most."

"We'd be there in one week if we'd just followed the coast."

Alden nodded. The quartermaster complained about the longer route every time they spoke of the course. Alden didn't blame the man. Of course he wished the voyage to end as swiftly as possible. Dobson had a family waiting in New Orleans.

Alden's belly knotted. *He* should have a family waiting in New Orleans as well. If only . . . He swallowed hard through a tight throat and pulled his thoughts from the past. "You know the reason for caution, Dobson."

"We're staying so far south the ship's likely to hit Cuba."

Alden smirked at the exaggeration. Dobson knew as well as anyone the wisdom in avoiding Florida. The war had spread across the southern border into the Spanish Colony. In spite of having trusted friends and associates in St. Augustine and Pensacola, Alden still decided to keep clear until hostilities ceased.

"We've seen no trace of the English fleet for months." Dobson scowled at the sea around them as if pointing out the lack of enemy ships.

"They're out there," Alden said. "Cochrane didn't give up that easily. And we're safer in the open sea. My darling is swift out here." He brushed a gentle finger over the bulwark rail. "Especially when her hold is filled with expensive cargo."

"Even if we were boarded"—Mr. Ivory crossed his arms, looking toward the sea as well—"they'd never find the tea. Too well-hidden."

Alden nodded. The *Belladonna's* secret compartments were so difficult to see that even he at times had difficulty locating the entrance to a few of them. "True. But cargo's not all they'd take. And some commodities are more valuable than tea."

The others nodded and turned their gazes from the sea to the crew. The British practice of impressing sailors from American ships was one of the atrocities that had led to this war in the first place.

"Speaking of the crew," Alden said. "Any concerns to discuss, Mr. Ivory?"

The boatswain shook his head. "We're still understaffed, but the men are managing."

"How is Charlie faring?"

Dobson's expression softened as he glanced at the smallest crewmember. The quartermaster definitely had a tender spot for the little swabbie.

"Works hard." Mr. Ivory shrugged. "Yancey said he's not complained, though I'd imagine his knees aren't pleased with the treatment."

"I know the crew's shorthanded, but one man scraping and swabbing the entire deck every single day?" Alden said. "Seems . . ."

"Brutal," Dobson said.

"Aye, it is at that. But you saw him in the rigging." The boatswain rolled his eyes. "Swabbing's miserable work, but the task never killed anyone."

The point was a fair one. Charlie was hardly suited for work as an upper yardman. Alden found it difficult to watch a young woman performing such labor, but he knew giving special treatment would result in ridicule by the other crewmembers, and she did not need that difficulty. He nodded and dropped the subject.

The three discussed their course heading based on Alden's equations, charts, and instruments' readings and then adjourned the conference, each moving on to their daily tasks.

Alden descended to the main deck and started below to his cabin, but before stepping down into the companionway, he changed course and crossed toward Charlie.

She sat against the gunwale on the portside in a scrap of shade, legs stretched out in front of her as she pulled apart old ropes to make oakum. The cords were untwisted and then rolled to loosen the fibers, which were pounded into the joints of the deck planks and sealed with a tar mixture to make the deck watertight. The task was mundane, but Alden was glad Charlie had a reprieve from the holystone.

He sat next to her, picking up a worn length of rope and drawing apart the fibers.

Charlie blinked and reached for the rope. "Captain, you don't need to do that."

"Nonsense. I've picked my share of oakum over the years." He smiled. "A dull task but rather relaxing, don't you think?"

She nodded, rolling a cord on her leg. "I don't mind it."

Her trouser legs were folded up, and Alden saw she'd wrapped scraps of cloth around her knees. He winced at the splotches of blood that had soaked through. Guilt tugged at his gut. Wounds like this looked so out of place on a girl, whereas he'd hardly have noticed the same on a boy. In his experience, females were delicate, gentle. His instinct was to care for a young lady, save her from anything that might distress or pain her. What would Elnora, his adopted mother, say if she saw the bleeding knees? She'd constantly stressed the importance of her boys behaving as gentlemen. Alden forced away his gaze, reminding himself not to think of Charlie as a young woman, but a crewmember.

"And swabbing?" he asked. "How do you find that task?"

She looked up at him, her brows pulled together as if she were trying to understand the intention behind his question. "It is not the *worst* task." She spoke slowly, choosing her words carefully. Her upper lip twitched as if it would curl.

Alden leaned back his head and laughed. "It *is* the worst task. The absolute worst." He laughed again, wagging a finger. "Your answer was very diplomatic, Charlie. How do you really feel about working with the holystone?"

She scowled. "I hate it."

Possibly without her notice, her lower lip pouted. Alden found it difficult to think of her as a lad when he saw the expression. "I don't blame you one bit."

She glanced upward, and her brow smoothed. "I could learn to go aloft, really I could. I just need practice."

He studied her. The hopeful expression in Charlie's enormous eyes was a powerful tool. Her parents must have had a difficult time resisting anything she'd asked, as, he imagined, had the young men in the Mississippi Territory.

"It is very dangerous," Alden said. "You climbed the rigging before when the ship was still, anchored in port. But the ropes are usually wet and slippery, the wind pushes and pulls without warning, and the sea is hardly calm, especially the higher you ascend. Can you imagine hanging on in choppy water or during a storm? Or in the pitch dark of night? You must not only climb aloft but also run along the yards and fight against an enormous flapping sail. More than a few experienced seamen have fallen into the ocean, never to be seen again."

Her shoulders straightened and her chin rose in a look of determination. "I could do it with practice. And I am a very good swimmer, you know."

"Swimming won't help you, especially not at night. In fact, I doubt many of the crew have even bothered learning the skill. The ship is moving faster than it appears. You'd be left behind before anyone even realized you'd gone overboard, and we'd never find you. The ocean isn't calm like a country pond." He was frightening her, but she needed to know the truth. Sailing was dangerous, and those tending the sails had the most dangerous job of all.

Her scowl returned, scrunching up her nose. *Ah, so she's a stubborn one.* Alden hid his smile, not wanting her to think he didn't take her seriously. He understood further Dobson's difficulty in turning her away in Savannah. There was something so *likeable* about Charlie's persistence.

"If you're not too tired after your work is done," Alden sighed, not believing the words he was saying, "And Stafford agrees to teach you . . ."

Charlie's face lit up.

"We could rotate duties," Alden finished.

She rolled the oakum fibers quicker. "I can do that." The dimple on her cheek made an appearance with her enthusiastic smile.

Alden shook his head, unable to keep a stern face. *An arbitrator? More like a persuader.* "In the end, the decision is the boatswain's, of course." He rolled a strand of rope between his hands.

"Of course." Charlie looked down, and Alden got the distinct impression she didn't want him to see her victorious grin as she gathered a handful of the loose fibers into a sack.

A persuader indeed.

Alden set aside the strand he'd been working on. He brushed the particles of rope from his legs and began to stand.

"Captain?" She glanced toward him and then down as she pulled apart another twist of rope. "I didn't mean to listen to your conversation the other day, but I overheard you talking to Mr. Dobson about Fort McHenry. What happened there? Were the British defeated?"

Alden settled back down, resting his forearms on bent knees. The fact that she didn't know about the famous battle and its result was a harsh reminder of her grim circumstance. Fort McHenry had been all anyone in America had talked about for the past months. Seeing her smile and the determination in her eyes nearly made him forget what Charlie must have suffered. Yet, somehow she didn't seem like a victim at all. The young woman was strong in spite of her hardships or perhaps because of them. And Alden felt an admiration he supposed few captains harbored for their swabbies.

"The British were not defeated at Fort McHenry." He held up a finger. "But they were also not victorious." He leaned back his head against the gunwale, glad for the slice of shade. "In September, Admiral Cochrane led a convoy of frigates and a half-dozen bomb vessels into Baltimore harbor."

Charlie opened her eyes wide.

"The American navy had sunk a number of its own ships in the channel in hopes of blocking the invasion and keeping the English out of firing range," Alden continued. "Nevertheless, the English launched mortar shells and rockets toward the fort for an entire day and night. The blasts could be heard and the red of the rockets seen from miles around, but in the end, they were unable to breech the armaments." He held his hands apart. "Thick walls."

"That is a relief," Charlie said.

"Very much so." Alden gave a nod. "The result was a stalemate and an enormous waste of English ammunition. The ships retreated, sailed out of the harbor, and left Chesapeake Bay altogether. The English navy clearly had the advantage of troops, weaponry, and experience." He ticked off the items on his fingers. "For them not to take the fort felt like an American victory, one we were in sore need of. In fact, an attorney, Francis Key of Washington City, witnessed the battle from a truce ship five miles away. He wrote a poem that was published in newspapers all over the country. Became quite famous. You've not heard 'The Defense of Fort McHenry'?"

Charlie shook her head.

"Well, I'm certain at least one of the crew must know it by heart. I've heard it sung to a catchy tune as well—a good rallying song."

"Where did the English ships go?" Charlie asked.

Alden shrugged. "Well, that's the question, isn't it? Some think they retreated altogether. Crossed the ocean back to foggy old England." He smirked. "But I don't believe Rear Admiral Cochrane would give up so easily. A fiery temper, that one." He lifted his chin toward the southwest. "They'll be massing somewhere in the Caribbean, planning to invade New Orleans."

Charlie dropped the piece of rope she was holding and leaned forward, turning to face him directly.

Seeing her in the sunlight and at such a close proximity, Alden noticed freckles dotted her cheeks and nose at nice intervals, as if they'd been carefully placed instead of flung like paint from a brush. Fifteen in all. A tidy sum.

"But, Captain, why?"

He focused on her eyes and the telltale furrow in her brow. "If the English were to take New Orleans, they would control the rivers and inland waterways, effectively halting any westward expansion, commanding trade throughout the states and territories, and trapping America on every side."

The furrow deepened into a crease above her nose. "I meant why are you going there? If you believe New Orleans to be the target of invasion, wouldn't it be wise to avoid the city altogether?"

"I never said I was the most intelligent of men." Alden gave a wry smile and a sigh. Why *was* he going to New Orleans? He'd asked himself the same question hundreds of times. What martyr returned to the site of his heartbreak? The mere thought of walking the streets brought a pain to his chest. If it were up to him, he'd avoid the city forever.

"Truthfully, Charlie, some things cannot be helped. I've lenders in the city, awaiting a return on their investments, and there's nowhere else a man can so easily sell—uh"—he flicked the lock of hair from his forehead—"creatively stowed cargo." New Orleans was notorious for ignoring American tariffs on imported products. In fact, pirates, smugglers, and "merchants with unorthodox business models," as Alden considered himself, sold their illegal goods openly in the city square. "If I am to fund my next voyage, I have no choice but to return to New Orleans. I expect the English will wait until the weather is more favorable to attack, and I hope to be gone long before they arrive."

Charlie nodded. "I see."

He studied her expression and decided she did not seem worried. Charlie, he was coming to find out, was a person who accepted the challenges life gave her and made the best of them.

Alden bid the swabbie farewell and made his way to his cabin. The conversation had opened a sack of worries and emotions he'd just as soon avoid, but today, pushing them back was more difficult.

He glanced to the drawer where he kept correspondence and important documents, his mind's eye seeing through the wood and to a neat stack of letters tied with a blue ribbon. Picturing them made his heart hurt, and he absently rubbed his chest as he sat at the desk and stared at the unrolled map. Bitter guilt rose in his throat, a typical companion to the heartache as the memories swept over him. Why had he insisted on one more voyage last winter? Why had he taken so long to return? If he'd only stayed, been there when she'd asked, Marguerite would be alive, and they would be happily together. But he'd been so obsessed, so driven by money and status, and—he'd give all of it, down to his last penny to go back, to change the outcome.

He rubbed his eyes, realizing they were wet. For an instant he thought to return to the upper deck, to sit beside Charlie and confide in her the entire story. Charlie was a good listener with a steady temperament, and—

Get ahold of yourself, man. The impulse was ridiculous. A captain did not go about confessing his mistakes and heartaches to a freckled escapee disguised as a sailor. He opened the ship's account book and took the cork from his ink bottle, needing a distraction from his thoughts.

He analyzed the columns, making certain there were no errors in his calculations. If he was smart, frugal, and lucky, he'd sell his cargo, pay his investors, and have just enough profit to fund a voyage to Calcutta. Tea was valuable throughout Europe and America, and his ship was fast enough to deliver the commodity before the leaves spoiled.

He sat back, pushing aside the curl from his forehead. With any luck, after this trip, he'd never return to or even think of New Orleans again.

Chapter 5

CHARLOTTE SAT ON HER STOOL at the table, eating slowly in an attempt to make the supper of pea soup last. As usual, she'd given the major portion of her meat to her messmates, and tonight she was hungry. She dipped a hard biscuit into the soup, letting it soak and hopefully soften.

The portholes were open to the night to dispel the heavy odor of sealant. She and Mr. Yancey had finally finished caulking the decks, and today the ocean was calm enough to apply what the ship's carpenter referred to as his "special brew": a hot mixture of beeswax, linseed oil, pine tar, and a splash of turpentine. The result was a paste-like varnish that hardened when cool and dry. Unfortunately, calm waters meant a lack of wind, and the crew complained endlessly about the smell. Charlotte and Yancey had only a small portion of the deck to finish sealing after supper, and Charlotte looked forward to a few days without the holystone as the sealant cured.

She had already spent quite a few hours climbing up and down the rigging with Mr. Stafford's help. Well, not his *help*, precisely, but he had been there and given quite a lot of criticism, which Charlotte had taken as instruction. Mr. Stafford still wasn't friendly or even slightly cordial, but Charlotte didn't take his rudeness personally. She'd never seen him act friendly to anyone.

She bit into the biscuit and chewed slowly, letting the bread crumble in her mouth, and watched her messmates. As usual, John Allred—she'd almost laughed out loud when she learned the red-faced man's name—was entertaining the group with a story.

". . . a calm night like this one. That unearthly dark that feels thick and heavy, like a wet blanket against your skin. I was on watch that night—somewhere below the equator in the China Sea— and after a few hours, far off in the distance, I could see flashes of light."

Allred paused for effect, opening and closing his hands. His eyes widened, and his features looked a bit skeletal in the shadows thrown by the lantern hanging over their table.

The men enjoyed Allred's stories, and Charlotte determined that they didn't question whether or not the tales were true but simply enjoyed them for the entertainment. She enjoyed them as well, and in spite of her initial unease around men in general, she had grown surprisingly fond of the four messmates. After a few days, they had started including her in their conversations and seeking her out when the crew gathered on deck in the evenings to listen to Mr. Gardner's fiddle or play at Crown and Anchor. She'd started to consider association with the messmates less of a precautionary measure and more of a friendship, which was something she'd not had for a long time. She wondered if they would continue treating her well if she stopped giving part of her meal but decided against tempting fate. She would remain wary. Trusting too quickly was unwise.

"Naturally I assumed I was watching a distant storm," Allred continued. "And the flashes were just lightning. But something about it seemed . . . wrong, somehow." He looked around the table, meeting each of the messmates' gazes in turn.

"What was it?" George Nye, the younger, hairier messmate's voice sounded apprehensive. Nye was a superstitious man and easily shaken. Charlotte decided his reactions were the reason Allred chose to tell frightening stories.

"Took me a little while to figure it out," Allred said. "But finally it occurred to me." He paused again. "The lights were . . . moving."

"Zis is not unusual for a storm," Marchand said, spooning soup into his mouth.

Allred nodded. "That's what I thought, at first. But you see, the lights were moving fast, and when they got near, I realized they were *under* the water."

"No." Nye froze with his spoon halfway to his mouth.

Charlotte glanced at the others. Mr. Stafford wore his typical scowl, Marchand watched the red-haired storyteller with an interested smile. But Nye looked utterly engrossed.

"Beneath the water and coming straight toward me." Allred leaned forward. "And that's when I saw it."

"What did you see?" Nye asked in a whisper.

"Don't know what exactly it was, only that it was big—longer than the ship—and covered in scales. Moved like a snake—a huge serpentlike beast, with spikes along its back."

"What did you do?" Charlotte asked, suppressing a grin at Nye's terrified expression.

"I froze, lad," Allred said. "Too petrified to move even my little toe. Watched, still as a statue, while the monster swam around the ship and then off into the night, just as fast as it had come."

The table was silent as the others pondered the strange tale.

Stafford grunted. He cut a chunk of meat and chewed.

Marchand watched Allred thoughtfully.

Nye glanced toward the porthole, as if worried he'd see glowing lights and a spiky, scaled monster swimming toward him.

"I imagine every seasoned sailor has a similar tale," Allred said. He spread his hands, wiggling his fingers spookily. "Ocean's vast. Full of strange phenomena." He glanced at Charlotte. "What about you, Swabbie? Seen something mysterious at sea?"

Charlotte shook her head. "I've only been at sea for two weeks. The strangest thing I've seen is Mr. Turley's tattoo."

Mr. Stafford snorted.

Nye grinned, pulled from his anxious mood. "He claims it's a mermaid—looks more like a deformed eel in a wig to me."

The others laughed.

Charlotte laughed as well. One thing she'd discovered in living in close quarters with fifteen men was that not all tattoos were created the same. The passage of time and lack of experience by the artist explained the worst offenders. But in Mr. Turley's case, she thought it must be both, as well as the thick hair on his forearms, that made the image look so strange.

"Marchand, you've been at sea for years. Have you seen something like that?" Charlotte asked.

"Like an ugly tattoo?"

"No." She smiled at his joke. "Something like Allred saw. Something you can't explain."

"*Oui*, Charlie." He spoke in his typical quiet voice, his accent making her name sound like *Sharlie*. "But I do not think you would wish to hear about it. The story is rather disturbing."

At his quiet tone the mood at the table shifted immediately. Charlotte could sense the sincerity in his words. He wasn't simply trying to get a reaction from the others as Allred had been. A chill moved over her skin.

Stafford's expression changed, his scowl softening and brows lifting in a look of interest.

Nye rested his gaze on Marchand, the edges of his eyes tight.

"Now you've piqued our curiosity," Allred said.

"Are you certain you wish to hear it?" Marchand looked specifically at Charlotte.

She nodded.

He leaned back, pushing his bowl away, and clasped his hands together in the space where it had been. "Zis was many years ago—at least twenty. I sailed on the *Canton* under Captain Bretrell." He rubbed his lip, as if deciding how to begin. "Well, at first it did not seem strange at all—simply a ship under half sail, moving with ze same wind and current as our ship." He glanced around the group then looked back at his hands. "We hailed her but received no answer and, thinking she may have been in distress, drew alongside and boarded." Marchand's face darkened, and he crossed himself. "She was a ghost ship."

The men around the table seemed to hold their breath.

Charlotte felt a stab of fear.

"We searched ze ship, but it was empty. Everyone—ze captain, ze crew—zey were all gone."

"But what happened to them?" Charlotte asked.

"I do not know. No one knows. They were just gone. All of zeir possessions and equipment remained, but ze people . . . I have never been as frightened as I was aboard zat silent ship. It felt lonely and very sad. Like a cemetery."

Nye shivered, and Allred swallowed hard, his Adam's apple bobbing. Even Mr. Stafford looked less certain than he had moments earlier.

Marchand stood. "I told you it was frightening." He glanced toward the galley and then opened his mouth to say something, but the ship leaned, and he grabbed on to the table to steady himself.

Charlotte reached out, stopping his bowl and her own from sliding onto the deck.

The ship leaned in the other direction. The board making up the table slipped, and a crash sounded from the deck above.

Charlotte caught herself before she fell off her stool, but doing so meant she dropped the bowls. Feeling foolish, she crouched down to gather them while the men centered the tabletop back onto the barrels.

"Fire!" A panicked voice called the warning from above, and without hesitation the crew left behind their suppers and rushed up the companionway.

Forgetting the dishes, Charlotte ran with them. Urgency and fear spread throughout the crew; panic felt like a stone pressing in her throat. On the upper deck, flames licked over the newly sealed boards, their brightness nearly blinding in the dark night. The ship pitched again as another wave hit it. Charlotte grabbed onto the companionway ropes to keep from falling. A sudden wind pushed her back, and the ship careened to the side. She held tightly to the ropes to keep from falling down to the lower deck, and looking up, saw immediately the source of the fire. The small stove where Mr. Yancey boiled his sealant burned in the center of the flames. The rough waves must have dislodged an ember into the combustible mixture. And the fire was spreading fast.

Charlotte didn't wait for orders. The idea of the wooden ship in the middle of the dark ocean going up in flames was even more frightening than Marchand's story. Terror spurred her into action. She grabbed one of the swabbing buckets and ran to lower it over the portside rail, taking care to twist her foot around a coil of rope to keep from following the bucket overboard. The sea that had been calm moments earlier sent the ship plunging and rising with shocking force. In the darkness, she felt rather than saw the bucket reach the water and grow heavy as water filled it.

Around her, men shouted and jostled against her. Her shipmates appeared only as shadows in the light of the flames. She pulled on the rope, and the instant she drew up the bucket, someone snatched it away into the darkness, leaving an empty one in its place. She lowered it quickly, scooping up more water, and the new bucket was snatched away as well. The smell of chemical smoke choked her throat. Men shoved and ran through the eerie darkness, yelling as they slipped on the sloping deck and fighting to push past one another to throw water onto the expanding ring of fire.

"Avast!" Captain Thatcher's voice cut through the noise like a shot.

Charlotte darted a look behind and saw him standing in the center of the deck, his face lit by the flames. Wind whipped his hair, and a spray of water drenched him as the ship pitched. He spread his legs to keep his balance but hardly seemed to notice the tilting deck or the blast of water as he called orders. Charlotte couldn't help but admire his control.

The chaos calmed, and the crew settled into their assigned posts, drawing water, passing buckets, and pouring it onto the deck. The urgency had not dissipated, but with the crew working systematically, the panic was managed and the fire doused.

The sudden dark made the rocking deck feel even more frightening. Charlotte held tightly to the ropes beside her, orienting herself and trying to keep from sliding down the wet deck when the ship tipped to the side.

Lanterns were brought on deck, and the crew gathered to inspect the damage.

Charlotte crossed the sloping deck and went below, returning with a mop. She held on to the companionway rail and, in the faint light, gazed around at the wet, ashy mess, uncertain of where to begin.

"Charlie!" Captain Thatcher yelled her name as he stomped across the deck. "What in the blazes are you doing?"

She waved a hand around, indicating the mess. "The deck, Captain. I—" A sudden pitch threw her off her feet.

Captain Thatcher caught her by the arms, holding her up. "Belay that. The deck is the least of our worries. A storm's approaching. Can't you smell it?"

He kept hold of her arms as he called orders over her head. "Furl the sails! Batten down the hatches!"

The crew hurried around the deck, some ascending the rigging, others pulling lengths of sail over the grates in the deck, securing them in place with nails.

Captain Thatcher looked back down at her. "Get below, Charlie."

"But I can help. I've practiced going aloft, and—"

"One strong gust will carry you away. You'll be no help to anyone if you're swept overboard."

A flush heated her chest. She could do this. She tensed her muscles, ready to argue, to do whatever was needed to prepare the ship to survive the storm. "But—"

"Help Turley secure the lower deck." In the faint gleam of lantern light, Captain Thatcher held her gaze. "That's an order, Charlie." The stern expression in his dark eyes left no room for argument.

She nodded. "Aye, aye, Captain."

He released his hold and started away, but Charlotte caught his arm. "Captain, please don't be angry with Mr. Yancey." She yelled to be heard over the waves and activity. "He was very careful with the stove." A blast of water crashed over her, and she wiped her eyes with a frustrated swipe of her hand.

Captain Thatcher's lips twitched. "Aren't you the little advocate." He studied her face. In spite of the severity of their circumstance, his expression turned gentle, and he leaned closer. "It was an accident, Charlie. I do not blame anyone. Set your mind at ease." He glanced up to where the men were fighting against the wind to pull up the sail and then back to her. He clasped her arms again—gently this time—then turned her toward the companionway, giving a little push. "Now, off with you, Swabbie."

His voice was soft, and though the words were spoken with a teasing tone, Charlotte also heard affection. Still carrying the mop, she stepped down the companionway, and a squirming feeling moved through her middle. It must be worry about the coming storm or the remnants of fear from the fire, she reasoned, but neither explanation felt right.

The captain's grip on her arms hadn't frightened her, which in itself was surprising, but his touch provided comfort—something she'd not felt from another person since before the Fort Mims attack. She was unused to the sensation and pondered on it throughout the long night.

Chapter 6

ALDEN KICKED THE CHARRED STOVE. The action hurt his toe, but he didn't care. He welcomed the pain, in fact, seeking for something to sharpen his thoughts. Even Turley's strong coffee couldn't help him shake the haze and exhaustion of a night spent fighting a Caribbean storm. His gaze moved over the scorched wood of the deck. Luckily the fire had been extinguished before anyone was injured, and none of the cargo had been damaged. But the same couldn't be said for his ship.

"I'm sorry, dearest," he muttered, rubbing his hand over the smooth wood of the rail. The sealant had accelerated the flames, burning a large section of the forecastle deck and part of the bulwark rail on the portside bow.

He turned his gaze upward, wincing at the jagged tear in the sail. In spite of the crew's best efforts, there were just too few of them and the storm had developed quickly. The pumps had been manned all night and the hatches covered. But the hold and lower deck had still been drenched. Alden rubbed his eyes, frustration and anger making his muscles tight.

A memory entered his mind. He was twelve years old, working at the shipyard with Jacob and their adopted father, Thomas Hathaway. The two boys had spent weeks constructing a scaffolding around the frame for a brand-new schooner commissioned by the governor himself. One morning they'd come to the shipyard to find all of the scaffolding in pieces, torn apart by a storm.

Recognizing Alden's frustration, Thomas had laid a hand on the boy's shoulder. "Feeling discouraged is natural," he'd said. "Allow yourself the emotion, and then push it away and get back to work."

Alden allowed himself a small smile at the memory. Thomas had been extremely practical, and his advice had remained with Alden long after he'd passed away.

Alden breathed deeply for a long moment, indulging in the emotions and then, with an effort, pushed them away. Straightening, he planted his fists on his hips and turned. Now was the time for action, and he needed to put on a confident aspect. Nothing would sink the crew's spirits faster than the sight of their captain looking overwhelmed.

He took stock of the situation. The deck could be repaired. Thankfully none of the damage was to the ship's frame, and he didn't think any of the beams beneath the deck were burned—Mr. Yancey would know soon enough, once he removed the damaged planks.

Glancing upward, Alden saw the torn sail was already being taken down. Not the main sail, luckily, and with Marchand's skill, it would be repaired within the day.

Dobson emerged from the lower deck and walked toward him. The quartermaster's jaw was tight; no doubt the man was frustrated at the delay the repairs would cause. "Lucky it didn't explode." He tapped the burned stove with the side of his boot.

"I'd hardly call this circumstance *lucky*." Alden scowled at the deck.

"Just came from talking to Yancey," Dobson said. "He assures me he took every precaution. Locked up the stove tightly before supper." He shook his head. "Terrible accident."

Alden glanced at the stove again. He didn't doubt for a moment the ship's carpenter took the threat of fire seriously, probably more so than any other person on board. The man had served on his ship for years, and Alden considered him responsible in his duties. He harbored no displeasure toward Mr. Yancey.

Dobson cleared his throat. "Just wanted to make certain you didn't blame him, Captain," he prodded.

Alden nodded. "Charlie already assured me Yancey isn't to blame."

"Oh." Dobson nodded, visibly relaxing. "Well, then. How shall we proceed?"

For an unexplained reason, Alden's anger returned. "We should stop worrying about everyone's tender feelings and fix the ship, Mr. Dobson." His voice was sharper than he'd intended.

Dobson blinked. "Aye, aye, Captain." He hurried away, barking orders at the crew.

Alden was surprised by his own response. He certainly wasn't angry with the quartermaster, nor did he hold the carpenter accountable for the fire. But his mental state was off-balance, and he was unsure why.

Charlie came up the companionway, carrying an armload of wet blankets and clothing. She and Mr. Turley strung a rope, tying it between the upper deck rail and the starboard rigging and laid the wet items over it to dry in the sun.

She rubbed her eyes, and even from his distance Alden could see they were red with dark smudges beneath. Charlie looked exhausted, much like the rest of the crew, but for some reason, this bothered Alden, and his frustration grew. He continued down to the lower deck and into his cabin, closing the door behind him.

He was surprised when he realized his anger had begun with the encounter with the young lady the evening before. The response was irrational, and he rubbed his neck, pacing across the deck as he considered what exactly had bothered him.

The idea of Charlie sliding over the rocking deck or going aloft in the storm had . . . frightened him. He wasn't prepared for the realization, and it took a moment to process the reasoning behind it. His anger had been caused by *worry*. What if she'd been swept overboard? Or hurt? She wasn't trained for the difficulty of a storm at sea.

The explanation was incomplete. He knew the concern had less to do with her skills as a sailor and more to do with the fact that she was a female. He let out an exasperated sigh. This was exactly the reason women weren't permitted to join a sailor's crew. They impeded a man's judgment, caused him to base decisions on feelings rather than necessity and reason. Women complicated things. They made a man worry when his focus should be on the voyage.

Alden hoped the others didn't find out Charlie's secret. A woman at sea was considered bad luck, and he suspected it wasn't just their presence but the men's irrational *reactions* to their presence that was the reason for the superstition.

Alden was still pondering this revelation as he made the calculations to determine the ship's location. The storm hadn't blown them far off course, he learned, which was extremely fortunate. The current stream around the tip of Florida would keep them from floating too far south while the sail was repaired. He sat back in his chair, allowing his eyes to close—just a quick rest.

The sound of arguing awoke him, and a moment later a knock sounded on the door of Alden's quarters.

He opened the door to find Mr. Ivory and Dobson.

"Captain." Mr. Ivory looked even more exhausted than the quartermaster. "We need your help with a . . . situation."

"And what situation is that?" Alden resisted the urge to rub his eyes, not wanting to reveal that he'd fallen asleep.

"A rearrangement of assignments is necessary in order to make repairs." Dobson scratched his cheek and glanced over his shoulder to the main area of the lower deck. "Some of the changes aren't . . . ah . . . sitting well with the crew."

Alden followed them out to one of the mess tables. Turley sat on one side of the table, arms folded as he scowled at Yancey and the red-haired carpenter's mate, Adam Day. Next to Turley sat his assistant, Paulo Nogales, wearing his usual blue kerchief. The four men looked as if they would burst out yelling at one another with the slightest provocation. And based on the noise he'd heard only moments earlier, Alden wouldn't have been a bit surprised if they did. The men were exhausted and strained, and the damage to the ship only added to their workload.

An unfamiliar source of light drew Alden's gaze. He glanced up. Sunlight streamed in from a hole overhead, where the damaged planks were being removed. His jaw tightened, and he looked back to the ship's carpenter. "What's the problem, Yancey?"

"Beg your pardon, Captain, but the deck's requiring more extensive repair than we'd thought. Day and I can't do it alone. We hoped Nogales could assist."

Alden looked to the opposite side of the table. Nogales was the only other crewmember with carpentry experience. The source of the discord became clear.

Turley leaned forward, resting his dark-haired arms on the table. "I still have an entire crew to feed, and some of the pantry supplies are soaked through. If I'm to save the food, put the lower deck back in order, and keep meals in the men's bellies, I need not only Nogales but more help as well."

Alden held his hands tightly behind his back, though he wanted to pinch the bridge of his nose against the headache forming. A beam from the hole in the deck above shone right into his eyes, a glaring reminder of the damage, which felt like a determined attempt from the sun to antagonize his already tense nerves.

He glanced upward and saw Stafford and Gardner pulling up the boards. Marchand was manning the ship's wheel and supervising the men sewing the tear in the sail, and the remainder of the crewmen were busy with their regular duties. And none had slept the night before. He clenched his hands tighter. There were simply not enough men on this ship.

He studied those around the table, considering how to use each crewmember's skills to the best advantage. Which duties were the most pressing? The damage to the pantry stores needed immediate attention in order to save all the food possible, but he couldn't focus on any other problem when *there was an enormous hole in the deck* directly above his head.

"If I may, Captain," Dobson said, his expression brightening as if he'd solved a complicated puzzle. "Shall I send for Charlie?"

The man must be suffering from lack of sleep. Alden looked at the quartermaster as if he'd just proposed they harness a team of dolphins to tow them to New Orleans. "Charlie? The boy can no more repair a ship than Mad King George."

"Aye, sir, but he's an *arbitrator*." Dobson appeared exceedingly proud of himself as he said the word. "He may be able to solve the problem."

The other men glanced at one another as if wondering whether the word was one the quartermaster had just invented but none wished to ask and sound foolish.

The hint of pain behind Alden's eyes burst into a full-blown headache. "Very well, then." He spoke in an agreeable voice that hid the resurgence of anger he felt toward the young lady. How was she so consistently at the center of the problems on the ship? "Let's see the *arbitrator* in action."

Dobson must not have heard the sarcasm in Alden's voice, or if he did, he chose to ignore it. "Fetch Charlie." He pointed at Nogales. "He's above, helping Nye with the sail."

A moment later Charlie descended the companionway. The line between her brows was the only indication she might be nervous at being sent for. Alden wondered if he was the only one who noticed the line. It was quite small.

"Come on over here, lad." Dobson gave an encouraging smile as he waved Charlie toward the table.

The quartermaster had most certainly noticed the line, then, and Alden had no idea why that irritated him. He wanted to get this entire ordeal finished—assign duties, repair the ship, and get on with it. Tapping his finger against his leg, he listened with increased agitation as Dobson explained to Charlie the dilemma of an excess of work and lack of capable men.

"We've been unable to reach a compromise that suits everyone." He shook his head, lips pulled to the side and eyes wide looking decidedly un-quartermaster-like as he and Mr. Ivory waited for the swabbie to do their job for them.

Charlie tapped her lip with her forefinger, the line between her brows deepening as she considered. From her expression, she took the problem very seriously. She looked between the various men, who all watched her with infuriating anticipation.

"Both duties seem very important," she said slowly. "I understand why you each need more than one person to get the work done." She glanced toward Mr. Ivory and Dobson, and then her expression cleared. "My own duties are much lighter with the newly sealed deck and the . . . damaged portion. If you'd like, Mr. Turley, I will help you in the galley, and Mr. Nogales can assist the carpenters."

The men looked at one another thoughtfully.

Mr. Turley nodded.

Alden rolled his eyes.

"And with Mr. Stafford assisting in the repairs as well"—she glanced to the hole above where Stafford was prying a nail from a burned plank—"I can help man the sails." Charlie very obviously kept her gaze from Alden, no doubt afraid he'd forbid it.

Yancey stood. "It's settled, then." He shook hands with Turley.

Alden returned to his quarters, a nagging feeling like an itch he couldn't scratch making him frustrated. Why was he so bothered? Had he wanted Charlie to fail? The smooth management of the ship benefitted everyone, most especially him. So why the irritation? Was it because Charlie had indeed turned out to be an arbitrator? Or because she planned to take on more-dangerous responsibilities? Or was the nagging feeling an indicator of something else? Something buried deep inside him beneath scars of guilt that he feared to examine too closely—that horrible regret that made bile rise in his throat? He pushed the thoughts away. The circumstance was different, he reminded himself. And being overprotective of this young woman wouldn't make up for the one he'd lost.

Chapter 7

CHARLOTTE SCOOTED BACK INTO THE corner on the portside of the upper deck where the gunwale met the bulkhead beneath the stairs of the quarterdeck. The night was clear, and the stars spread overhead, bright against the velvety blackness. She would never fail to be captivated by the sight of the night sky over the open sea. Without a tree or a hill to obstruct the view, it wrapped all around, glistening on the water.

On the other side of the deck, the crew gathered, cheering and laughing while Mr. Gardner played jolly dance tunes on his fiddle. Usually Charlotte clapped along or even joined in singing. But tonight she just wanted to watch the sky. She encircled her arms around her legs and leaned back her head.

In the three days since the fire, she'd been busy, but every single moment of her day wasn't occupied with physical labor, and the respite, while welcome, had the *un*welcome effect of giving her time to remember. Her chest ached, and every bit of her felt heavy as she missed her parents. If only they'd gone somewhere other than Fort Mims when the Red Sticks had threatened. If only they'd found a hiding place or escaped into the woods, or General Jackson's soldiers had arrived earlier. If only . . . She closed her eyes, tears streaming from the corners of her eyes into her hair and ears.

And little Will. Where was he? Finding him was her only reason to push ahead, though it seemed she'd faced pain and discouragement at every turn. Would she find him? She squeezed her arms tight and shook off the negative thought. Of course she would. She had to.

The creaking of the ship reminded her of the sound of her mother's rocking chair, and she was pulled into a memory of sitting on the family porch in the cool of the evening. Will played with a stick, swishing it like a sword. Pa sharpened farm tools, scraping the blades against a whetstone, and Ma hummed softly as she sewed by lantern light. Stars spread over the sky, mirrored below by fireflies in the trees. Frogs croaked and insects buzzed, and a breeze brought the smell of flowers and freshly plowed earth.

"Why do I always see you sitting here?" Captain Thatcher's shadow covered her, and Charlotte jolted from the reminiscence. She sniffled and swiped away her tears.

"Is this section of the deck secretly more comfortable than the rest? Or perhaps you have a stash of sweets hidden beneath the stairs." He settled down onto the deck, stretching his legs out before him.

They sat at a strange angle to one another. If Charlotte straightened her own legs, they would cross his. She kept them bent and close.

"So," Captain Thatcher said. "What is the answer?"

Charlotte thought back, trying to remember his question. Oh yes. This particular spot on the deck. "It's where I finish scraping with the holystone," she said. "And this spot is shaded during the day."

"And it is one of the few places you can be *almost* alone on this ship." The stars gave enough light that she could see Captain Thatcher's expression clearly, though he was shadowed. His forehead wrinkled as he waited for her answer.

"It feels secure, I suppose," she said. "The roof of my father's barn had a similar spot where the eaves came together. I liked to go there to think and to see the stars."

He leaned back his head and looked up at the sky. "Beautiful tonight, aren't they? I'll never tire of the sight."

Charlotte nodded, though he wasn't looking at her. She glanced at him, wanting him to remain and, for reasons she didn't understand, wanting to confide in him. "Tonight the music makes me nostalgic."

He rolled his head to the side, studying her. "I suppose you went to dances and assemblies back in Mississippi."

She smiled, remembering. "Every chance I got."

"And I imagine all the young ladies lined up to dance with you."

She opened her mouth then closed it. The question was so strange that Charlotte didn't know how to answer. She considered herself as Captain Thatcher must see her: a small young man with narrow shoulders who wore a knit cap pulled tightly over his hair—hardly a person young ladies were hoping to take a turn around a ballroom with.

"In New Orleans, they have grand dance halls, and the music plays all night." He glanced at her. "The city is a blend of French and Spanish culture, and the Creole people refuse to learn English, even though Louisiana has technically belonged to America for more than ten years. There are disputes over the proper dance steps, and I've seen swords drawn between French and Spanish dancers." He smiled and shook his head. "There really is no place like New Orleans."

"Is that where you live?"

Captain Thatcher was quiet for a moment, and she could see his shoulders stiffen in the darkness. "I'd . . . hoped to make the city my home. But even the best-laid plans can go off course."

"I know."

He glanced at her. "I imagine you do. Life has a way of surprising us, doesn't it?"

The cheerfulness was gone from his voice, and Charlotte felt sad that she hadn't been able to keep the conversation pleasant. "My father used to say, 'A person often meets his destiny on the road he took to avoid it.'"

"And does that comfort you?" he asked.

Charlotte again tightened her arms. Her father's words were trite, and how could they possibly be true? Surely her parents' destinies hadn't been to die pleading for their lives. "I don't know."

"A man makes his own destiny." He pushed himself up. "I'll leave you to your stargazing."

A lump grew in Charlotte's throat. She'd hoped to lift his spirits. Captain Thatcher had suffered some tragedy. She recognized loss and pain in a person. The evidence was right there in his eyes. And she'd made it worse.

Resting her chin on her knees, she stared down at the deck. Tonight not even the stars could chase away her gloom.

***

Three days later Charlotte stood on the footrope, balancing by leaning her legs forward onto the yardarm while she reached forward with the other members of the crew to set the sail. She pulled on a gasket, untying the reef knot, and then moved to the next, loosening a clewline as she passed. The footrope beneath her bounced with the movements of the other sailors, but she'd gotten used to the motion and moved with it, pacing her own steps to follow the up and down motion instead of fighting against it, like a sort of dance.

Though she'd never admit it, especially to Captain Thatcher—whom she could feel watching every time she went aloft—she was still utterly terrified by the height. From beneath, the tops of the sails didn't look nearly as far away as the deck did from above. But over the last few days, the terror had been joined by elation at her accomplishment. Going aloft was frightening and difficult, and every time she looked out at the sea and then all the way down to the deck, a swell of pride spread from her chest.

When the last gasket was released and the sail fully dropped, she held on to the yardarm and studied the activity below. From this distance, the hole marred the shining wood of the deck, although the charred wood had all been removed. Mr. Yancey was still worried about the integrity of one of the beams. He didn't want to set the new planks until it was replaced.

That issue had become a source of tension for the crew. Replacing a beam was difficult, Charlotte had learned. While planks were easily taken up and laid down, the beam needed to be a particular length, and solid. Mr. Yancey claimed none of the beams in the hold were exactly right, Captain Thatcher didn't want a less-than-perfect repair to his ship, and most of the crew just wanted the ship repairs finished so they could get to New Orleans.

Along with the damage to the deck, a section of the gunwale was being replaced. Charlotte smiled at the small figure of Mr. Stafford leaning over the edge of the rail, nailing a fresh board into place. Seeing him from so far above was possibly the only time the man would be considered small.

Sail set, the others on the line moved to the rigging, climbing down, and Charlotte followed, stepping carefully between the knots and shuffling to the side as she'd been instructed. Many of the more experienced men ran along the tops of the wooden yards, somehow managing to keep from slipping as the boat swayed. But Charlotte was not that brave. She moved cautiously along, placing her feet carefully, and making certain she had a strong handhold. Her progress was slower than the others', and for the moment, she was alone on the highest point of the ship. Hearing a yell, she stopped.

"Man overboard!"

She recognized the words as the crew below rushed to the portside of the ship. Looking into the water, she saw him, and a jolt pierced through her heart. Mr. Stafford had fallen into the sea!

Heart and mind racing, Charlotte remembered what Captain Thatcher had told her. Most of the sailors on the *Belladonna* didn't know how to swim. Did Mr. Stafford? From this distance she couldn't tell if his motions were controlled or not. She looked back down at the crew gathered at the rail. They pointed, yelled, and even at this distance, she could see their motions were panicked, which frightened her more than the man in the water. There was no time to waste. With the sails set and filling with wind, the ship was moving away from her messmate. She had to save him.

Charlotte scooted to the edge of the yardarm, her breath coming in spurts as she realized what she was about to do.

A voice below called her name. It was Captain Thatcher. He must know what she intended to do. "No, Charlie! Don't—"

Before she could change her mind, she jumped.

Charlotte's stomach flew into her throat as she dropped. She plunged feet first into the water, sinking deep. Her thoughts turned to frenzied confusion for an instant as she floundered around, uncertain which way led to the surface, but she calmed and got her bearings and then with a firm kick pushed upward toward the light. She emerged into the air and took a deep breath, coughing out a mouthful of salty water and wishing she'd thought to plug her nose.

The sea rose and dipped, and she twisted around, kicking her legs and stirring with her arms as she searched for Mr. Stafford. Behind her, the ship moved away, but she imagined the crew was at this very moment reefing the sails to slow it then sending a small boat after them. She could remain afloat for a long time, she reasoned. And she hoped Mr. Stafford could as well.

She turned in each direction seeking him, but the enormous waves rose and dipped, and she was so low that the moving water felt like mountains surrounding her. How would she ever find him? "Mr. Sta—" She tried calling his name, but a wave covered her, filling her mouth. She sputtered as she broke through again.

Mr. Stafford had to be close. She'd jumped directly toward him. Had he gone under? If he'd sunk, she didn't think she would find him, but should she try? She took a breath and dove down, kicking her legs and slicing her hands through the water just like she'd done in the pond on her father's farm. Around her, the water was clear, but the sea floor was so far beneath that she saw only darkness. The panicky feeling returned, and she fought it away, peering in each direction. Then, not knowing which way to go, she followed a school of silver fish until her air ran out. Emerging again, she twisted, looking over the water.

If Mr. Stafford was attempting to swim, thrashing his arms, she thought she'd see motion, but the waves were too big. She could only glimpse a small distance at a time. She again turned in a circle, wishing for a sign or even a hint of an impression to show her the way to go.

Her legs were tiring, her clothes heavy, and she couldn't even see the ship. She twisted around again, looking for the *Belladonna*, and caught a glimpse of something white. Not the sails—the object was low, in the water. She started toward it, heart pounding. Had she imagined it? Or was it truly Mr. Stafford's shirt?

The wave under her rose, lifting her higher, and she saw the mass of white again. It *was* him. But she couldn't see clearly enough to know if he was keeping himself afloat or if the waves were moving him. As she swam toward him, another fear arose. If Mr. Stafford couldn't swim, he might grab onto her in his panic, and she wasn't strong enough to get out of his grip. Would he take them both down? She shivered but kept her eyes on the man instead of glancing down into the bottomless depths.

When she reached him at last, she saw he was floating, facedown, bobbing limply with the movement of the waves. The sight was horrifying. The strong, large man hung in the water, lifeless. She dove down, swimming beneath his chest, and pushed him upward, turning him over. She pulled his head back against her shoulder, holding his face out of the water as well as she could while she kicked her legs to keep them afloat, but it was much more difficult to swim with the extra weight. Waves continued to wash over him, and she couldn't tell whether he was breathing or not.

Charlotte scanned the endless sea, feeling helpless. Her legs burned, and she still couldn't see the *Belladonna*. Despair filled her. Hot tears pressed behind her eyes, and her throat was tight. She wouldn't be able to hold the two of them up for much longer. She concentrated on keeping Mr. Stafford's head above the bobbing waves and not allowing the frightening thoughts to enter her mind, but it became more difficult as her arms and legs tired. *Remember Will. I can endure this to find Will.*

She kicked harder with her legs, letting one arm rest, then switched, churning the rested arm and allowing her exhausted legs to still. How much longer could she do this? The image of a dark scaled shape beneath the water came into her mind, and she pushed it out.

A faint noise reached her ears. A voice? Or just a seagull? She listened closely over the swishing sound of the waves, afraid to hope.

The noise came again, louder this time. It *was* a voice, and it shouted her name.

"Over here!" Still holding Mr. Stafford's head, she found a reserve of energy and kicked her legs, raising herself up and waving an arm as high as she could. "We're over here!"

"Charlie!" Mr. Dobson yelled as a small boat came into view, rowed by four crew members. A moment later strong arms grabbed her beneath the arms, and she was hauled onboard, followed by Mr. Stafford. Mr. Dobson and Mr. Allred laid Mr. Stafford flat on a bench.

Limbs shaking, she crawled over the bench to the unconscious man, laying her hand on his chest. Mr. Stafford didn't move. His face was pale. "Please, Mr. Dobson. Help him. I don't know if he's breathing."

Her throat clogged as the fear she'd held at bay flooded over her— fear for her friend as well as the realization of the peril she'd put herself in. The tears came now, and sobs shook her.

"There, there, lad." Mr. Dobson patted her back. "You're safe now, and we'll see to Stafford."

While they rowed back to the ship, the quartermaster pushed down on the large man's chest and breathed into his mouth.

Finally Mr. Stafford coughed, spewing a fountain of water.

Charlotte continued to weep, even after she was on the *Belladonna*'s deck. She wrapped her arms around her legs, burying her face against her wet knees. She felt foolish but could no more stop her sobs than she could use her knitted hat as a soup bowl. Thinking of her hat, she felt her hair, but of course she'd lost the hat in the ocean. Tremors shook her, and she realized she was cold, but her thoughts were muddy. It seemed the only thing she was capable of was crying like a child whose pet had died.

With Nye and Allred's help, Stafford sat up against the gunwale. The large man pressed a hand against his chest, wincing with every cough. His skin looked bluish, and Charlotte could see he was shaking as well.

Steps sounded behind her, the noise made by boots on the wooden planks. Only Captain Thatcher and Mr. Dobson wore boots aboard the ship. Charlotte peeked over her shoulder, feeling a burst of fear.

What would the captain do? She had no doubt she'd be punished for disobeying him.

"Take Stafford below," the captain said in a calm voice. "Remove his wet clothes and cover him with blankets." He pointed. "Nye, you stay with him."

"Aye, aye, Captain." The men led Stafford away, leaving Charlotte and the captain alone on the starboard side of the deck.

She didn't dare look up at him.

"Can you stand?" he asked.

Glancing up, she squinted against the sun and searched his expression for a sign of compassion but could see nothing in his expression—not even anger, which made him seem angrier. The fear spread, tingling in her fingers.

She pushed herself to her feet, wobbling just a bit on her tired legs. She shivered. Water dripped down her back and puddled on the deck at her feet. Her first thought was to fetch the mop, but beneath Captain Thatcher's gaze, she was afraid to move.

His expression remained stony as he looked her over. He gave a sharp nod then turned toward the companionway, motioning with a flick of his finger for her to follow. "Come with me, Charlie."

Chapter 8

ALDEN'S JAW WAS TIGHT. HIS muscles ached, his skin was hot, and he was so supremely angry he could hardly form words. He led Charlie down the companionway to his quarters, his pulse thumping in his ears.

She followed quietly, and he knew she was afraid. Well, good. It was about time the girl felt a good hearty dose of fear. Maybe it would teach her once and for all to exercise caution, to actually listen to his orders and not to believe herself incapable of coming to harm. What on earth had she been thinking, diving off the tops of the yards?

He stormed into his quarters and took a pair of trousers and a shirt from his sea chest, tossing them onto the chair. "Change out of your wet clothes."

He stormed past, leaving Charlie alone in the room and closing the door behind him without even giving her a glance. He didn't think he could actually look at her right then. He had never been so . . . furious in his life. Furious didn't even come close. Furious was a huge hole in the deck of his ship. But this . . .

Unable to remain still, he paced in front of the door, seeing Charlie drop again and again in his memory. He'd already been tense this morning, watching her move up the rigging and along the yard, but that fall from so high above and losing sight of her among the waves as they'd fought to slow the ship . . . Every nerve in his body hummed, and he paced faster. What had gone through her mind? Did she imagine she'd just take a pleasant dip in the ocean, find Stafford, and then swim at their leisure back to the ship?

He imagined her alone and afraid, out of sight of the ship, surrounded by endless waves, the sheer terror she must have felt. Alden's anger resurged, making him clench and unclench his fists.

He wanted to hit something or scream or strangle someone or hold Charlie in a tight embrace and not let her go— The thought stopped him short, foot in the air. He stared at the door as a realization hit him with the tenderness of a cannonball.

It wasn't anger he felt, but fear. He set his foot down and leaned his back against the door, rubbing his eyes. Now that he'd identified the emotion, he experienced it fully. Limbs shaking, heart feeling like it would explode, he fought to breathe steadily.

Charlie had jumped without a second thought into the sea to save her shipmate. As frightened as Alden had been, her fear must have eclipsed his by a hundredfold. But she'd done it anyway. And with that thought the last bit of his anger dissipated, leaving in its place a jumble of confusion. He wasn't certain exactly how to feel. Fear and guilt and admiration swirled around inside him like leaves caught in a river's eddy. Even more perturbing, he was uncertain how to act. The dichotomy of Charlie being both a woman and a crewmember was one Alden had never dealt with before. He had no idea how to approach the situation.

Anger was much more convenient, he decided.

He knocked then entered, finding Charlie standing in the center of the room, one hand holding her wet clothes and the other gripping the waistband of Alden's trousers, lest they fall off. Without her hat her honey-colored hair stuck to her head like damp straw. Her eyes were red from both salt water and weeping and still leaked tears onto her freckled cheeks.

He took the dripping clothes from her and called from the doorway for Turley to take them to dry.

When Turley had whisked the clothes away, Charlie said, "I'm sorry, Captain."

Seeing that she was shaking, Alden sat her on the chair.

She released the trouser waist and wrapped her arms around her middle. "I know you're angry, but I just couldn't let him drown."

The line was firmly entrenched between her brows, and Alden was finding it nearly impossible not to comfort her like he would a weeping child. He sat on the berth, facing her, and rested his forearms on his knees. "Did you think the crew would leave Stafford behind without attempting a rescue?" he asked.

She pursed her lips, glancing at him. "No . . . that is . . . I didn't know. You said most sailors can't swim."

"Charlie, we would have done all we could to save him." He sighed, wanting to ease her misery, but she needed to understand the magnitude of what she'd done. "When you jumped in, *two* crewmembers' lives were at risk instead of just one. And having to save two people halves the chance of rescue for each."

Her lower lip trembled, and she looked down, more tears slipping from her eyes. "I didn't think of that. I . . . made the situation worse, didn't I?"

Alden rubbed his eyes again, briefly wondering if they looked as red as hers. "Well, on one hand, you acted with unbelievable bravery, selflessly risking your life, and saved a crewmember. But on the other . . . yes. Your actions increased the danger to both of you."

"I'm so sorry."

Her voice was hardly more than a whisper.

"Charlie." He sighed again, wishing some of the anger would return. It was much easier to discipline a sailor who didn't incite such compassion. "The sea south of Florida is filled with sharks. The two of you are more than lucky."

Her face paled and eyes widened. "I'm glad I didn't know that before."

Alden shook his head against the "what if" images that came into his thoughts.

She pulled her arms tighter around herself. "Captain, are you going to punish me?"

He tapped his chin, considering. "Well, typically, I'd send you to scrape the deck with a holystone, but for you, that would hardly be a punishment." He fought to keep a teasing tone from his voice. Discipline had a more lasting effect when he didn't wish to comfort the offender. He stood, motioning for her to remain seated. Charlie understood the significance of what she'd done, and Alden thought the girl needed a reprieve from danger and fear and reprimand.

"I'm afraid discipline will need to wait," he said. "At the moment another much more pressing matter requires our attention." He moved aside the maps, charts, and inkbottle from his desk, lifting the top to reveal the mirror and washstand beneath.

Charlie frowned, looking uncertain. "What matter?"

"Your haircut."

Her hands flew to her head. "Oh, my hat!"

"Yes." He shook his head dramatically. "Saying goodbye to such a treasured headpiece is a pity indeed. But now you must be brave and go on without it." Crouching to her level, he took hold of her wrists, pulling her arms down. He looked over her hair. Stick-straight didn't even begin to describe it. There existed not the slightest hint of a curl, and the haircut . . . "Charlie, who is your barber? Because the man deserves to be terminated—and by that I mean not just removed from the hairstyling profession—actually terminated." He shook his head. "This is simply a disgrace."

She pulled away her hands, covering up her head again. "I cut my own hair."

That uncomfortable feeling of compassion returned and, with it, the need to set her at ease, even make her smile. "Are you certain?" He moved away her hands and then made a show of walking around her in a circle, rubbing his chin between his thumb and forefinger and studying the haircut. "In my opinion, this barbering job was done by . . . well, it could only have been a . . . blind monkey."

Charlie gasped, her cheeks going red.

"During an earthquake," Alden finished.

A sound that was some combination of a sob, a laugh, and an insulted choke came from the young lady as she stared at him, clearly not knowing how to react to such a preposterous statement.

Alden smiled. After the past hour, he'd consider it a positive noise.

"I didn't have a mirror," Charlie said, her tone sounding less defensive and more like an apology.

"If there is one thing a gentleman must take seriously, it is his presentation." He took a comb from the washstand and pulled it through her hair, noticing where the shears—or whatever blunt instrument she'd used—had hacked away the hair unevenly. Some patches were so short they were shorn nearly to the scalp. Others hung in longer strings. The overall effect reminded him of a stray cat who'd been in fight after fight. Pity made his eyes itch.

He imagined the young woman hiding away in a barn or deep in the woods, cutting off her long braids and then, by feel alone, trimming the remainder. A lump pressed in his throat. Young ladies took particular pride in their hairstyles and pretty clothing, and her lack of either was just another reminder of what must have been taken from Charlie.

Using his own scissors, he carefully trimmed away the longer strands, trying to blend away evidence of the harsh cuts. But in the end he decided to make all of it evenly short. It would grow, eventually, and would look much nicer if it were all the same length.

Charlie sat disconcertingly still as he worked. A few times he caught her gaze in the mirror, but he wasn't sure if she actually saw him or not. Her expression was serious as she stared into the mirror, and he wondered what she saw there. How had her time in captivity changed her?

"I don't think monkeys can cut hair," she said after a long a moment. A small smirk tugged at her mouth.

Alden shrugged. "That was my assumption as well, until I saw . . ." He moved the scissors in a circling motion, indicating her hair.

Her smirk faded. "I frightened you, today, didn't I, Captain?"

He paused in his cutting, surprised she'd so quickly come to the conclusion it had taken him an hour to reach. "You did."

Charlie's shoulders dropped. "I didn't mean to. I had hoped to do the opposite."

"I know."

She looked at him in the mirror, chewing on her lip as if uncertain whether to continue. Then she looked down at her hands. "You lost someone, didn't you? I . . . I can tell. Your eyes are sad and sometimes haunted." She glanced up then looked back down. "Nearly losing your shipmates today reminded you."

Alden stared at the young woman in the mirror. He would never have thought Charlie to be so perceptive. He pulled away his gaze and continued to cut.

"Do you want to tell me about it?" She asked the question with such a tone of understanding that Alden was surprised to find that he did. It may have been relief from the safe rescue or the aftereffect of his worry, or perhaps cutting a person's hair made a man wish to confide in her. "Her name was Marguerite LaFontaine." Alden hadn't spoken the name aloud in more than a year, and the sound startled him.

"You loved her," Charlie said softly.

He nodded.

"And she lived in New Orleans," Charlie guessed.

He nodded again. "Marguerite was elegant, more beautiful than any woman I'd ever met." He was looking at Charlie's hair, but in his mind he was in a dance hall in the hot city. He'd been walking toward the entrance, hoping to step outside for some fresh air. The door had opened, and the smell of magnolias floated inside along with a dark-haired beauty. He blinked and kept cutting.

"She belonged to an old Creole family. Her parents didn't even speak English. They were traditional—very French and very religious. They wanted their daughter to find a man in their social circles, but for a reason I will never understand, she found *me*."

"And you planned to marry?" Charlie asked.

"Yes, but I wanted to wait before declaring my intentions. I didn't feel . . . worthy . . . of her. Not until I had enough money to provide the lifestyle her father had given her. She assured me we'd be happy no matter my financial situation, but . . . my pride wouldn't allow it."

He stepped to the other side, combing over Charlie's hair, and glanced at her in the mirror. She watched him, listening to his story attentively. "Marguerite begged me to stay with her in New Orleans, but I was determined to take another voyage—a short one. Through the Lafitte brothers I learned of a silk shipment stashed away in a cave on Hispaniola. Acquiring it involved great risk, but the payoff was a fortune grand enough that I could propose. So I left."

He blew out a heavy breath. "When I returned, she was gone. A fire had destroyed an entire section of the city. Marguerite's house had suffered some of the worst damage. And she . . ."

"She died," Charlie said.

He nodded.

"Captain, I'm so sorry. But you mustn't blame yourself. The fire wasn't your fault."

"Not being with her when she needed me—that was my fault." He had never spoken to her father, never made his intentions public. Marguerite had died not knowing he would have married her.

Charlie spun around in the seat to face him. She touched his arm. "You forgave Mr. Yancey so readily, but you cannot forgive yourself." A tear leaked from her eye.

He took her shoulders, turning her back to face the mirror. "How is forgiving myself any different than justifying my actions?"

Charlie did not answer, though he could sense she did not agree with him.

The room was silent, save for the sound of scissors. And Alden contemplated whether he'd been right in telling her something so personal. He pushed away the memories and their pain, focusing on the job he was doing, and considered the young woman sitting in his chair.

Since he'd met Charlie, Alden had reminded himself constantly not to think of her as a young woman. She was a member of his crew, nothing more. But seeing her, studying her face, he couldn't help but wonder what she'd been like before. Had she been a quiet, thoughtful girl, or had she flirted and giggled? As hard as he tried, he couldn't imagine her in a dress, her hair long. But even wearing his shirt, with her hair shorn, he found it impossible not to see her as a young lady, and a pleasant-looking one at that. Wide eyes, a teasing dimple, rounded cheeks and freckles—while not a devastating beauty, Charlie's look was fresh and pretty. Especially when she smiled.

Once he finished, Alden stepped back, turning her by the shoulders to face him, and he studied the result. Charlie's hair was longer on the top, brushing over her forehead and in front of her ears, but he'd not been able to salvage the back and sides. They were very short. But the style wasn't unattractive, making her neck look long and slender, and somehow her eyes looked even larger.

She watched him, and he saw nervous anticipation in her gaze as she waited for the verdict. A very ladylike reaction.

He nodded, rubbing his chin thoughtfully as he had earlier. "Much better."

Charlie's cheeks turned pink, and she smiled self-consciously. The compliment—though it was a meager one—had pleased her. "Thank you."

Alden smirked, raising a brow. "Now, back to the matter of your punishment."

Charlie blinked and drew back.

At the sight Alden laughed. "I am only teasing, Swabbie."

Chapter 9

CHARLOTTE AWOKE THE NEXT DAY, wincing at her sore muscles. Swimming had made her legs and shoulders ache. She stretched, wished she hadn't, and then blinked herself fully awake. Only then did she notice the sun shining through the hole in the deck was full in her face. She jolted, realizing she'd overslept—something she hadn't believed possible aboard the ship—and scrambled out of the berth, landing on her feet, and grabbing on to Captain Thatcher's trousers as they slipped down off her hips. Why hadn't anyone woken her? She glanced around and saw all of the other berths were empty.

She started to roll down the waist of the captain's trousers in an effort to keep them from falling but stopped when she saw her clothes had been folded into a tidy pile at the foot of her berth. When she put them on, she found patches had been sewn over the holes in the knees and elbows. She ran her fingers over the thicker material and the stitching. The color wasn't exactly the same, but it was close, and the stitches were small and even. She glanced around, feeling nervous prickles on her skin. She wondered at the act and the reasoning behind it. Was she being manipulated? What would be expected of her in return?

The smell of mush reached her nose as she hurried to the galley. She should have been awake hours ago to help prepare the morning meal and set the peas soaking for luncheon. She winced as she approached the cook, bracing herself for a stream of criticism. "Mr. Turley, I am so sorry. I overslept this morning."

He was scrubbing out the large cooking pot, and Charlotte's stomach sank when she realized she'd not only missed preparing the meal but the meal itself as well.

Mr. Turley looked up then motioned with his bearded chin toward a wooden bowl covered with a cloth on the preparation table. "Not to worry, lad. Figured you needed your sleep after yesterday."

Charlotte stared at the man. Mr. Turley's voice was almost . . . kind. When she lifted the cloth, she discovered he'd saved breakfast for her. She glanced back at him, suspicious and wondering what his intentions could possibly be, but he simply continued scraping.

Taking the mush, she stepped out into the common area and saw the tables had already been cleared and the lower deck swabbed. The fact that someone had done her duty confused her, and she could come up with no reason behind it other than worry that she'd slept too deeply and the others had been unable to wake her. Whom did she owe? And how was she expected to repay? She sat on a barrel, eating quickly, then cleaned her bowl and measured peas into the large pot for the midday meal.

She searched for her mop and bucket, and unable to locate either, finally ascended the companionway. After only a few moments of searching the upper deck, she discovered the mop. It was in Marchand's hands as he swabbed the boards near the stern.

Charlotte hurried toward him. She grabbed on to the mop's handle, pulling on it. "Marchand, you don't need to do this."

"It is almost finished, Charlie." He spoke in his quiet voice, holding firm to the mop.

"But it is *my* duty. You have other work to do."

He pulled the mop away and then dipped it into the bucket, spreading the water over the boards. "I think you have earned a day free from swabbing." He motioned toward the companionway with his chin. "You should rest."

Charlotte's suspicions lessened, and her heart felt warm at the unexpected kindness. Could the shipmates possibly have done her work without expecting anything in return? She grinned, wanting to throw her arms around her messmate. But the action was decidedly unmanly, so she patted his shoulder as she'd seen other men do when they wished to express a deep, heartfelt emotion. "I believe I have a story even stranger than your ghost ship, Marchand."

He stopped mopping and raised a questioning brow, perhaps wondering if she'd seen something strange when she was overboard the day before.

Charlotte pointed to the wet boards at his feet. "It is about a man who voluntarily swabs decks."

He chuckled. "Go rest, Charlie."

As she passed the others on the deck, Charlotte was met with nods and greetings. Her actions the day before had apparently earned respect, and she began to accept that the services performed for her were done in gratitude for saving a fellow shipmate.

Charlotte was grateful for the day of respite, and knowing her shipmates took on extra duties to ensure she recovered touched her. Truth be told, she hurt everywhere, and her limbs felt incredibly weak. Moving to the starboard side of the deck, she leaned against the gunwale, watching a flock of gulls high overhead.

A gust of wind moved over her, stirring her hair. She ran her fingers up the back of her neck and over the spiky bristles. The feel of it was so strange but also rather liberating. She'd worn the knitted cap for so long, hiding away the embarrassment of her shorn hairstyle. But now that it was gone, she didn't miss the old thing. Over the weeks of the voyage, it had stretched out, fitting poorly, and it had also taken on a strange smell.

Charlotte shivered, pulling the coat tighter around her. Mr. Ivory had mentioned that this winter was even colder than usual for the Caribbean. She ran fingers through the hair above her ears, still not used to the new style, and she thought of Captain Thatcher's fingers doing the same. A blush moved over her.

She remembered his story, his pain making her heart ache. She knew the same crushing sorrow of losing loved ones. The pain of losing her family had been nearly more than she could bear, and she wished he didn't have to feel it as well.

She considered what the captain had told her about the woman from New Orleans. The story was so wonderfully romantic: a beautiful heiress who'd defied her parents to love a handsome merchant captain. Marguerite LaFontaine no doubt had thick glistening curls and a porcelain, freckle-free complexion. She must have spoken with an enchanting accent and worn beautiful gowns. No wonder Captain Thatcher adored her.

A sour taste came into Charlotte's mouth and, with it, an emotion that made her hot with embarrassment.

She was *jealous*, and though she didn't want to delve deeper into the reason behind the emotion, she did it anyway. Was she jealous of the luxurious curls? Or the romantic story? Of course. What eighteen-year-old girl wouldn't be?

But as she considered, the full truth was much worse, and the realization made her ashamed. She was jealous of the woman Captain Thatcher loved.

Charlotte didn't like the feeling at all. It felt like a betrayal of Captain Thatcher's confidence.

"Charlie?"

She whipped around, her cheeks burning at the notion that someone might read her humiliating thoughts.

Mr. Strafford was walking toward her.

Seeing him upright, looking strong and healthy, was such a change from his bluish complexion and lifeless limbs of the day before that Charlotte gasped. She put her hands to her heart, feeling a wave of relief. "I'm so glad to see you well."

The large man joined her at the rail, his gaze moving over the water. He took something from his pocket and held it out toward her.

Charlotte glanced at his expression and then accepted the object, leaning close to study it. The item appeared to be a large tooth of some kind—a shark's? Or maybe it was from a whale—with a picture carved into the flat side. A hole was drilled through the wide part of the tooth, and it was strung with a leather cord. She supposed it was to be worn like a necklace. She examined the carved image—a bird with enormous feet and an oversized beak. Though the carving wasn't colored, she could tell the bird's body was white and its wings black. It looked as if it were wearing a gentleman's formal coat, complete with a collar. "I can see it's a bird," she said. "But I don't recognize it."

"A puffin," Mr. Stafford said. "They live in the north."

"Puffin," Charlotte repeated, looking at the bird's face. Its cheeks were round, and its eyes looked comically sad. The picture made her smile. "I didn't know you were interested in birds."

He shrugged, and she thought he looked a bit embarrassed. "Just make a record of those I see."

"And you travel the world, so I imagine you've seen quite a variety."

He shrugged again. "I keep a notebook of drawings if you ever want to look at it."

His cheeks were red, and he shuffled his feet. He was definitely embarrassed by the admission. Charlotte wondered why. Was the man just shy? Or did he think drawing birds a pastime unbefitting a sailor? "I would be very pleased to look at your book." She handed back the carving. "Thank you for showing this to me. It is beautiful."

He jerked away his hands, as if she were offering him something hot. "It is for you."

Charlotte looked back down at the necklace. "Thank you. But I can't accept such a—"

He shook his head, the red on his cheeks spreading down his neck. "I'm not by nature a . . . friendly person, Charlie. I fear my . . . disposition could be considered . . . ah . . . unpleasant. For that, I apologize." He cleared his throat and folded and then unfolded his arms.

Charlie could see how uncomfortable the admission made him. "An apology is unnecessary . . ."

He shook his head. "Let me finish." His voice was a growl. He clasped his hands behind his back, looking down at the deck as if unable to meet her eye. "What you did yesterday . . . I can't begin to thank you. And after how I treated you . . ."

Charlie felt the man's discomfort coming off him in waves. What she'd taken as rudeness she could see now was shyness and an awkwardness when talking to people. The enormous man looked anything but threatening as he struggled to find his words, and she loved him for it.

"Mr. Stafford—"

"Tom."

"Oh." She smiled and patted his arm. "We are shipmates, Tom. Please do not be uneasy for a moment longer."

He nodded, looking relieved to have gotten the uncomfortable conversation over with.

Charlotte tied the leather behind her neck—using a reef knot, of course—and touched the pendant where it hung below her collarbone. She was reminded of how touched she'd been when her parents had presented her with the turquoise ring. Both pieces of jewelry, each so different, were more valuable to her than any chest of pirate treasure. Happiness spread down to her toes, a feeling she'd not experienced since before the attack on Fort Mims and one she'd definitely not expected when she boarded the *Belladonna*.

The two turned to watch the sea. Charlotte wondered if Tom was remembering his nearly fatal accident, and she looked around for something to take his mind off it. Flying overhead was a sleek white bird with a long beak. She pointed. "Is it a crane?"

Tom squinted and shook his head. "A heron. Cranes fly with outstretched necks and herons with their necks tucked."

They watched the heron circle and fly off.

"It means we are not far from the coast." Tom pointed with his chin toward where the bird disappeared.

"Surely we are not near New Orleans," Charlotte said. Only yesterday Captain Thatcher had said they were south of Florida.

Tom frowned. "Not yet."

A strange expression moved over his face. It seemed to grow darker, as if his thoughts bothered him. He glanced to the side. "You should be resting today, Charlie."

She wasn't quite ready for the conversation to be finished, not when the dark look remained. "And you should as well."

He shook his head. "I didn't swim yesterday. Just floated."

Charlotte's Promise 83

"When we reach New Orleans, I will teach you to swim."

He raised his brows, and something very near a smile pulled the corners of his lips. "Not in New Orleans. The whole place is a swamp. Gators, cottonmouths . . . you'll not see me in that water."

Charlotte smiled. She'd seen her share of snakes and even a few alligators near her parents' farm. But the large reptiles weren't considered a threat. They avoided humans, and if one was foolish enough to come near a populated area, it was turned into a pair of boots for a rich gentleman before it even knew what happened.

"Well, you must learn somewhere. But we will avoid the swamp."

Tom held out a hand, and when she took it, he enclosed her small hand in his larger and shook, giving the first real smile she'd seen on the man. "You have a deal."

***

The next evening Charlotte leaned over the boiling pot in the galley. Satisfied the meal was finished, she scooped fish stew into a bowl and set it onto a tray beside a cup of grog and a few biscuits. She carried the supper through the lower deck to Captain Thatcher's quarters. She hadn't spoken to him since the day before, when she'd returned his trousers. Remembering the afternoon in his cabin, her haircut, and the intimate nature of their conversation made her pause. She was not entirely certain how to act around the captain now that he'd shared such personal things with her. She found herself feeling a funny mixture of apprehension and anticipation at seeing him again. Balancing the tray on her hip, she raised her hand to knock but stopped when she heard raised voices inside.

"The beam simply cannot be repaired with the supplies on board," Captain Thatcher was saying. "We're running out of options."

"Plenty of beams in New Orleans," Mr. Dobson said.

Charlotte thought she could hear Captain Thatcher let out a frustrated breath and imagined him rubbing his eyes. "If we arrive in Barataria Bay with a damaged ship, Lafitte will charge us double to fix it and tax the cargo while he's at it. With the impending invasion . . ."

"*Possible* invasion," Dobson interjected.

"The English *will* attack," Captain Thatcher said. "It's just a question of when. And I don't want that when to be while we are there. We need to get in and out of the city as quickly as possible."

"But Pensacola?" Mr. Ivory's voice piped up. "The Spanish won't be friendly toward us after the skirmishes with the American armies."

"All in the past," Alden said. "I have contacts in Pensacola. Good people."

"And what if we arrive and the entire British navy is amassing in the harbor?" Mr. Ivory said.

"If it makes you more comfortable, we'll drop anchor to the west of the city—avoid the harbor altogether and leave ourselves an easier escape. It does mean dragging a heavy beam overland, however. And if we see any sign of trouble, we'll land in Mobile instead."

Charlotte's skin went cold. *Not Mobile.* The city was less than forty miles from her home and deep in Red Sticks territory. And Pensacola—that's where the Red Sticks got their weapons. She wished she could burst into the room and tell the men to avoid both cities. She leaned closer, hoping someone would offer another option.

"You know what the English will do, Captain," Mr. Ivory said. "What we stand to lose—if they don't blow us out of the water first."

"I understand the risk, gentlemen," Captain Thatcher said. "But we have no other choice. We can't risk another storm with the deck in this shape. The repairs need to happen as soon as possible, and Pensacola is the closest city."

"Understood," Dobson said.

"I understand your reasoning as well," Mr. Ivory said. "But that doesn't mean I like it."

"I don't like it either." The captain's voice sounded pensive. Or maybe discouraged. Charlotte couldn't fully tell.

She knocked, and when the door opened, she acted surprised at seeing all of the men gathered. "Oh, I beg your pardon, Captain. Mr. Turley told me you wished to take supper in your quarters tonight."

He accepted the tray, setting it onto the chair since papers and maps covered the desk, the berth, and the trunk. "Thank you, Charlie."

She hadn't seen the captain since the day before when he'd cut her hair. A flush rose from her chest, even though he spared her hardly a glance. Hurrying back to eat with her messmates, she considered what she'd overheard. What had Mr. Ivory meant? What did they stand to lose? Had he been speaking about the cargo? Or would the English confiscate supplies? Weapons?

She sat beside Tom, who showed her the bird pictures in his notebook. He was a talented artist, and she was pleased to see a larger picture of a puffin. Once she had Will, perhaps she'd take him north, somewhere far away from the Creek tribes, and they would watch puffins all day long.

That night as she tried to fall asleep, the worried voices of the captain, quartermaster, and boatswain haunted her.

Why had the men sounded so worried when they'd discussed Pensacola? Would the crew be safe there? If the English were amassing a fleet to attack America, was anyplace safe?

Chapter 10

ALDEN SPREAD THE ROLL OF parchment over his desk, holding it flat with his hands. He tapped his finger on the dot that marked Pensacola. The ship should be in sight of the Florida coast anytime now.

He rolled his neck, kneading out the stiffness from days of strain. The plan to stop in Pensacola for lumber was not optimal, but he couldn't think of a better one. He'd thought through the contingencies of every option, discussed them with Dobson and Mr. Ivory until the men were so tired of the speculation that they'd thrown up their hands and told Alden they'd do whatever he chose.

But how could he choose for the entire ship? He was responsible for the men's safety, but during wartime there were simply no guarantees.

He sighed. When he'd dreamed as a child of captaining a grand ship, he hadn't taken into account the difficult decisions he'd have to make, thinking only of the adventure and exciting destinations that awaited him.

The advantage to Pensacola, aside from the city's closeness to their current location, was familiarity. He knew the city. He had friends there—one in particular whom he knew he could trust. Well, mostly.

He leaned back in his seat. Though he considered Sebastián Delgado a friend, he'd not seen or spoken to the man for years. And so much had happened between their countries in that time. Pensacola was technically in enemy territory, although Alden had traded peacefully with the Spanish settlers for years. But for all he knew, the English controlled the city and the harbor now, in which case, he was leading his men into danger.

Alden rubbed his eyes and turned back to the map, tracing his finger west along the Gulf Coast.

Alden had considered Mobile, a logical choice, as it was in the American territory of Mississippi. But sailing to Mobile worried Mr. Ivory. The city sat at the very top of an enormous bay. If the English had taken the city and controlled the bay, Alden and his crew would not know until they'd sailed far up into it. By then retreat would be impossible.

He studied the map, wishing some new place he hadn't thought of would materialize. But it remained just as it had been every time he'd pored over it.

If the English were indeed gathering in the Caribbean, they could be in any of the cities or even on an island somewhere. And not knowing their location made every port a risk.

Alden stood and paced across the small space. He'd already decided the greatest risk to his crew was sailing with a damaged beam and deck. If they met another storm, the pumps couldn't work fast enough to empty the lower deck and hull. Their cargo and supplies would be ruined and the ship damaged further. And even more concerning was the structural integrity of the vessel. A damaged beam was not to be taken lightly.

A knock sounded—an appreciated distraction from his concerns. He would almost welcome a trivial complaint or dispute. He opened the door and discovered Dobson and Tom Stafford on the other side. Both men wore concerned expressions, and Alden thought he might have to reconsider his wish for a distraction.

"Might we have a word, Captain?" Dobson glanced behind him and leaned closer. "In private?"

Surprised and a little apprehensive, Alden opened the door wide. "Of course."

The men entered, turning to the side to scoot past him in the tight space.

Alden closed the door behind them. "You're recovered from your mishap the other day, Stafford?"

"Aye." Stafford shuffled his feet, a strangely childlike action for such a large person. He was unsettled, making Alden even more curious. Stafford was a steady man. In fact, in the years he'd known him, the man had never complained or caused any trouble.

Alden waited, but neither man seemed to wish to begin the conversation. He clasped his hands behind his back and cleared his throat. "Well, then. How can I help you gentlemen?"

Dobson and Stafford shared a glance.

Stafford looked down at his hands.

Dobson cleared his throat. "Yes, you see, Captain . . ." He looked to the side and cleared his throat again. "Stafford came to me this morning with a . . . question. No, it was rather a concern, one that's been on my mind as well."

Alden looked at Stafford, but the larger man didn't meet his eye.

Alden wasn't going to wait all day for the two to muster the courage to voice their worry. He had a ship to manage. "Out with it."

"Captain, we think Charlie is a girl."

Alden looked between the men and barked out a laugh. "Of course she's a girl." He'd wondered how long it would take for others to realize what to him had been evident from the start.

The two stared at him.

Dobson's mouth actually fell open. "You knew?"

Alden shrugged. "Well, it is fairly obvious."

"Those men at the docks in Savannah." Dobson scowled. "They were looking for a girl. They were looking for Charlie."

"They were . . ." Stafford's lip curled, and an angry frown darkened his eyes. Identifying the repulsive men's profession was unnecessary. Alden was glad not to be on the receiving end of Stafford's glower. He almost felt sorry for the men in Savannah. If Stafford ever came upon them, Alden couldn't imagine them leaving the encounter in one piece.

"You sent them away to protect her . . . ," Dobson said slowly. "That is why you kept her on, even though you intended to dismiss her from the crew."

Alden nodded as the men put together the pieces.

"I'm mighty glad you did," Stafford said in a quiet voice.

Dobson frowned. "What should we do, Captain? Don't know if the other crewmembers would approve of a woman on board the ship. Some are suspicious, and others might . . . take advantage of the situation."

Alden tensed, realizing again the protection Charlie's disguise gave her and how afraid she could become if she was revealed.

"We should continue exactly as we have been—treat Charlie as we would any crewmember. She has certainly proven herself deserving in that respect."

Stafford nodded.

Dobson pursed his lips, looking thoughtful.

Alden spoke slowly, wanting the men to understand the importance of what he was saying. "We will keep Charlie's secret and keep her safe. Do you understand?"

"Aye, aye, Captain." The two stood straighter, their expressions looking solemn. Alden knew they'd not take the charge lightly.

***

Alden led a party of his crewmembers through the tall grass along the Florida coastline. He'd left the rest of the men behind under the command of Dobson to guard the ship, bringing Yancey and Day to select a beam; Stafford, Marchand, and Allred to help the carpenters carry it; Mr. Ivory to oversee the purchase; Paulo Nogales, who was fluent in Spanish; and Charlie. Alden had received curious looks from the crew when he'd selected Charlie to accompany them. Of course, she would serve no practical purpose on the errand. She could hardly carry a heavy beam five miles over sandy ground. But Alden preferred having her close, where he could keep an eye on her. And he thought she might like to visit the city.

Most of the men walked in silence, but he could hear Charlie and Stafford chattering away. Alden slowed to listen.

"I thought it was a duck," Charlie said.

"Definitely a cormorant," Stafford said. "Just watch . . ."

Alden glanced to the side, looking over the mossy pond as they passed. A fat black bird swam toward the far bank.

"It still looks like a duck," Charlie said.

Alden glanced back. The tone of her voice sounded like she was teasing. The sound made him resentful of Stafford, a feeling he shook off immediately. Why should he begrudge the man a friend? The chill in the air and the long walk were making him bad-tempered.

He looked to the right, admiring the view of the sea from the white sand beach. The sea was tranquil today, and with the clear sky, it was a magnificent aqua color. A pity the weather was so cold this winter. He stuffed his hands into his coat pockets.

"There," Stafford said. "See that?"

Alden looked back toward the bird. It stood on the bank, holding its wings outstretched but bent down at a strange angle.

"What is it doing?" Charlie asked.

"Unusual, isn't it?" Stafford said. "Don't know why they stand like that. But it makes them easy to identify."

"A cormorant," Charlie said. "I would never have known."

"If we are lucky, we will see a blue heron," Stafford said. "Some are enormous—almost as tall as you, Charlie."

Alden's sullen mood remained.

The party neared the city, and he led them inland, wanting their approach to be less obvious, especially if the English had scouts watching the beach. Though they tried, they couldn't completely avoid the swamps, but he'd prefer an encounter with a gator or a wild pig to one with an English battalion.

He motioned for Marchand to take the lead. The Cajun used a long stick to poke into the ground as he walked, determining the best route. At times he claimed they were following a path, but Alden thought one bit of the swamp looked the same as every other.

The cold fortunately kept the insects away. Marchand assured the group again and again that alligators didn't hunt in the winter, but the men still held their weapons at the ready, startling and cursing when they spotted one of the large reptiles or even a log that looked like one. Marchand also explained the difference between a bayou and a swamp, but after so many hours slogging through the marshland, Alden didn't care what the place was called. The air was heavy and wet, and combined with the cold, Alden felt like a heavy, damp blanket covered him.

There were, however, an abundance of waterfowl in the swamp and in the tall trees overhead, much to Charlie and her friend's delight.

Stafford identified quite a few from their calls, pointing them out in the undergrowth or the trees.

Charlie asked question after question about the various birds, which the large man appeared delighted to answer.

Alden had never seen the sailor so friendly. He supposed diving into shark-infested water after a person could soften a gruff disposition. He was grateful Stafford took the responsibility of Charlie's care seriously. But that didn't ease his irritability over their newfound friendship.

"We should keep quiet," Alden told them, though he knew very little chance existed of them being overheard this deep in the swamp.

They pushed on, beneath trees heavy with moss and over rotted logs, sometimes retracing their steps when the route they followed was blocked. The trek led them over enormous tree roots and through heavy, wet underbrush, until all of them were sweaty and exhausted.

Grimacing at the muck on his boots and having no idea how much farther they had to go, Alden was nearly ready to risk walking on the beach, but when he emerged from a patch of tall grass, Marchand motioned him forward.

The Cajun pointed to a rise ahead. "We should be able to see ze harbor from atop zat hill."

They waited for the group to regain their strength and then started up the rise, crouching when they reached the top.

Alden let his gaze travel over the harbor and the city, trying to discern whether it was safe for a group of Americans to enter. The city appeared quiet. But on the island at the very tip of the harbor, Fort Barrancas was nothing but a charred ruin. What had happened?

Alden looked around for any clue as to the situation. Ships bobbed in Pensacola Harbor, but they were fishing boats and private vessels. Only a few Spanish Navy sloops and one galleon were among them.

"No English ships," Marchand said.

Alden nodded. "And no American ships." He lifted his chin to the remains of the fort. A Spanish flag flew over rubble of blackened rocks and wood. "I'd feel better if that flag had white stars and red stripes, but at least it's not the Union Jack."

He turned to the group of men, still uneasy about entering the city with no knowledge of how relations stood between their countries. "The English have departed, and I take that as a good sign. But be on your guard, and stay close."

Stafford took a protective step toward Charlie.

Alden led the group to the main road, his eyes scanning ahead for any sign that a band of American sailors weren't welcome. Pensacola was a small settlement with just more than a hundred houses and some outlying farms.

Life for the city's inhabitants seemed to be going on as usual. Alden saw farmers tending to their crops, women hanging clothes on a clothesline, and children playing. Nothing appeared out of the ordinary, save for the burned fort, which stood out like a blemish against the white sands and blue ocean.

The group approached an Indian settlement on the edge of the city. Alden had heard stories of injured and hungry Red Sticks fleeing to Pensacola, hoping for assistance after the tribe's defeat at Horseshoe Bend. From the looks of it, the group consisted of mostly women and children, and the majority hid away, peeking from their grass-and-mud dwellings as Alden's crew passed.

"Charlie? What is wrong?"

Alden turned when he heard the concern in Stafford's voice.

Charlie stood frozen, her face ghostly pale and eyes wide. She trembled all over, shaking her head. "No. No. No."

"Zere is nothing to fear," Marchand said. He extended his hand to coax her forward.

Charlie gasped for breath, sinking down to sit on the path. "I can't. I have to go back to the ship."

Stafford looked worriedly at Alden. "Captain? I don't—"

Alden motioned with his chin for the men, including Stafford, to go on ahead. "Give us a moment." His stomach was ill as he saw the young woman's panic and understood the reason behind it. This must be the same tribe that had attacked her family and taken her prisoner. No wonder she was afraid to continue. Just seeing the Red Sticks must be an enormous shock. He crouched down beside her, setting a hand on her shoulder. "Charlie, you're safe with us."

She pressed a hand to her chest, shaking her head back and forth. "The ship. I must return—"

"Charlie." Alden moved around, facing her directly. He lifted up her chin—her very soft, unwhiskered chin—holding her gaze. "I will not let them—or anyone—hurt you. Do you understand?"

Charlie's lip trembled, and tears fell from her eyes. She wrapped her arms around herself. "I'm just . . ." Her voice choked off.

Alden's throat constricted, and he felt a strange combination of anger toward the people who had hurt her and a swell of compassion for the girl. "You're afraid. I know. And it's all right. I'm here." He gestured behind to the other men who waited ahead on the road. "We're all here. You're safe."

She continued to tremble. "I know . . . I just can't."

"Then, we'll wait until you can." He sat, knowing it wouldn't do for him to embrace a crewmember. But if he couldn't comfort her, perhaps a distraction would help.

"Have I ever told you of the time the *Belladonna* welcomed an elephant onto her deck?"

She didn't respond, so he continued. "It was about three years ago. A large cargo ship had run aground on a sandbar near a small island off the coast of Madeira. We were cautious about approaching.

The Barbary pirates set traps to capture Christian ships in that part of the world, you see. But we determined the ship was truly in distress and decided to extend our aid."

Charlie continued to stare at her boots.

"As we drew near, the crew heard strange noises coming from the ship. Shrieks and screams and something that sounded very much like a roar." He leaned an arm on his knee, twisting toward her. "You can imagine the response in some of the crew. Nye in particular was certain the ship was haunted." He chuckled and thought he saw a flicker of a smile on Charlie's lips.

"But we continued on and, upon boarding, discovered the ship full of African wildlife: monkeys, birds, a cheetah, two giraffes, their long necks poking out of the hatch in the deck. There was even an elephant in the hold. The ship was apparently delivering the animals to a wealthy Venetian conte for his personal menagerie."

Charlie glanced at him, and her shaking seemed to calm somewhat.

"The captain attempted to lighten the ballast and loosen the ship from the sandbar, and the easiest way to do it was to jettison the heaviest cargo—which was, of course, the elephant."

"He didn't throw the elephant overboard, did he?" she asked, her voice still unsteady.

"Hardly." Alden shook his head. "That one animal was worth more than the rest of his shipment combined." He was relieved to hear her speaking again. "The ship had a special crane with a sling made of ropes and heavy canvas that he'd used to load the elephant onto his ship—ingenious device. So we drew the *Belladonna* as close as possible, attached the great beast to the crane, and swung the animal over the waves for a visit." He made a sweeping motion with his arm as he described the operation.

"You are joking."

Alden grinned. "You should be glad you weren't cleaning the decks that day."

Fifteen minutes later Alden and Charlie walked toward the other crewmembers. She was still pale, but her shaking had subsided and she was walking on her own, though her hand clasped his arm.

"I'm so sorry, Captain Thatcher. I don't know what came over me."

"You've nothing to apologize for, Charlie." Alden turned his shoulders, deliberately blocking her from the view of the village.

"I don't know what I'd have done if you hadn't been here."

They reached the others, and she released her hold.

"Charlie, are you all right?" asked a worried-looking Stafford.

"Yes. I'm sorry. I was just—panicked, I guess. But Captain Thatcher calmed me." Her cheeks regained a bit of color, and she looked down at her twisting fingers. "I'm sorry I made everyone wait."

Alden motioned them toward the city, his mood lighter than it had been all day. "On we go, then."

Chapter 11

CHARLOTTE WALKED THROUGH THE CITY of Pensacola, hardly giving a glance to the Spanish-style buildings with their wrought-iron balconies and arched doorways. She still shook from the attack of panic that overtook her upon seeing the Creek Indian encampment. Her body felt wrung out, and she was utterly humiliated that her shipmates had seen her fall to pieces. But even more upsetting were her muddled feelings when it came to Captain Thatcher.

Her cheeks heated when she remembered his gentle touch and the patient way he'd soothed her fear. His humor, his kindness, his fingers in her hair . . . She glanced up, certain she had a longing expression on her face and hoping none of the others noticed her blush.

Annoyed, Charlotte shook herself. She was acting foolishly, letting her emotions get out of hand. Captain Thatcher thought of her as a boy, treated her as he would a younger brother. That was the extent of his affection for her. Brotherly kindness.

But on her part . . . She sighed then glanced around to ensure nobody had heard her do it. She felt confused. Was she simply reacting in this way because so much time had passed since anyone had shown her kindness? She didn't think so. Tom and Marchand both treated her well, and she didn't feel anything more than friendship toward the two of them. What was she to do? She clenched her fists tightly and reprimanded herself. She was not a silly young girl but a woman with a responsibility. She was not simply on an adventure but a mission to find her brother. She would leave the *Belladonna* and Captain Thatcher behind as soon as they reached New Orleans. And in the meantime she'd keep on as she was doing: perform her duties on the ship and avoid spending any unnecessary time with the man. Perhaps then the feelings would not be so complicated. With her mind made up she felt much better, though a part of her was sad the voyage would end. She had been unexpectedly happy working aboard the *Belladonna*.

Captain Thatcher led the party up a street lined with palm trees to one of the grander homes in the city. The walls were made of whitewashed stucco and the roof of red terracotta in the Spanish style. They followed the captain past a low wall and along a flagstone path through a nicely maintained flower garden.

The main door made Charlotte think of the entrance to a castle. It was arched and constructed of thick, sturdy-looking planks. Within the door was a small window.

Captain Thatcher stepped up to the door, brushed the dirt from his coat and trousers, straightened his hat, and knocked.

After a moment the small window opened, and a man spoke in what Charlotte recognized as Spanish, but she couldn't understand the words. Captain Thatcher answered, though his speech was much slower. The window closed, and Nogales whispered to the group that the servant had gone to fetch his master.

Charlotte wondered why Captain Thatcher hadn't asked Nogales to do the speaking for him. He was clearly more fluent in the language, having Spanish parents.

A moment later the door was flung open and a man with dark hair and a white smile strode through.

"Alden Thatcher! *¡Qué sorpresa!*" He clasped Captain Thatcher's shoulders and kissed both of his cheeks. "I wondered if I would see you again, *mi amigo*." He stepped back, and his smile grew even wider. "Your timing is terrible, as usual."

Alden smiled, inclining his head. "I am nothing if not consistent."

"Please, enter." He made an elaborate bow, gesturing for Alden and his party to come inside.

They entered into another courtyard, but this one had a pool in the center, lined with painted tile. A fountain sprayed water into the pool, and a wooden table and chairs sat in a shady spot created by potted trees. Other wooden furniture was arranged around the area, decorated with colorful pillows and cushions.

Along the far side of the courtyard, arches led to what Charlotte supposed were the family's private rooms. An ornate wrought-iron cross hung on the wall.

As the party filed inside, Charlotte studied the Spaniard. He appeared to be close to thirty years old. A finely tailored coat fit perfectly on his slender body, and on one finger, he wore a golden ring with a red gemstone. His face was handsome, with high cheekbones and dark eyes. Though he acted friendly, Charlotte thought his manner was rather pretentious.

Alden clapped the man on his shoulder. "You look well, Sebastián."

"*Gracias*, my friend." Sebastián sniffed and raised a brow as his gaze traveled from Alden's hat to the tips of his boots. "You, however . . ." He made a tsk noise and shook his head at Captain Thatcher's weathered clothes and dirty boots.

Charlotte frowned, not liking the man's way of making insults sound polite just because he spoke them with a charming accent. Captain Thatcher looked perfectly presentable, especially for a man who'd spent the greater part of the day hiking through a swamp.

The Spaniard glanced at the other members of the crew as if just noticing eight other people stood in his house.

Alden lifted a hand toward the other crewmembers. "Allow me to introduce my companions."

Sebastián nodded a polite greeting to the men as Captain Thatcher presented them and related their specialty aboard the ship. Charlotte was surprised that, while he introduced the others by their full names, he referred to Paulo Nogales as Paul. She wondered if the captain was just speaking quickly or if he did not want Sebastián to know Nogales was Spanish as well.

The captain introduced Charlotte last of all. He gestured toward her. "And this is Charlie Bower, the newest member of our crew."

Charlotte nodded her head as she'd seen the others do, relieved he'd not called her the swabbie.

Sebastián's brow lifted when he looked at Charlie. His gaze lingered, but after a moment he turned back to Captain Thatcher. "Alden . . . *por favor*, do not tell me you are in trouble."

"Me? In trouble?" The captain put his hand on his chest as if insulted by the implication, but his smile remained. "I am here on business." He smirked as if the two shared a private joke. "*Legitimate* business. One of the beams below my deck is damaged, and I have simply come to purchase a new one on the way to New Orleans."

"Ah, the *Belladonna, tan hermosa*. You do not deserve such a ship if you cannot care for her." He made the tsk sound again, and Charlotte became more annoyed with the man's criticism of the captain.

Sebastián's expression grew serious and his voice low. "You take a risk coming here, Alden. Americans are not welcome in the city."

Charlotte's breath caught.

Alden winced. "I was afraid of that."

"But, of course, I will not deny hospitality to an old friend and his shipmates." He waved his hand through the air as if to banish the thought. "Although I would prefer to be less . . . conspicuous. For your safety."

"And *your* reputation," the captain said.

"*Sí, naturalmente*." Sebastián maintained his pleasant smile, and Charlotte didn't like that he said one thing while his expression said another. She was leery of trusting this Spaniard.

Sebastián called out toward the arched doorways, and three men joined them. He spoke to them in Spanish, gesturing toward the crew, and the men nodded their understanding.

"Alden, these men can be trusted."

Captain Thatcher lifted his chin in acknowledgement, though he watched the men carefully. He glanced at Nogales, and the man gave a small nod.

"I have ordered them to feed your crew and escort them to the lumber mill—by a less obvious route. Once a beam is selected and purchased, at a slightly inflated cost, of course"—he grinned—"they will escort your men safely from the city." He spoke again to his men and then turned back to Alden. "It is a dangerous time to be an American in Pensacola. Soldiers patrol the streets. It is fortunate you met none on your entrance, but they will not bother your crew with my men accompanying them."

"Thank you," Alden said. He glanced at Nogales again, and the man gave another slight nod.

Apparently Sebastián told the truth about the orders he had given his men, but Charlie still wished Captain Thatcher had chosen a different person to do business with. The man was blatantly extorting the captain, knowing they needed both protection and the lumber—things only he could provide.

"Alden, por favor, join me for drinks and tapas. So much time has passed since we last spoke." Seeing the captain's hesitation, he continued. "I know you are anxious to return to your ship, but one hour only, and I will personally see you safely to your crew."

Captain Thatcher smiled. "How could I reject such a gracious invitation?"

Sebastián dismissed his men, and the crew followed toward one of the doorways. When they neared, the smell of food cooking made Charlotte's stomach grumble.

"Charlie." Captain Thatcher motioned her toward him. "Remain with me."

Sebastián looked surprised at the unexpected request but covered it quickly with a gracious smile. He led them to the table, extending his hand in a sweeping gesture. "Please, *señores*, be seated."

A woman wearing a wide-necked white blouse and lace-trimmed skirt brought drinks and plates of food.

"Gracias," Charlotte said to the woman, feeling a hint of jealousy at seeing her thick curls and beautiful clothes. She wondered how different it would be to sit at this table as a lady in an elegant dress and chat with the men.

Sebastián gestured to the food. "Please, eat."

Charlotte took a piece of toast with a slice of meat and tomato on it.

Captain Thatcher offered another of the plates to her. "What happened here, Sebastián? We saw the fort. Was it the American army?"

Sebastián let out a theatrical sigh, shaking his head. "No, but they were the reason the English destroyed it."

"Ah." Captain Thatcher wiped a crumb from the corner of his mouth. "They could not defend it, so they made it unusable to their enemies."

"Sí."

"It was an invasion, then?" the captain asked.

"Led by General Jackson." Sebastián took a bite of fruit. "The Americans claimed the English were using the city as a headquarters for arming the Creeks."

Charlotte's insides turned cold at the word.

"Were they?" the captain asked.

Sebastián shrugged. "What difference does it make now? English, Americans, Indians, Spanish. One loses track of who is an ally and who is an enemy from one day to the next." He took a drink from a metal goblet. "In the end the only people who profit are weapons dealers."

"And lumber mills." Captain Thatcher gestured with his cup at the beautiful house around them.

Sebastián leaned forward, clinking his cup against his friend's and grinning. "Sí, people must always build. It is one constant here in the colony. Houses, forts, ships . . ." He nodded toward the captain as he mentioned the last item. "Materials will always be in demand."

The captain took a deep drink. "This is delicious, Sebastián. Not that I expected anything less." He glanced at Charlotte and slid a piece of quiche and some fruit onto her plate.

"Thank you," she said. He was right. The food was delicious. She took another small bite, out of habit, chewing slowly to make the meal last.

"Where is Jackson's army now?"

"Gone," Sebastián said. "Hurried off to defend Mobile, or so I heard."

"The American and English armies invaded Pensacola, fought, destroyed the fort, and then both deserted the city?"

Sebastián gave a wry smile. "Leaving us to rebuild."

"I am sorry, my friend," the captain said. "Tell us what happened to the Upper Creeks—the tribes antagonistic to the Americans. Are they still a threat?"

Charlotte swallowed through a suddenly dry throat. She took a drink to keep from choking.

Sebastián set down his cup. "You do not know?"

Alden shook his head. "I've only heard rumors. Your information will be more accurate." He glanced at Charlotte. "Charlie will particularly wish to hear. He had a personal encounter with the Red Sticks."

Stunned, Charlotte gaped at Captain Thatcher. She had no idea he'd guessed this detail from her past. Realizing the men were both watching her reaction, she blinked and turned her gaze to Sebastián. "I was at Fort Mims," she said quietly. She held herself tightly to keep from shaking.

"A survivor." Sebastián tipped his head, studying her. "You did not hear what happened after?"

Charlotte shook her head.

Sebastián settled back in his chair. "In the spring General Jackson and his army, along with Lower Creeks, Cherokees, and the Tennessee Militia took their revenge for Fort Mims at a Red Stick fortification on the Tallapoosa River. Horseshoe Bend." He took a drink. "The tribe was obliterated—all the warriors were killed, the women and children were taken prisoner, and the chiefs surrendered. It was a massacre."

Charlotte stared at her plate, taking in Sebastián's story and sorting through the myriad of emotions it elicited. She should have felt relief. A part of her did. The Upper Creek Indians had threatened the settlers

in the Mississippi Territory for as long as she could remember. The
saying "The good Lord willing, and the Creeks don't rise" was second
nature to those who lived in daily fear of the hostile tribes.

But she thought of the frightened faces peeking from their shelters
on the outskirts of Pensacola—the women who'd watched their loved
ones killed and taken away just as she had. Along with the relief
Charlotte felt a deep sadness. Her eyes burned, and she rubbed them
with her fingers. The terror that to this day woke her in the night
with a racing heart and paralyzed her with panic . . . knowing others
had to feel it as well, had to live with the aftermath . . . She choked
back a sob.

"Charlie . . . ?" Captain Thatcher pulled a handkerchief from his
coat and held it out.

"It is the innocent who suffer when governments fight," Sebastián
said in a quiet voice.

Charlotte swallowed away the tears and wiped her face. "I just
didn't know . . . it was . . ."

"A shock," Captain Thatcher said. "I'm sorry."

She took a few deep breaths. The man she was pretending to be
had openly wept twice in one day. She needed to control herself if
she was to maintain her identity—hold the emotions in until she was
alone. She cleared her throat and drank the cool juice.

Sebastián took a bite of the toasted bread and then used it to
point at the captain. "Now that you are fully informed of martial
affairs in the area, tell me, Alden . . . what is it you have in your
cargo hold? It must be something of great value, if you'd risk sailing
through a war zone."

Captain Thatcher pulled his gaze from Charlotte. He gave a
smile, though it looked forced. "Tobacco, a little sugar, coffee . . ."
He shrugged.

Sebastián lifted his brows, looking away. His expression indicated
he didn't believe the captain was telling the full truth. "You'll never sell
the sugar. Not in New Orleans or anywhere. The entire coast has more
sugar than we know what to do with, thanks to the English." His eyes

narrowed. "I know you. There is more." He spoke thoughtfully, and then his eyes went suddenly wide, and he leaned back in the chair, laughing. "You have a woman in New Orleans." His gaze flicked to Charlotte.

She stared, shocked at the Spaniard. He had no idea the hurt his words caused.

Captain Thatcher went stiff. His expression shifted around as if it wasn't certain which emotion to take on. After a quick moment he smiled, shrugging as if modesty prevented him from answering.

"You always did follow your heart instead of your brain, Alden." The Spaniard wagged a finger. "Not a particularly wise habit for a man in your profession. But it makes me even fonder of you."

The captain's smile didn't waver, but he swallowed hard.

Still grinning, Sebastián looked at his pocket watch. He snapped it closed with a click. "*Qué lastima.* An hour has passed already." He stood. "Night will fall soon, and your men will be waiting."

"A pity indeed," Captain Thatcher said, standing as well.

Charlotte followed them from the courtyard through a large kitchen. The woman she'd seen before gave Sebastián a cloth sack.

He handed it to Charlotte. "For the crewmembers who remained behind."

"Gracias," Charlotte said. She lifted the strap over her head and inhaled the smell of fresh bread from inside. She grudgingly admitted to herself that the gesture was very thoughtful.

They left through a rear exit and wove through the streets of the town, toward the harbor.

Sebastián stopped at a bridge that spanned a small stream. He pointed along the road toward where it curved behind a cluster of trees. "Your men will be waiting in the trees," he said, glancing up the road behind. "The patrols do not come this far from the city. You can follow the road safely."

Captain Thatcher extended his hand, but Sebastián ignored it, grasping his friend's shoulders and kissing his cheeks as he had when they'd first arrived. "Until we meet again, mi amigo."

He turned to Charlotte, and she pulled back, bracing herself and praying he wouldn't kiss her as well. "A pleasure to meet you, Charlie."

"And you, *señor*."

Giving a final wave, Sebastián spun and walked back toward the city.

They watched him go and then turned, following the road in the other direction toward the trees.

"You do not like him," Captain Thatcher said.

She scowled. "He is likeable, but I don't trust him. Just because he's handsome and has a grand house and a shiny ring doesn't mean his intentions are unselfish."

"Handsome?" Captain Thatcher said.

Charlotte turned red. She shrugged, reminding herself again that as a man she should hardly mention such things. "Some might think so."

He pushed together his lips, glancing back at the city behind them. "Sebastián Delgado is rather . . . slippery. But he has been a good friend."

"You don't trust him either," she pointed out. "That is why you didn't tell him Nogales speaks Spanish. You wanted to make certain he wasn't telling his men one thing and you another."

"Just a precaution." He looked at her. "You don't trust many, do you, Charlie?"

She considered. When was the last time she'd truly trusted? As a captive she'd learned quickly that people—even fellow prisoners— would betray her in an instant if they stood to gain. She'd become cautious, weighing all of her words and actions, lest they were turned against her.

"Your trust has been broken, hasn't it?" he said. "You've been hurt."

"I trust you." She said the words without thinking then gasped, wishing she could catch them and push them back into her mouth. What was she thinking, speaking so intimately? "And Tom and Marchand," she amended, hoping to soften the intensity of her declaration.

"It is a start," he said.

Charlotte needed to change the subject—immediately. "You knew about Horseshoe Bend."

"I did."

She frowned. "Then, why did you ask Señor Delgado to tell me about it?"

"Like I said, I'd heard only rumors. I knew his account would be accurate. The man is a magnet for information. And I wanted you to hear it."

His reasoning made sense, but why had he gone to the effort just so she could hear the story? Why had he kept her behind instead of sending her with the rest of the crew? It must be because of her spell of panic in the road; he wanted to help her heal from the trauma. Her chest grew warm, but her thoughts were still confused. And the numerous emotions of the day were taking their toll. She needed to think.

"How did you know I was at Fort Mims?"

He tapped his temple and winked. "Captain's intuition."

Charlotte smiled, but she did not ask further questions. She had plenty to ponder as the crew walked back along the moonlit beach.

Chapter 12

THE DOOR TO ALDEN'S QUARTERS banged open. In an instant he went from sound asleep to standing on the deck, fully alert. *Charlie!* His first thought was that something had happened to the girl. He blinked in the darkness, seeing the outline of the quartermaster standing in the doorway.

"Captain!" Fear laced Dobson's voice. "You must see this."

Alden glanced at the porthole opening. Dawn was near. He'd have woken soon anyway to take the bearing to calculate the ship's latitude. "What is it, Dobson?"

"Warship," Dobson said. "Two points abaft the beam, starboard. Too dark to see her colors." He was already out the door, headed back to the upper deck.

Alden pulled on his trousers and boots and rushed to join him, snatching up his coat from its hook as he passed. Above decks, sunrise was in its full splendor. Soft clouds blushed lavender and rose, and hints of waves were beginning to glimmer in the east. A glow on the horizon showed the sun would be up within a quarter hour. Normally this was Alden's favorite time of day. The sea was calm, the sky indescribably beautiful, but marring the scene was the dark silhouette of a ship, right where Dobson had said. The vessel was near enough that there was no doubt its crew had seen them as well.

Dobson stood with Marchand and Nye—fresh from their night watch—at the starboard rail. The men stared anxiously toward the top of the unknown ship's main mast, waiting for light to illuminate the colors of the ensign.

Alden studied the ship: three-masted, square-rigged, and from the size of it, he judged the vessel to be a corvette, smaller than a frigate, with likely no more than twenty guns on her deck. Sleek, fast. A favorite of the English and American navies alike.

"No running lights, Captain," Nye said. "Or we'd have spotted her sooner."

Alden muttered a curse. Sailing at night without running lights to alert other ships of one's position was either foolhardy or, in this case, showed a devious arrogance. The vessel's inhabitants, whether English or not, hoped to come upon ships unawares in the darkness. Their intentions could be nothing short of malicious.

"Do you think she's English, Captain?" Nye asked, a tremble in his whispered voice.

"Pray she is not," Alden answered.

The sky lightened gradually, and the four men kept their gazes upon the limp piece of cloth that would reveal the ship's origin and thereby determine the *Belladonna*'s destiny. Alden's stomach turned with worry, and his mind with different scenarios. If the ship was indeed English, he had no doubt *Belladonna* would be boarded. If she was Spanish, French, or even a privateer vessel, he didn't imagine there was much chance they'd be left alone with a salute and a wish for a happy voyage.

He thought through various plans, his eyes flicking to the tell tail, a hanging light rope that indicated the wind's direction. The unidentified ship was upwind, which made outrunning her the *Belladonna*'s best option. And they would be ready to do so before the ship was close enough to be a threat.

"Make ready to hoist the sails," Alden said. "On my command. But silently."

Dobson left to wake the crew.

For the next few moments, shadows moved about the *Belladonna*'s deck, climbing aloft, running along the yards, and loosening knots. The only voices were whispers, but in them Alden still heard worry.

Finally a beam of sunlight broke the horizon, brilliant as it shone over the rippling water.

A breeze fluttered the ship's ensign, and Alden's stomach dropped. The Union Jack.

He squared his shoulders. There was no choice but to outrun her. "Set sail," he called, not bothering to remain silent. With the morning light, the English sailors had no doubt seen them as well. They would recognize the set of the canvas, and the *Belladonna*'s course would be known immediately.

The sails dropped, swelling with the northeast wind as they were adjusted to the right angle.

"Captain! Off the port bow." Dobson pointed.

Another ship sailed toward them from the southwest—directly in their path. The second ship was downwind, and her progress would be slower as she tacked back and forth in a zigzag motion. But she was definitely moving in their direction.

A cannon blast sounded, sending men scrambling as the first ship fired a warning shot across their bow.

"Lie to!" Alden yelled the order to bring the ship to a stop. He balled his fists and glared toward the English ship. Smoke from the cannon blast blew toward him. He clenched his teeth. "And prepare to be boarded."

The English ships drew closer, and the crew of the *Belladonna* could only watch, glancing nervously between the two ships and one another. The morning meal was forgotten, and the night watch didn't go to their berths. None of the deckhands began their morning duties. And Alden didn't bother to give orders. Dread settled heavily onto the crew, dispelling the frantic energy they'd felt moments earlier as they'd prepared to flee, and they all waited silently. Charlie stayed close to Stafford's side, her eyes wide with worry.

The nearer ship drew alongside, just over fifty meters off the starboard.

Dobson offered a spyglass, and looking through it, Alden saw the golden letters on the arch board that read *Falcon*. The *HMS Falcon*. He recognized the name. The ship had been stationed at Fort Albion, an English fortification in Chesapeake Bay on Tangier Island. Both Alden's pride and his ship been wounded when Alden and his brother, Jacob, had joined Joshua Barney's flotilla to attack the island nine months earlier.

Alden paced, watching as dinghies filled with redcoat marines were lowered over the side of the *Falcon*. The English sailors took their time, knowing the *Belladonna* had no choice but to wait.

One man stood in the bow of the lead ship, the brass buttons and epaulets gleaming against his blue coat and identifying him as a captain.

Alden turned to the portside, looking through the glass toward the *Falcon*'s sister ship, *HMS Lark*. She drew nearer, but sailing against the wind kept her moving at a slow rate. Unfortunately, she was still within firing range.

He motioned for Dobson to join him at the portside rail and spoke to the quartermaster in a low voice. "Hopefully all they're after is supplies. The instant they leave this ship, bear away. Use the wind and aim directly for the *Lark*."

Dobson nodded, squinting toward the ship off the portside. "Aye." A glint came into his eyes. "We'll overbear her. Steal the wind from her sails."

"It will give us an advantage, though a brief one. They'll be windbound until they adjust their sails." He ran a finger over the rail. "And a head start is all my beauty needs to outrun those corvettes. Neither will fire when the dinghies are still in the water or when we are still between. They won't risk shooting one another."

"A good strategy, Captain." Dobson nodded. "We should sustain, at worst, minimal damage."

Aiming the bow directly for the *Lark* would make the *Belladonna* a narrower target. They'd be more difficult to hit, especially if the *Lark* was still on a tacking course.

Alden grimaced, his hand tightening on the rail, wishing he could protect the ship and the crew on it. "Let us strive for *no* damage."

The *Belladonna*'s crew drew back toward the stern as English marines armed with cutlasses and muskets clambered over the side and boarded the ship. The redcoat soldiers aimed their guns, bayonets shining, at the frightened sailors.

Alden was furious. "Cowards," he muttered through clenched teeth. They'd brought the larger weapons—utterly impractical for boarding a ship—for no reason other than to frighten his crew.

Charlie shook as she held on to Stafford's arm.

"Stand down," Alden called. "You can see we offer no resistance."

"You, sir, are hardly in a position to be giving orders," said an arrogant voice. The *Falcon*'s captain stood on the deck, one hand in his jacket's breast and the other lying limply over his sword as if he were posing for a portrait. The man was young for a captain, in his early forties, Alden guessed. His powdered hair was held back in a silk ribbon, his uniform immaculate. The captain glanced around the deck, his gaze lingering on the spot where the deck was still undergoing repairs. He sniffed and brushed lint from his jacket sleeve.

Alden folded his arms. "There is no excuse for honorable men to point bayonets at unarmed sailors."

The captain waved a hand, and the marines stood to attention, weapons held at their sides. He crossed the deck to Alden, walking with graceful steps, and Alden didn't consider that assessment of his movements to be a compliment.

"You must be the leader of this . . . ah . . . company." He motioned toward the crew with a jerk of his chin.

"I am."

The English captain looked back to the marines. "It's doubtful they carry anything of value." He motioned toward the companionway with a flick of his fingers.

Half the redcoat soldiers went belowdecks while the others remained to guard the *Belladonna*'s crew.

The stuffy captain turned back to Alden, giving a sniff as if he were quite bored with the whole process of raiding and plundering merchant ships. "And what is your name, sir?"

"Alden Thatcher, Captain of the *Belladonna*."

"Charmed." He glanced over Alden with a curled lip. "*Captain*, are you?" He smirked at the title, bent his wrist, and touched his fingertips to his chest. "Captain Sir Percival Alfred Harrington, at your service." He spoke the words slowly, letting Alden know they were important.

Alden kept his arms folded and simply watched Captain Harrington. He was no doubt expected to bow or show some sort of deference to the man's name and title, but he didn't care one fig who the man was or how important he thought himself. He just wanted the prancing buffoon off his ship.

Captain Harrington shook his head. "Such poor manners. Not wholly unexpected, as you are American." He sniffed again, adjusting his sleeve. "But as a guest, I did expect a more courteous welcome."

"An uninvited guest hardly warrants such treatment," Alden said.

The smirk returned, followed by what Alden could only describe as a giggle. "Ah yes, we did just *pop* on over without warning, didn't we?" He waved his hand as he spoke.

One of the marines strode from the lower deck—a heavyset man with a scar crossing his nose and down his cheek to his jaw. "Only tobacco, sugar, and coffee, Captain." He spoke in a croaky voice that sounded like it came from the back of his throat.

Captain Harrington lowered his eyelids and shook his head sadly. "Oh well. I was wrong to get my hopes up. What I wouldn't give for a warm cup of Darjeeling."

Now it was Alden's turn to smirk as he thought of the Indian tea hidden behind the secret panels in the hold. He glanced toward where the marines still guarded his crew, saw Charlie's fearful eyes, and felt a resurgence of anger. He was grateful Stafford stayed with her.

"Take whatever you like," Captain Harrington said to the marine. "I imagine the crew will be pleased with the tobacco. Heaven knows we have plenty of sugar and coffee in Jamaica." He darted a quick glance at Alden, as if he'd said something he shouldn't have.

Alden kept his gaze on his crew, pretending he hadn't heard. He wasn't surprised to learn the English fleet was gathered in Jamaica. The island was a British colony, after all, and Negril Bay was the perfect place to assemble an invading force. But apparently the fact was one the English navy wished to keep secret.

Captain Harrington took a few steps to the side and looked to the bow, studying the figurehead. "The *Belladonna*." His voice was thick with sarcasm. "Another name for the poison nightshade, the beautiful yet deadly flower. What a dramatic moniker, Mr. Thatcher." He turned back toward Alden, resting one hand on his hip, the other drooping limply once again over the hilt of his sword. "I seem to remember your ship. She was at the battle off Tangier Island, was she not? Sustained a few well-aimed shots, I believe."

The man was attempting to raise Alden's temper. And it was working. Alden clasped his hands behind his back and watched the marines taking the smaller barrels from the lower deck. He guessed they weren't interested or equipped to remove the hatches for the larger hogshead barrels.

The men eased the barrels over the side and onto their small boats and then returned to the *Belladonna*'s deck, standing to attention and awaiting orders.

Captain Harrington's haughty smirk grew into something much more sinister, and an evil gleam sparked in his eye. "Now, let us have some fun, shall we?" He walked toward the crew.

The back of Alden's neck prickled.

The marine with the low, croaky voice followed him toward Alden's crew, bayonet fixed and pointed. He used the weapon to spread the men apart as they backed away from the sharp blade.

Charlie hung on to Stafford's arm until the bayonet was aimed at her, and then she moved away, her eyes wide and face chalky.

Alden had seen the same terrified look on her face twice before, and this time it not only hurt his heart but spurred his anger. "That is enough, Captain."

Captain Harrington didn't acknowledge Alden. He pointed toward Stafford. "I think this one, don't you?"

The marine nodded, motioning two others forward.

They took hold of Stafford's arms, pulling him away from the crew.

"Tom!" Charlie started after him, but the marine's bayonet swung toward her again, and she froze, eyes darting in panic between the blade and her friend.

"Maybe one other?" Captain Harrington tapped his chin, as if considering. "But not the scrawny boy."

Alden marched forward, pulse pounding in his temples. "You will not take my men."

A dozen muskets were lowered, forcing him away from the English captain.

Captain Harrington pointed at Gardner. "Escort them to fetch their belongings," he said in a bored voice.

The marines pulled Gardner away from the other crewmembers to join Stafford.

The man's face was terrified as he looked back at the crew then to Alden for help.

"You can't take them!" Charlie screamed.

The captain walked slowly toward her. "What did you say, boy?"

Alden's heart clenched. "Charlie, don't." He started forward but was repelled once again by the bayonets.

Tears shone in lines on Charlie's cheeks as she looked up at the English captain. "Please, don't take them."

The sound of desperation in her voice and the tears on her cheeks made Alden's throat tight. "Charlie, step back."

"Perhaps I shall change my mind about this one," Harrington said to the leader of the marines. He studied Charlie then raised his fist to deliver a blow. "The navy would teach the brat some respect."

Alden's heart thrashed in his chest. Terror and anger pushed energy through his veins with painful force until he shook. "Captain Harrington!" he roared.

The captain spun, fingertips pressed to his breastbone. His eyes were wide. "Oh my. I believe we touched a nerve." He motioned the marines to step aside and walked toward Alden. "So angry, Mr. Thatcher."

"You will leave this ship immediately." Alden ground out the words. Red tinted the edges of his vision. "You have the tobacco. Leave my men alone. They are Americans. You have no claim on them."

Captain Harrington tipped his head and puckered his lips as if seriously contemplating what Alden had said. "You know, you're right."

Alden blinked.

"Except for the fact that *my* men hold the weapons. And you . . . you are a bit helpless." His malevolent sneer returned. "Oh, and I almost forgot about this . . ." From his breast pocket he drew a pistol and straightened his arm, pointing it at Alden.

"No!" Charlie screamed, but Marchand drew her back, whispering frantically.

"I had thought to take the ship," Captain Harrington said in a conversational voice. "Though she is poorly maintained"—his gaze flicked toward the hole in the deck—"she would still be a valuable prize. As would all of these prisoners." He pointed backward with a flick of his fingers, though his gaze and his pistol remained on Alden. "But then I remembered Chesapeake Bay and how gratifying it was to blast holes through this vessel." He stamped his foot on the deck. "Don't you think there is just something so satisfying about completing a task?" He gave a shrug. "I admit, I am a perfectionist."

"You are a coward," Alden said.

"And yet I don't feel cowardly at all." Captain Harrington shrugged and cocked the pistol. "I shall enjoy this."

From the corner of his eye, Alden saw Charlie sobbing, comforted by Marchand. Helplessness made him want to scream. He was so angry he'd led his men into this trap that he could hardly see through the fury. They had depended on him for protection, and he had failed.

He straightened his shoulders, lifted his chin, and gave his men a nod that he hoped they found encouraging. He believed in them, trusted them. They were his shipmates. If this was indeed the end, he would stay strong for them. He wouldn't shame all of them by breaking down or begging for his life. He most certainly wouldn't give Captain Sir Percival Alfred Harrington the pleasure.

Alden pulled his gaze from his crew and glared at Captain Harrington. "You would shoot an unarmed man?" He shook his head, his expression disappointed and taunting. "I was right. You truly are a coward."

"Unarmed?" The captain closed an eye and sighted along the barrel. "I thought all Americans were armed with self-righteousness and moral superiority."

"Don't forget a razor-sharp wit." Alden flicked the curl on his forehead. "And devastating good looks."

Captain Harrington fired.

Chapter 13

THE PISTOL'S BLAST ECHOED ACROSS the deck.

Charlotte froze, watching in shock as Captain Thatcher fell. *No.* Her insides went cold, and she looked at the others, searching for support or help or someone to tell her she was only imagining it, but the rest of the crew just stared as well.

She pulled away from Marchand and ran across the deck to the captain. No one stopped her. She didn't know whether the marines had been told to allow her to pass or whether they simply didn't care now that the *Belladonna*'s commander had fallen.

"Captain." She fell to her knees, feeling helpless. Blood covered his shoulder and pooled on the deck beneath him. Charlotte patted his face. "Captain, can you hear me?"

He opened an eye and groaned. "That really hurt."

"Lie still," Charlotte said.

Captain Thatcher's eyes rolled, and his head lolled to the side.

"Oh drat." The English captain peered down at them, his lip curled. He shook his head. "I'd meant to kill him. Would have made for a much more sensational exit." He sniffed and handed his used pistol to a marine. "I have such a flair for the dramatic."

Charlotte glared at him, her tears turning to anger. She opened her mouth to tell the horrible man exactly what she thought of him but stopped when she felt a hand on her arm.

Marchand knelt next to her. "Remain silent, Charlie. You cannot help Captain Thatcher if you are dead." His voice was sharp.

Charlotte was taken aback. She'd never heard the soft-spoken man speak in anger. But as her temper cooled and she saw the situation clearly, she realized the need for the reprimand. Feeling a calm determination, she held Marchand's gaze and nodded to tell him she had control of her emotions.

The English captain gave another sniff. "Farewell, Mr. Thatcher. I suppose it is destiny that you will still be alive when I blow your ship from the water." He strode away to supervise the marines. Charlotte searched for Tom among them but caught only a glimpse of him in the commotion as the redcoats moved to the gunwale. Some had already climbed over, descending on ropes to their small boats. She wiped a sleeve over her face. Now was not the time for tears. She looked back at Captain Thatcher. His face grew pale as he lost more blood. "What do we do for him?"

Marchand pulled back Captain Thatcher's coat and unbuttoned his shirt, exposing the bloody wound in his shoulder then rolled him to the side, looking at his back. "Ze bullet went clean through."

"Is that a good thing?" Charlotte asked.

"*Oui et non.*" He shrugged. "We do not need to remove a bullet, but he bleeds from two wounds."

Following the Cajun man's direction, Charlotte helped remove Captain Thatcher's coat and shirt completely.

Captain Thatcher groaned again as they laid him back, flat onto the deck.

"Don't worry, Captain," Charlotte said in a comforting tone. "We'll take care of you."

Marchand wadded the shirt against the wounds on the front and back of the captain's shoulder. "Press here and here," he told Charlotte. "Do not worry that you use too much force. We must stop the bleeding."

Charlotte scooted closer, hardly noticing the blood that soaked into the knees of her trousers. She slid a hand beneath the captain and pressed his shoulder between both palms. She glanced up and saw that only a few redcoats remained on the ship and they were preparing to climb over the rail. Her heart was heavy when she saw that Tom had gone.

"*Oui.* Just like that, Charlie," Marchand said, placing his hands over hers, and pushing with even more force. "When the bleeding stops, we will stitch closed the wounds."

Charlotte nodded, grateful the man kept a cool head in an emergency. Seeing Captain Thatcher pale and unconscious made her insides shaky. She was glad to focus on a task to keep from panicking.

Mr. Dobson yelled a command, startling her. The *Belladonna*'s crew jumped into action, scampering up the rigging, pulling on ropes, and calling out to one another as the canvas shifted to catch the wind.

Marchand glanced up at the sails and then to the quartermaster, his eyes narrowing thoughtfully. "Excellent plan," he muttered. "Overbear the *Lark.*"

The quartermaster supervised the crew, hands on his hips as he looked over the sails, then gave a nod and strode toward Charlotte and Marchand. "Get the captain below." He called for Mr. Nye to assist.

The ship surged forward, and Mr. Dobson's jaw tightened in a look of determination. He started toward the stern, calling back over his shoulder. "Stay with him, Charlie. And be prepared. We may be fired upon."

Mr. Nye and Marchand lifted Captain Thatcher, and Charlotte kept the shirt pressed against his wounds as they made their way awkwardly down the companionway and to the captain's quarters.

The men heaved him onto the low wooden berth, putting his right side to the wall, so Marchand could doctor the injured shoulder, and then Mr. Nye left to help the rest of the crew.

Captain Thatcher groaned again.

Marchand opened the portholes to lighten the room. He stepped next to Charlotte and motioned for her to move her hand. "Ze blood is slowing, but it still has not stopped completely." Setting back the wad of shirt against the wound, he pushed her hand over it. "I will return in a moment."

Alone with the captain, Charlotte studied his face, worried he was growing even paler. Or did she imagine it? She knelt beside the berth, keeping the pressure on his wounds. "You must heal, Captain." She spoke in a quiet voice meant for his ears only, resting her cheek against his. "Please. I could not bear to lose you too."

Marchand returned with two lanterns, a bucket of water, and a surgery kit. "We need more light if we are—"

A blast from outside stopped his words. It was followed closely by another.

Yelling and running feet sounded above.

"Marchand . . ." Charlotte's gaze darted to the porthole. She could smell smoke. "They are shooting at us."

"Do not pay attention to what happens above, Charlie. We have a job to do. One that requires focus."

Charlotte forced her breathing to calm, though it was difficult as another volley of blasts sounded.

A crash came from the upper deck. The ship shuddered. Men yelled out. They'd been hit.

Charlotte wanted to scream, but Marchand put a hand on hers. "Focus, Charlie."

"Focus," she repeated, looking back at Captain Thatcher. She drew in a jagged breath and then another until the trembling inside her stilled.

Another cannon blast sounded, but this one was most assuredly behind them and seemed more distant.

Marchand pulled the chair close and set one of the lanterns on it. He held the other over Captain Thatcher and motioned for Charlotte to lift the bloody shirt.

Marchand bent close. He pinched the edges of the wound together with his fingers. "Hold ze lantern," he said. "But do not release the pressure on his back."

Charlotte obeyed, holding the light steady as Marchand stitched the injury closed. She listened, trying to perceive what was happening above. The shouts had stopped as well as the cannon blasts. She hoped they were out of danger from the other ships.

When he finished, Charlotte helped him turn the captain onto his side and held the lantern again as Marchand stitched the exit wound.

"How is it you can do this, Marchand?" she asked. "Do you have surgeon training?"

Marchand did not look away from the task. "If a man lives long enough, he learns a skill or two."

"Have you sewn a bullet wound before?"

"Oui. Many."

"And the injured men—did they . . ."

"No, Charlie. They did not all survive," he said quietly.

She swallowed through a dry throat. The thought that Captain Thatcher could still succumb to infection or fever or lack of blood terrified her. And the sadness in Marchand's voice made her ache inside. He'd known loss, seen people he cared about die, just like she had.

Once the wounds were stitched, Marchand dipped a rag into the water and cleaned the blood off the captain.

Charlotte assisted, noticing the bunched, discolored scars on Captain Thatcher's torso and side. "He's been injured before." She pointed to the marks. It was a good sign, wasn't it? He'd mended before, which might be an indication that his body was able to do so again.

"Captain Thatcher is a complicated man," Marchand said. He smiled fondly, dropping the rag and Captain Thatcher's bloody shirt into the bucket. "Somehow he manages to be extremely lucky and extremely unlucky at the same time."

"He was very brave today," Charlotte said. "Standing his ground against that horrible Englishman the way he did."

Marchand's expression turned sober. "The English captain is a coward who thrives on intimidation. Captain Thatcher knew this and kept the man's attention on himself to spare the crew." He looked at the captain. "He knew fully the risk to himself."

Charlotte gazed at the captain as well. Her admiration for him grew. He was an honorable leader who cared for his men and was willing to put himself between them and danger. "He must recover," she said in a soft voice. "He simply must."

Marchand returned to the partitioned wood box that held the thick thread, hooked needle, and other surgical instruments. He opened a jar of strong-smelling ointment and smeared it over the stitches and then pulled out clean strips of cloth and, with Charlotte's help, bound the wound and wrapped Captain Thatcher's arm snug against his body. "This way, when he wakes, he will not use his arm and tear ze stitches," Marchand explained.

The smell of fish stew wafted through the door to the captain's quarters. Charlie felt a twinge of guilt that she hadn't helped prepare the meal. "Should I fetch you something to eat?"

Marchand shook his head. "Dobson ordered you to remain with ze captain, and so you shall. I will fetch food for you. And something for his pain." He glanced toward the captain.

"I still need to do my duties. The lower deck must be swabbed after the meal, and with less men to do the work . . ." Charlotte spoke halfheartedly. She was reluctant to leave Captain Thatcher.

Marchand gathered the bucket of bloody clothes and the surgical kit. "Your most important duty is to care for our commander." He opened the door and then turned back, glancing down. "Your clothes will need to be cleaned as well." He pointed with his chin toward the sea chest. "The captain will have spare trousers for you to wear."

When he left, Charlotte made certain the door was closed and peeked into the sea chest. She snatched out the trousers she'd worn before and closed the lid quickly, not wishing to intrude on the captain's privacy, and hurriedly changed from her own blood-soaked trousers before Marchand returned.

While she rolled down the too-wide waist, the sound of the captain's voice made her jump and spin around. Her cheeks burned at the thought that he'd been awake while she changed her clothes. But his face was turned away, and when she got closer she saw his eyes were shut. He was muttering in his sleep.

Charlotte knelt back on the deck. She brushed the curl from his forehead, noting that his skin was cool. "Hush now," she said, in the same singsong tone her mother had used when she or Will had been sick. "Rest yourself and heal, Captain."

Marchand returned with a bowl of stew, a biscuit, and a tin cup and indicated for her to eat. He showed her a small bottle. "Laudanum," he said, pulling out the stopper. "Only a few drops now and again at sunset." He lifted Captain Thatcher's head, dripping two drops onto his tongue. Then he held a cup of water for the captain to drink. When he swallowed, Marchand laid the captain's head back down.

"He feels cold," Charlotte said. "Should he be covered? Or will it bring on a fever?"

"Keep him warm," Marchand said. He yawned and rubbed his neck, bending his head from one side to the other.

Charlotte noticed his eyes were red. "When did you sleep last?" Charlotte asked.

Marchand didn't answer.

"You were on night watch," Charlotte said. She took the bottle from him. "Go on, now. It is time for you to sleep. I will care for the captain."

Marchand gave a small smile. "Do you give orders now, Charlie?"

She shook a finger at him. "Mr. Dobson and Captain Thatcher would tell you the same thing. You need to sleep."

The Cajun man yawned again. He glanced at the captain.

"I will wake you if anything changes," she said, giving him a push toward the door.

"Aye, aye, Charlie." He looked pointedly at the bottle in her hand and then wrapped her fingers tighter around it. "It is all we have."

"I understand." Charlotte made certain the stopper was tight and then slipped the bottle into her pocket.

Marchand pointed to the tin cup. "And he must drink. As often as possible."

He started through the door, but Charlie stopped him. "Was anyone else hurt?" she asked. "In the cannon fire?"

"No, Charlie."

She let out a relieved sigh.

Once Marchand had gone, Charlotte closed the portholes to the cool breeze and hung the lanterns from the hooks on the deckhead. She covered Captain Thatcher with the wool blanket on his berth, tucking the edges around him, and deciding he was not warm enough, she put aside her scruples about trespassing on his space and opened the sea chest wide. Inside she found two more carefully folded coats.

As she took them out, she saw a small pile of books. One was a Bible, one had to do with winds and sea currents, and the last appeared to be a picture book of India. She didn't investigate, already feeling as if she'd been too nosy. But she wondered about the books. Had the Bible been a gift from his mother? Or a friend? Was the captain interested in India? Charlotte realized she knew hardly anything about the man. She closed the sea chest, feeling a guilty relief that it hadn't contained a painting of the beautiful Marguerite LaFontaine. She draped the coats over him and held his head up as Marchand had done, dribbling a bit of water into the captain's mouth and waiting for him to swallow before laying his head back.

She sat on the chair, feeling utterly exhausted. How much time had passed since she was awoken by Mr. Dobson's whispered command of "Beat to quarters"? She listened to Captain Thatcher's deep breathing, thinking the laudanum must be taking effect. She hoped he felt no pain and no worry about his crew or the condition of the ship.

And what was the condition of the ship? She'd heard and felt a cannonball's impact somewhere. She had no idea of the extent of the damage, but she would take it as a good sign that the ship wasn't filling with water.

She rested her head back, touching the pendant at her neck, and her throat tightened. *Tom.* In the chaos she'd lost track of her friend. If only she could have bid him farewell, told him what his friendship meant to her . . . The tightness turned into a choking, and she covered her face with her hands so her sobs wouldn't wake the captain.

What was Tom doing on the *HMS Falcon*? Were his new messmates cruel to him? Did he have to swab the decks? Or was he climbing aloft to the upper yards where he belonged? Was he looking for sea birds to add to his book? Did he miss her?

That feeling of helplessness as a person she loved was pulled from her arms, the ache and desperation it left behind, was becoming far too familiar, and her heart couldn't handle the strain. It was simply too much.

***

Charlotte jolted from sleep. She blinked, getting her bearings as her heart calmed and her familiar nightmares receded. Overhead, a lantern swung. She glanced around, pulling herself into a sitting position. She'd fallen asleep on Captain Thatcher's sea chest.

From his berth, Captain Thatcher watched her.

She grimaced, imagining she'd cried out in her sleep. "I'm so sorry, Captain. I woke you, didn't I?"

"Could have been you." He shifted, wincing, and his already-pale face turned even whiter. "Or it could have been this infernal hole in my shoulder."

He rubbed his eyes. "My head feels like it weighs a hundred pounds. Did you give me the laudanum? We have only a small amount on board."

"Stay still." Seeing that he was trying to sit up, Charlotte brought the cup. "Marchand said you need to drink since you lost so much blood." She held up his head as he drank and then eased him back carefully.

Captain Thatcher groaned, closing his eyes. "I really didn't think he'd shoot me."

Charlotte pulled up the blanket to cover his shoulders. She touched her hand to his forehead. He didn't feel fevered.

"Did they take Stafford?" Captain Thatcher asked.

"Yes," she said quietly. "And Mr. Gardner."

His eyes squeezed. "I'm sorry, Charlie."

Her eyes burned. "You have no reason to apologize."

He opened his eyes, taking a moment to focus. "I led us into danger. I didn't protect my crew."

"You couldn't have predicted—"

"It's my job to predict. As the captain I am responsible." He clenched his jaw tight.

Charlotte worried becoming upset would hinder his recovery. She considered giving him more laudanum but didn't know how long it had been since sunset. She thought she should wait until Marchand approved another dose. She sat on the chair. "Marchand said you purposely diverted the man's attention from the rest of the crew to protect us." Charlotte spoke in a calm voice meant to soothe. The captain's eyes were drowsy, and she hoped he would fall back asleep. His cold skin and pale face worried her. "You acted very bravely."

A small smile pulled at his mouth, and he closed his eyes again. "Apparently Marchand—and you—have a much higher opinion of me than does Captain Sir Percival Alfred Harrington."

Charlotte settled back into the chair, sliding down to rest her head against the back.

Captain Thatcher's eyes opened again. "Who's Will?"

She didn't ask how he'd heard the name. She must have said it in her sleep. "My little brother."

"He was at Fort Mims as well?"

"Yes."

Alden winced. "How old was he?"

"He was seven years old. Now he's nine." Seeing the question in his gaze, she continued. "We were both captured but, soon after, separated."

"And you're searching for him."

Charlie folded her arms. "I heard the other group was being taken to New Orleans. So that is where I must go. I have to find Will. I promised him."

Captain Thatcher's blinks became longer. "I know . . . people in New Orleans, Charlie." His voice sounded slurred. "I will help you find your brother."

His eyes closed, and this time he didn't blink them open. His breathing deepened.

Once she was utterly and completely certain he was asleep, Charlie brushed a kiss on Captain Thatcher's forehead.

Chapter 14

ALDEN STRETCHED HIS ARM, PULLING his coat around his back and over his shoulder. He grimaced at the pain as he twisted. Where was Charlie? She knew just how to adjust the sling or maneuver his sleeve without sending bursts of pain through his shoulder. After another painful attempt, he just fastened the clasp at the neck.

He sat back on the berth, feeling light-headed from the exertion of putting on his coat and frustrated with himself for not healing quicker. It had been three days, after all. How long did one require to mend from a fancy little pistol's bullet wound? He rubbed his eyes, feeling sullen. He hadn't slept well the night before, and he blamed the restlessness on Charlie's absence.

Since the moment Captain Harrington's bullet had dropped him to the deck, Charlie had scarcely left his side. She and Marchand had even fashioned a small pallet—or rather a nest—of blankets so she could sleep on the scant deck space in Alden's quarters and remain near should he need her during the night.

She had returned the day before to her regular duties. And while she checked on him often, he missed her constant presence. He'd grown used to the sound of her breathing and the little noises she made in her sleep. He glanced at the deck, feeling guilty. The space was so small, he didn't think anyone but Charlie—or perhaps a beagle—could have slept comfortably in it.

He stood again, pushing a hand against the bulkhead as his head swam. He ran a hand through his hair, wishing Charlie were here to comb it and tie it back. He didn't like to appear unkempt in front of his crew. He wanted them to have confidence in their leader, especially after being boarded by the enemy. A captain with unmanaged curls who couldn't even put on his own coat was hardly inspiring to morale.

The lower deck was empty, save for the night watch crew snoring in their berths. When he emerged onto the main deck, he glanced around to assess, but the sunlight made his headache flare. Keeping his gaze downward, he made his way to the stern and climbed up the steps to join Dobson and Mr. Ivory on the quarterdeck.

"Good to see you up and about, Captain." Dobson moved his hand as if to slap Alden's shoulder, but fortunately, he stopped before making contact.

"Morning, Captain." Mr. Ivory picked up a bundle that leaned against the quarterdeck rail and started to pull it apart.

"What in blazes is that?" Alden's headache wasn't letting up, and he was irritated to see the strange bundle of what appeared to be broom handles and canvas on his quarterdeck, which he expected to be kept in pristine condition. He leaned against the rail.

"Charlie found it in a storage closet." Mr. Ivory set the contraption onto the deck. It was a chair. "Thought you'd need a place to sit."

Alden sneered at the chair. "I am not an invalid, and a captain does not *sit* on the quarterdeck."

The instant he finished the sentence, Charlie joined them. "Captain, you're up early. I didn't expect you to be dressed and on deck." She took his arm and gave a tug. "Come, have a seat."

Alden sank into the chair, surprised to find it so comfortable. He rubbed his eyes, deliberately avoiding the gazes of the quartermaster and the boatswain, both of whom he fully expected to be repressing a laugh at his expense. If only his head would stop spinning.

"You're still a bit pale." Charlie bent down to look at his face. "But much improved." She unhooked his coat and removed his sling, sliding his wounded arm carefully through the coat sleeve, then retied the wrappings. "I'll return in just a moment with some breakfast."

As she hurried below Alden glanced up at the other two men. Mr. Ivory looked away quickly, and Dobson coughed into his hand to hide his smirk.

Alden was too fatigued to feel angry, and he knew they were still worried about his health and would not tease. He was fully aware that the swabbie was being a mollycoddling nursemaid, but the thought of making light of the situation or defending it was exhausting. He lifted his head, the motion making him dizzy. Walking onto the deck had taken all of his energy, and he wasn't certain how he was going to make it back down to his cabin. He imagined he could rest in this chair for a long time. Perhaps even take a nap in the sunlight.

He looked back to the main deck, squinting as he appraised the state of the ship. The hole in the deck was fully mended, thank the heavens. Mr. Yancey and Adam Day were painting the gunwale on the portside, where he'd been informed the *Belladonna* had taken a hit from the *Lark's* cannons. That the ship was in one piece and none of the crew injured—except for himself, of course—was nothing short of a miracle.

Charlie brought a bowl of mush and a cup of grog, but instead of setting it onto Alden's lap, she handed the tray to Dobson and spread a blanket over the captain's legs instead.

Alden opened his mouth to protest the treatment. If he'd had enough blood for a blush, he was certain his face would be red with embarrassment. A captain should command respect from his crew, inspire confidence, and here he sat wrapped in a blanket, eating mush.

"The crew is pleased to see you on deck." Charlie tucked the blanket beneath his legs. "Everyone has been so worried." She set the tray onto his legs. "It is a comfort to all of us to have you back where you belong."

She left, and Alden took a drink. Her words were exactly the comfort he'd needed. Perhaps it *was* encouraging for the men to see that he was recovering. Even if the healing was frustratingly slow.

"We're approaching the city, Captain," Dobson said. "A decision must be made soon. By tomorrow at the very latest."

Alden nodded, chewing on the thick mush. He and Dobson had discussed at length over the past days precisely how to approach New Orleans. As Alden saw it, they had three options.

If they were to land at Barataria Bay, the *Belladonna* could berth safely among the small islands. Jean Lafitte and his men would see to all of their needs. Lafitte would help to smuggle the tea into the city and even sell it. At a cost, of course. Alden liked the idea of the pirate's protection, but the bayous between Barataria Bay and the city of New Orleans could take days to cross, even in the preferred barges, pirogues. The water would be low in the winter, impeding their passage further, and the weather was unseasonably cold this year. Alden worried he was in no condition for the journey.

A further concern was the recent discord between Governor Claiborne of Louisiana and the Barataria pirates. Jean and his brother, Pierre, had already been jailed once, and Alden had no way of knowing if the governor had followed through on threats to drive the Baratarians from the bay.

Another approach to the city was from the east, through Lake Borgne. But this route posed problems as well. The lake would be low this time of year, and again reaching the city would require travel through miles of cold bayous. And Alden didn't like the idea of leaving the *Belladonna* unprotected in the large lake.

He imagined Andrew Jackson's defenses were already set in the swamps leading to the city, making the passage even more difficult.

The most obvious route, of course, was directly up the Mississippi River. The ship would berth in a safe port, and entering the city proper would require no extra travel. But his primary concern in that approach was the English invasion. If the city had already been taken, his ship would be seized as a spoil of war, and he had no idea what would happen to his crew. They might even be fired upon on their approach.

But, as Dobson had argued numerous times, the English could be anywhere. They did not know the enemy's strategy. Perhaps they had taken the lake already, or Barataria Bay. There seemed to be no safe answer.

"We'll take the river," Alden said. "If we are fortunate enough to reach New Orleans ahead of the English, we'll be able to help in the city's defense."

Both men looked at him with surprise.

Alden shrugged his one shoulder. Until three days ago, he'd been primarily concerned with the wellbeing of his ship, the selling of the cargo, and preparations for another voyage. He'd sought to avoid the conflict completely, having experienced quite enough of the war in Washington City. But recent events had changed his mind.

Dobson nodded, relief filling his expression. He was a loyal first mate, not allowing his personal feelings to color the decisions made in behalf of the crew and the voyage. But Alden knew the man was anxious to get home to his family.

Alden sent away the breakfast tray and settled fully into the chair, closing his eyes and listening to the sound of the waves against the ship's hull. And as he fell asleep he allowed himself to imagine how satisfying it would feel to accept Captain Harrington's surrender.

***

Hours later Alden sat heavily on his berth. He'd managed an entire day on the deck and even taken a meal with the crew. And doing so had taxed his energy more than he would have believed possible. His head ached, his shoulder throbbed, and he felt like every time he opened his eyes, the room spun around him.

A knock sounded at the door, followed by Charlie's voice. "Captain, do you need anything?"

He nearly sobbed in relief when he heard her. But he kept his voice nonchalant. "I could use help removing my boots."

"Oh." Charlie came near and touched his forehead. "Captain, you look dreadful."

He gave a wry smile. "I *feel* dreadful."

She knelt and took hold of his boot, one hand across the toe, and the other behind the heel. "You really should have rested more today. But I am happy you came on deck."

Alden braced himself for the pull, but he should have known Charlie would move carefully. She gently tugged off one boot and then the other, setting them beside his sea chest.

Charlie bent down, looking closer at his face. "You overexerted yourself." She untied the sling and set the cloth strips aside then pulled one arm from his coat, easing out the other without moving his shoulder.

"I was tired of lying here all day," Alden grumbled.

"Do you want to heal?" she asked, hanging the coat on the back of his door.

"Of course I do." While he didn't particularly appreciate the reprimand from his swabbie, he knew she was right. He hadn't done himself any favors today.

Charlie scooted the chair closer and sat facing him. "I'm sorry, Captain. I didn't mean to snap at you. I just worry. If you were to take a fever . . ."

"I will rest tomorrow."

"Good." She took out fresh cloths from the surgical kit and lifted down a lantern from the hook on the deckhead. "Now, I am going to check your wounds, if you don't mind. Would you like some laudanum first?"

He lifted a brow. "Are you going to poke at them?"

She laughed, showing her dimple. "No, just make certain they are healing. Marchand is on night watch tonight. I could have him do it, if you would prefer."

"You are a hundred times gentler than Marchand," Alden said. "And I would like my mind clear. No laudanum."

"Very well." She unbuttoned his shirt, slipping it over his shoulder and tugging softly at the cuff to pull his arm from the sleeve. She unbound the bandages and brought the lantern close, inspecting the wound on the front and then moving around to look at the other.

"How does it look?" he asked.

She touched the backs of her fingers to the stitches. "They are red. But neither wound is hot. Or seeping."

"Seeping?" Alden wrinkled his nose and pretended to shiver, looking revolted.

"I'm glad they are not. Of course, I do not want you to have an infection. But also . . ." She scrunched up her nose and shivered, mimicking his exaggerated expression.

Alden grinned, knowing laughter would hurt his head. He sat obediently still while she bound the wound, enjoying the gentle feel of her touch.

"You've been injured before," Charlie said.

He nodded.

Charlie helped him into a clean shirt. "What happened? Did you anger another English captain?"

"Well . . ." He glanced down, pointing at the different scars between the sides of his unbuttoned shirt. "These were caused by an English knife." He pointed to two of the wounds on his ribs.

Charlie blinked, her mouth forming an *o* that emulated her round eyes.

He shrugged his good shoulder. "And here"—he pointed to a puckered scar on his side—"a musket ball. Luckily it was only a scratch."

"It doesn't look like a scratch." Her brows knit together as she fastened his buttons. "Did they happen in the war?"

"Yes, but not in the way you're thinking."

Charlie tipped her head.

"A few were the result of an ambush while I carried a message to Washington City, but the others are byproducts of my profession." He held still as she secured his arm once again in a sling she tied. "The blockades and the war in Europe have forced merchants to become smugglers." He shrugged again. "I just happen to be good at it."

He studied her face, hoping for a clue as to what she was thinking. Though it was not piracy, smuggling was not typically considered an honorable profession. Did Charlie think less of him?

She adjusted his pillow and helped him lie back.

He closed his eyes, thinking he'd not been so pampered since he was a young boy with a bellyache, and he was not ashamed to admit he savored the sensation. Quite a lot of time had passed since he'd felt so cared for. He was reminded of Jacob's wife, Lydia, tending to her husband when he'd been injured. She'd been so caring. Perhaps it was a quality all women possessed.

"You are quiet," Alden said after a moment. "Have I disappointed you?" He was surprised by how much her opinion of him mattered.

Charlie shook her head. "Of course not. I was just thinking."

"About . . . ?"

She fussed with the wrappings and his soiled shirt, and he got the impression she didn't want to meet his eye. "I hope you do not feel shame, Captain," she said. "Not for something forced upon you." She glanced up quickly then looked back down, her hands shaking as she dropped the wrappings into a bucket.

Charlie's words were not only meant to comfort him; he could see she sought reassurance herself. His heart felt heavy, and he wished he knew what to say to ease her pain. But any words he thought of felt trite. A surge of anger flared inside him, and an urge to punish violently the men who had hurt Charlie.

She pulled the blanket over him, tucking it around him. "Shall I extinguish the lantern?" Her voice sounded cheerful again, but he thought it was forced. "Or would you prefer the light?"

He would prefer for her to remain, at the very least until he was certain she was not upset. He grasped for a topic that might keep her there. "Tell me about Will."

Charlie looked surprised. She sat on the chair and rested her hands in her lap. Her gaze was far away as she looked past him. "Will is clever and silly and has an enormous heart. He is fearless. My parents and I spent most of our time trying to keep him from hurting himself. He is full of questions, just like any seven-year-old boy." Her shoulders sagged. "At least he was. I don't know what he will be like when I find him."

"And does he look like you?"

Charlie shrugged. "I've been told our eyes are the same. But his hair is thick and full of curls—like yours. His cheeks are soft and round, and I used to sneak up and grab him so I could kiss them."

Her smile held fondness as well as sorrow, and Alden's stomach went hard, knowing there was little chance her quest would end happily. If Will was still alive, if she managed to locate him . . . Alden didn't think there existed any possibility she would find the boy she'd lost.

"I have a brother as well. Jacob." Alden shifted, grunting at the pain in his shoulder, and closed his eyes. "We met in an orphanage in Washington City and were adopted by the same couple." He shook his head. "Jacob was the serious one. The protector. And I always managed to find trouble."

"Oh my. That is a surprise."

He kept his eyes closed but smiled at her teasing tone. "I suppose some things will never change." The two sat in silence for a moment, a silence that felt surprisingly comfortable. Alden hoped she was thinking of happy memories with her brother.

"Do you remember your parents?" Charlie asked.

"Distantly," Alden said. "I was six when they died, so the memories feel more like dreams."

"How did they die?"

"Smallpox."

"I'm sorry to hear it."

Silence again. Alden cracked open an eye and glanced at her.

Charlie twisted her fingers, and her lip shook. "Captain?"

"What is it, Charlie?"

"At Fort Mims everyone around me was killed. Everyone." She swallowed. "Mothers, fathers, children, babies . . . It was so . . ." She squeezed her eyes shut and shook her head. "I think about them all the time. Remember their faces. Their screams." Her voice had dropped to a whisper. "I don't know why . . ." She pulled up her feet onto the chair and wrapped her arms around her legs. "Why was I spared?" Her knuckles turned white as she held her legs tightly. "What made that Indian brave decide to take me as a prisoner instead of killing me too?"

"I wish I knew."

"It shouldn't have been me," she whispered. "Others deserved to live more than I."

Alden felt ill hearing her confession, her guilt over surviving, and the shame of her ordeal. "You lived so you could find Will," he said. He glanced at her hand, wanting to reach for it, but he couldn't move his arm in that direction. "Charlie, listen to me. I don't know whether it was divine Providence or destiny or simply luck that you and I were both spared when others around us weren't. But I do believe we owe it to those who died to make the most of our lives. To make the world better. To move past the things that hurt us. These people—our families—they loved us, and they want us to be happy."

Charlie brushed at her eyes. She looked at him and seemed to consider what he said. After a moment she stood. "Thank you for listening, Captain. I've not spoken to anyone about Will for more than a year. I was happy to tell you about him."

She tucked the blanket around him again and then picked up the lantern. "Your parents would be very proud of the man you've become, Captain Thatcher. And so would Marguerite."

Alden lay back and thought about Charlie's words long after she'd gone. The sound of Marguerite's name had taken him off guard. But the feeling didn't come with the shower of guilt that usually accompanied his thoughts of her. And the thing that surprised him most was that during the conversation, he'd not thought of her at all.

Chapter 15

"SORRY TO LOSE YOU, CHARLIE." Mr. Ivory frowned as he counted out coins from the ship's coffer.

"I am sorry as well," Charlotte said, feeling a tightness in her throat. She was nervous, uncertain of what lay ahead in the unfamiliar city, and she would miss the *Belladonna* and its men.

He laid a heavy hand on her shoulder. "Despite my initial . . . misgivings, you turned out to be a fine sailor."

Charlotte accepted the wages and smiled. "Thank you, sir."

"If you ever care to return, you'll be welcome on the crew."

Charlotte bid Mr. Ivory farewell, descended the gangplank, and stepped onto the New Orleans dock. Loud noises assaulted her from every side. A cold wind blew from the river, making her pull the coat tighter. Her toes felt uncomfortably smashed in boots she hadn't worn for weeks, and the land seemed to be swaying beneath her feet. After only a few weeks at sea, Charlotte felt like a fish out of water.

Captain Thatcher and Mr. Dobson stepped from a small official-looking building. The captain folded a paper and slipped it into his coat pocket. He stood tall, his face no longer pale and drawn. Aside from the sling on his arm, one would never know the man had been shot ten days earlier. He looked superbly handsome in his clean coat and polished boots as he gazed up at his ship and then along the docks. She thought it incredible that all the other people on the riverfront didn't stop what they were doing and stare at the man. When his gaze fell on her, he smiled.

Charlotte's heart flopped over, and everything inside her went soft. She walked across the dock to join him and the quartermaster.

The two men shook hands. "A good voyage, Captain," Mr. Dobson said.

"Aside from a barrage of bad luck and misfortune . . ." Alden tipped his head thoughtfully. "It was indeed memorable."

"And how would we have managed without our arbitrator?" Mr. Dobson gave Charlotte a warm smile. He shook her hand. "A pleasure to have you aboard, Charlie."

"The pleasure was mine, sir." She swallowed, feeling a wave of melancholy as she bid another of her shipmates farewell. "Thank you for taking me on."

"Best decision I've made in a long time," Mr. Dobson said. He squeezed her hand between both of his. "Good luck to you, Swabbie." He released her and stepped back, glancing between her and Captain Thatcher. "Now, if you will excuse me . . ."

"Go," Alden said. "Enjoy your family."

"Aye, aye, Captain." Mr. Dobson grinned, and, with a final wave at Charlotte, he was gone.

"He's right, you know," the captain said. "Your presence was a bright spot on an otherwise disastrous voyage."

He could have no idea how his words made her heart melt. She watched the dock workers with great interest until her blush cooled. "You said Marchand is coming with us to meet with your friend?"

Captain Thatcher nodded. "New Orleans is an interesting city, Charlie. Complicated. Marchand understands the politics and social nuances better than anyone I know. He grew up nearby and lived in the city for years before he went to sea. He's trusted in different communities, and having a native French speaker with us will go a long way to winning trust."

"And your friend is the one who will know about Will?"

Captain Thatcher's brows pulled together. He nodded. "If Pierre Lafitte doesn't know, he will tell us whom to ask."

Marchand joined them, and the three set off. Armed soldiers stopped them at the edge of the city but allowed them to pass once they'd inspected the captain's papers. The ship had been stopped twice by the American soldiers on their way up the Mississippi as well. Charlotte had felt a sense of heightened security as the ship was searched both times. The soldiers were preparing for invasion.

Charlie and her companions started down the dirt road that ran along the river. A high man-made bank rose between them and the water.

"Mr. Dobson went in the other direction," Charlotte said.

"Oui," Marchand said. "He lives in the American sector of the city. Above Canal Street."

"What sector is this?"

"Vieux Carré," Marchand said.

The word—or words—was French, Charlotte thought. She didn't think her mouth could form the sounds that made it. "Voo cahay?" she said.

"Oh, Charlie." Marchand closed his eyes, looking pained as if her inability to pronounce the word was a personal insult. "In English it is called the Old Quarter, where the wealthiest Creole families make their homes."

"When they're not on their plantations downriver," Captain Thatcher said.

Charlotte glanced at the captain and wondered if Marguerite LaFonatine had lived in the Old Quarter. Was he thinking of her now?

They walked past stucco and brick houses with shuttered doors and windows. On some blocks, structures were built directly against each other as if they were all part of one enormous building, but an occasional gate showed paths and carriageways leading behind the individual houses. Grand balconies hung over the walkway below, surrounding the upper stories and filled with potted plants. The roofs were sloped and made of red tile. Many of the doorways were arched, with columns between. Other homes stood alone, grand mansions surrounded by walls or iron fences. Charlotte wished the men would slow so she could study the stained-glass windows and filigreed ironwork of the gates and railings.

They stepped to the side as a company of soldiers marched past.

"Farther in zat direction is the Faubourg Marigny neighborhood." Marchand pointed with his chin.

"Is that where you're from?" Charlie asked.

"My people are Cajun," he said. "From French Canada. I was born in a small village on the bayou."

Charlotte nodded, moving to the side of the street as a carriage passed. "Do you plan to visit while we're in port?"

"I have not returned for almost thirty years."

She turned toward him, studying his face, but she couldn't read his expression. "Why not?"

"Ze woman I loved married another. So I left."

Charlotte tried to imagine Marchand as a young man in love. She wondered if he'd been brokenhearted like Captain Thatcher. Or had he been angry? He spoke now matter-of-factly about what had once, no doubt, caused him pain.

"But your family," Charlotte said. "Surely . . ."

"I have no one zere," Marchand said. "Not anymore. Ze sea is my home now, and ze crew my family. I intend to sail as long as my body is able."

What did Charlotte intend to do? She wished she had a set course like Marchand did. She would of course find Will, but then what? Where would she go? She would need to find work to support them. Would she remain in New Orleans? Since her family had fled their farm to the safety of Fort Mims, no place had felt like home . . . until the *Belladonna*.

They passed a tree-lined park, and Charlotte stopped, gazing up at the massive church beyond it.

"St. Louis Cathedral." Marchand crossed himself. "She burned down twenty years ago and has been rebuilt."

"Beautiful," Charlie breathed, studying the columns and spires. She'd surely never seen a building so grand.

The group continued on, nearing an area with shops and an open market on high land overlooking the river. As they drew closer, the street became more crowded.

Captain Thatcher glanced back at her. "Stay close, Charlie," he said. "And watch your pockets."

She kept a hand in her trouser pocket, clasping the pouch of coins and the silver ring as they walked, but she lost sight of the men more than once because she could not stop staring at the mixture of people around her. She recognized immediately the wealthy Creoles in colorful gowns and elaborate hats. The men accompanying them seemed to prefer wearing military uniforms with various medals and decorations. Among the crowd there were also working-class people tending shops, carrying children and bundles, or pushing carts. Their clothing looked more like what Charlotte was used to. Some moved in groups or families, others alone. She saw a group of rough-looking men, and her stomach tightened. She looked away quickly, not wanting to draw their attention.

Servants, soldiers, slaves, and even Indians gathered among the shops, but what surprised her most were the beautifully dressed dark-skinned women mingling among the wealthy crowd. In Mississippi she'd only known blacks as slaves. It seemed that in New Orleans the same rules didn't apply.

The sounds of music, of voices speaking various languages, the colorful clothes and people, and the smells of fish and butcher shops were new and fascinating. Charlotte craned her neck, wanting to see everything, to take it all in. Children ran through the crowd, and she looked closely at each face, searching for her brother.

"Charlie, there you are." Captain Thatcher took her arm and steered her though the crowd. They walked past the rough men into a small dimly lit shop.

Charlotte squinted as her eyes adjusted. It appeared the shop didn't specialize in one type of merchandise but sold everything from bolts of silk to weapons to exotic spices. She even saw a box of assorted shoes.

Captain Thatcher kept hold of Charlotte's arm as if worried she'd get lost again. And she kept hold of her coin pouch and ring, thinking this place looked rather disreputable.

Marchand spoke in French to a man on the other side of the counter. The man glanced at Captain Thatcher and Charlotte and then went into the back room. A moment later he returned and motioned for them to follow.

When they stepped through the curtain that separated the small shop from the back room, Charlotte gazed around, realizing they were in a warehouse of some sort, lit by sunlight filtering through high windows. Dusty boxes and barrels surrounded them, some partially opened or in the process of being unpacked. An assortment of wares was piled up haphazardly.

The French-speaking man disappeared behind a stack of crates and reappeared a moment later accompanied by another.

The new man raised a hand and grinned. "Alden Thatcher. Wondered if I'd ever lay eyes on you again."

When the man drew closer, Charlotte saw he was much older than she'd envisioned an overseer of a smugglers' warehouse to be. His hair was white, his back stooped, and wrinkles covered his face like cracks in a rock.

Captain Thatcher smiled and shook the man's hand. "I just keep turning up, don't I, Jim?"

"Like a bad penny," the older man grunted as he sat on a crate. He motioned for the others to do the same.

The captain touched Charlotte's arm, motioning with his head for her to sit near him.

"Jim, you remember Henri Marchand."

"I do." Jim nodded toward the Cajun man.

"And this is Charlie Bower, another of our crewmates."

"Charlie." Jim nodded to her.

"We'd hoped to see Pierre," Captain Thatcher said. "Is he—"

"Arrested," Jim said. "And, naturally, he's already escaped, but he's lying low for now. Governor Claiborne sent the navy after Lafitte's island in Barataria Bay."

Alden raised his brows. "Destroyed?"

Jim shrugged. "Parts of it. But of course Jean Lafitte is too crafty to store all of his valuables in one place." He turned a shrewd gaze to Captain Thatcher. "And to what do I owe the privilege today? You've something for me to sell, no doubt."

"Indian tea," Alden said.

"Always in demand," Jim said. "And possibly more so, should the city be taken by the English."

"You believe New Orleans will be invaded?" Alden asked.

"I do. English ships have already taken Lake Borgne."

"They think to invade through the bayous?" Marchand snorted. "An ambitious and foolish plan."

Jim gave a cruel chuckle, showing a mouthful of missing teeth. "I imagine the area looks much easier to traverse on a map."

"A pity the Americans drove away the Baratarians," Alden said. "They could have used their expertise. Nobody knows the bayous like the Lafittes."

"And that's just where things get interesting," Jim said. "In spite of the governor's offense, Jean Lafitte has thrown in his lot with Andrew Jackson. Made a bargain for the pardon of his men and gave the American general an enormous stash of weapons."

"Jean must think the Americans have a chance of holding the city," Alden said. He rubbed his chin. "What do you think, Jim?"

Jim scowled. "I think the English army is the most powerful in the world. They've not been defeated and have the advantage of troops and experience."

A slice of fear moved through Charlie's stomach.

"But . . ." Jim held up a crooked finger. "I also trust Lafitte's instincts. The man is never wrong."

Voices from the front of the store made Jim look up. The French-speaking man leaned through the curtain and asked a question Charlotte couldn't understand.

Jim gave an answer in French. He turned back to them and sighed. "Always work to do."

Captain Thatcher stood. "Thank you for your time."

The others rose as well.

"Glad to see you again, Alden," Jim said, shaking his hand. "Thought you'd stay away from New Orleans for good, hoping to avoid a certain lady."

"There is just one more matter, if you don't mind." Captain Thatcher motioned toward Charlie then stopped and tipped his head as if just registering what Jim had said. "I beg your pardon? What lady?"

"Mademoiselle LaFontaine," Jim said. "Don't imagine you'd want to chance a meeting with her, not after leaving the way you did."

Alden's brow furrowed. "Marguerite? But she died . . . the fire . . ." His voice trailed off.

"The Fontaine house was indeed burned, but all the family came through just fine," Jim said. "Away at their plantation house, I hear." He gestured over his shoulder with his thumb. "I saw Marguerite this past Sunday at mass looking hale and hearty."

Charlotte felt cold.

Alden pressed a hand on a crate as if he needed it to keep from falling over. He shook his head slowly back and forth. "René de la Croix told me she . . ."

Jim barked a laugh. "René de la Croix? You believed him? That man's tried to court the mademoiselle for years. The lady won't give him a second glance." He shook his head. "Looks like René pulled the wool over your eyes, my friend."

"I . . ." Alden's head snapped up, and his glassy gaze sharpened. "I must go." He spun and ran from the room.

Charlotte's heart shattered to bits.

Chapter 16

ALDEN STOOD BEFORE THE MANTEL in the drawing room of Chez LaFontaine trying to comprehend what was happening. He'd occupied this exact spot on numerous occasions, waiting for Marguerite, but this time . . . He shook his head.

This couldn't be real. How was it even possible? At Jim Stewart's words, Alden had felt like he'd been dropped into the ocean depths, and he'd still not found his way to the surface.

His mind was sluggish as he tried to make sense of it all. He glanced around the room, a room he'd never thought he'd enter again. A room he'd thought no longer existed. Much of it looked the same: a faux marble mantel with Vieux Paris style vases, ornate furniture on plush rugs, carved mahogany, and gilded gold frames surrounding expensive artwork. A newspaper lay on the table, printed in both English and French. But the wall color was different, as well as the carpets. Likely they'd been damaged in the fire.

The fire. He rubbed his eyes. He'd imagined the horror of that day so many times, pictured this house burning, flames licking the walls, windows shattering, beams collapsing and trapping Marguerite. He'd heard her frantic cries in his dreams. Could the entire tragedy have been nothing but a fabrication created by a jealous rival?

He paced to one of the balcony doors, looking at the street below. People gathered, he supposed for an event of some sort. He'd not even noticed as he passed by half an hour earlier in a daze.

Footsteps sounded behind him.

Alden's chest tightened. He drew in a breath and turned.

Marguerite LaFontaine stood in the doorway, her dark curls cascading over her shoulders. She looked complete and perfect, and very much alive. She also looked furious.

Alden had been away for months, almost a year, after promising to return within a few weeks. What could he possibly say to fix this?

Marguerite entered the room accompanied by the smell of magnolias. She moved with the grace of an aristocrat. One brow lifted. "I see you have returned, Alden Thatcher."

"Marguerite." He whispered her name, unable to convince his mind that what he was seeing was real. "It *is* you. I can't believe . . ." He reached toward her, wanting to touch her, to prove she was not an apparition.

"Can you not?" She glared at his outstretched hand and held his gaze with flashing eyes.

"I thought you were dead."

She tipped her head and blinked, watching him. The fire remained in her eyes, but her gaze was more curious now than angry.

"Last winter, when I returned from Hispaniola, René de la Croix met me at the docks. He told me you'd perished in a fire."

She faced fully toward him. "Last winter? You returned?"

"Of course I did. I promised I would."

Marguerite studied his face, and bit by bit, her expression softened as the anger dissipated. She crossed the room, taking his hand and laying the other on his cheek. "Oh, my poor Alden, *mon amour*. How sad you must have been." She dropped her hand to his chest. "Your dear broken heart."

She frowned, and the flames flashed in her eyes once more. "René is a villain. To go to such lengths to keep us apart . . ." She huffed out a breath. "But you are here now, and we can resume where we left off." She gave a slow blink, looking up at him through dark lashes. "I have missed you, Alden."

He knew that look and felt the familiar pull. He glanced at her soft lips and waited to lose himself in her gaze, but all of it was wrong somehow, like this moment belonged to his past. Marguerite's touch, her flirting glances had once filled his heart with warmth and desire but now felt . . . flat.

What was wrong with him? He'd dreamed of this, ached for it, mourned its loss, but now, looking into her eyes, he felt nothing but a friendly affection. "I—"

Marguerite stepped back, but she didn't release his hand. Her gaze took on a sharp perceptiveness as she studied him. "Alden, what is it? Your eyes." She pouted her lower lip. "You do not feel the same as you once did."

"I—" Did he? He loved Marguerite. He was certain he did. His memories of dancing with her, laughing . . . they filled him with a fondness. Seeing her alive was utter relief. Her smile made him happy; her beauty still astonished him. But the quickening heartbeat, the breathlessness, the longing to hold her . . . was gone.

But why? What had happened? Did it have to do with his mourning her death? The guilt he'd felt? The anxiety of a problematic voyage? His injury? He couldn't for the life of him figure out what had changed.

"Oh. I see." She dropped his hand. "You love another."

Another. Of course not. Alden dismissed the notion immediately. *I don't*— A memory washed over him. He lay in a semiconscious stupor, shoulder on fire, and felt her cheek on his, heard her whispered plea. He thought of the funny noises she made when she slept, her stubborn determination to climb the rigging, the line that appeared above her nose when she worried . . . The realization hit him with the force of a fancy pistol's bullet.

I am in love with Charlie.

The instant the thought came into his head, his nerves buzzed and his heart pounded. He knew with a surety it was true, and an urgency overcame him. He needed to find Charlie Bower, to be with her, to hold her and tell her—

He looked up, remembering he wasn't alone, and became aware of how very inappropriate it was to have such an epiphany in the company of his former beloved.

Marguerite watched him. And she knew. Her lip trembled, and her eyes were wet.

Alden's stomach turned into a rock. "I am so sorry, Marguerite. You must know I didn't leave you. I never would—"

"I know. I should have never doubted you, Alden." Her voice faltered, but she held up her chin.

He was hurting her, and he didn't know what to say to make it right. "I should not have come."

"You think it would be easier if you still thought me dead and I believed you'd abandoned me." She shook her head, blinking hard. "Love is not always easy, Alden."

He swallowed hard. Leaving behind his past was difficult. And knowing he was hurting her made his heart ache. He reached for her, pulling her into a one-armed embrace, and prayed she would find a man who adored her as she deserved.

"She must be very special." Marguerite pulled away and dabbed at her eyes with a handkerchief.

"She is," Alden said.

"And beautiful?"

Alden grinned, remembering when the swabbie with her shorn hair, shabby hat, and oversized clothes fell to the deck in front of him. Was Charlie beautiful? He'd hardly thought of her in those terms. But when he pictured her wide eyes, the one dimple, and her fifteen freckles, his heart felt like it might explode.

The urgency to find Charlie returned. "I should go."

"I am glad you came." Marguerite gave a sad smile. "I have truly missed you."

He winced.

"Do not worry for me, Alden Thatcher." Marguerite lifted up her head in her most dignified pose, but her eyes still looked sad as she forced an overconfident smile that held just the slightest tease. "I am young, beautiful, and very rich, *bien sûr*. I shall manage."

A moment later Alden closed the door to Chez LaFontaine, feeling the significance of leaving behind his old life. While he still felt sorrow, hopefulness lifted his despair. Ahead lay Charlie and their future together. He hurried back through the crowded streets toward the French market, realizing he'd left her and Marchand with hardly an explanation. They would understand, wouldn't they? Realize why he'd gone?

He wondered what Charlie must be thinking. Had his leaving to find Marguerite hurt her? Did she even care? He pulled up short. Did Charlie love him? He'd just assumed . . . The question opened the floodgates to countless others, and they tumbled through his thoughts.

If he declared his feelings for Charlie, she would know he'd guessed her secret. Would she feel deceived? Embarrassed? Angry? Would she believe herself to be the second choice since he'd left her behind to go find Marguerite? He could have kicked himself for behaving so carelessly. Why had he confided in her his love for another woman? Could Charlie trust his feelings for her were true? His stomach twisted with urgency. He needed to reach her, to explain. The crowd grew denser the closer he got to the city's central square, and Alden found it more difficult to move through the streets. Townspeople lined the upper-story balconies and crowded together in windows. Some even gathered on rooftops.

Finally he inquired of a passerby the source of the commotion.

"General Jackson's announced a procession in the Place d'Armes," the man responded, motioning toward the square in front of the cathedral. "A military parade."

Moments later the roll of drums was joined by a cheering crowd as two regiments of militia marched into the square. Local militia, Alden assumed, based on the cheers and waving handkerchiefs of the women in the crowds as their husbands, sons, and fathers marched past. Most of the militia were dressed in civilian clothing, and they carried an assortment of weapons: fowling pieces, rifles, muskets. And among them Alden recognized some of Lafitte's pirates.

Behind the militia marched the uniformed companies of the active army regulars, wearing full parade dress uniforms. The townsfolk continued to cheer, and martial music played as another regiment marched in—a battalion of freemen and, following the black soldiers, a company of Choctaw Indians.

Another line of men marched into the square wearing blue hunting shirts and wide-brimmed black hats. The men shouldered long Kentucky rifles, sharpshooters. "Beale's Rifles," the man beside Alden said in an excited voice.

Alden studied the gathered army, amazed by the brilliance of its commander. New Orleans was a city divided along racial and cultural lines. By parading freed slaves, Indians, farmers, pirates, woodsmen, militiamen, merchants, and colonials through the streets and gathering them together, General Jackson was making a statement. Uniting the various groups into one army, he showed the people who their defenders were, and the townspeople rallied behind them.

The crowd quieted as the general himself rode into the square. Sitting tall atop his horse, Andrew Jackson drew all eyes to him. He was a thin man with long legs and a shock of gray hair, whose sharp eyes and authoritative manner demanded immediate respect.

The general spoke to the gathered soldiers and the surrounding townsfolk in a commanding voice, and a translator repeated his words in French. He began by complimenting the people of the city for their bravery then urged them to continue the course as they prepared to meet the enemy. He promised the city not only safety but victory and then spoke to each of the military groups in turn.

The speech was inspiring to the soldiers and reassuring to the civilians. Alden was impressed by the man's poise and his strategy in unifying the city. It seemed simple, but it was imperative that prejudices and animosity be set aside if the army had any hope of standing against the English.

Alden walked through the square as the crowd dispersed. He imagined Charlie and Marchand would have come to the parade as well. If he didn't find them here, Marchand had a favorite inn where he would go for food and lodging while the ship was in port. Alden hoped Charlie would stay with him and not head off on her own in search of her brother.

He gritted his teeth, wishing he'd not acted so impulsively and left her. Hadn't he promised to inquire about her brother?

Not seeing either of them, Alden started toward the French market, planning to search there first and then go on to the inn.

He turned down a side street and saw ahead of him a group of soldiers.

The leader motioned toward Alden then strode toward him. "If you would please come with us, sir." The man was tall and slender, with a crooked nose. He spoke in a firm voice, as if anticipating an argument.

"Come with you?" Alden asked. "Where? Who are you?"

"Grant Harker, Provost Marshal." The man inclined his head. "You're a sailor?"

"I am."

The other soldiers moved to either side with slow movements as if to cut off an escape.

Alden's skin prickled, but he kept his posture casual. He'd done nothing wrong—well, aside from the illegal tea, but that was a matter for customs agents, not military police.

The man with the crooked nose watched him. "And you've not volunteered for service?"

"I arrived in the city only today."

The man nodded. "Perhaps you don't know, then. General Jackson has instituted martial law. You and every man capable of bearing arms are to register for service or face imprisonment."

But Charlie. Alden glanced behind him, gauging his chances of escape.

The flanking soldiers tensed.

"What is your name, sir?" the man asked.

Resigned, Alden sighed. "Captain Alden Thatcher."

"Welcome to the United States Militia, Captain Thatcher."

Chapter 17

CHARLOTTE SAT BACK ON THE crate—hard. Her insides felt like they'd been turned into cold water, and she hurt too badly to even weep. Captain Thatcher was gone. He'd rushed back to Marguerite without even a backward glance.

Marchand slipped an arm beneath hers and pulled her to her feet. "Jim, Charlie wished to inquire about his brother." He gave her a little push.

Charlotte looked at him, her mind taking a moment to understand what he'd said. *Oh yes. Will.* She forced aside her hurt feelings and remembered why she'd come to New Orleans in the first place. "Mr. Stewart, my brother was taken from Fort Mims by the Creek tribe. I believe he was brought to New Orleans." Her thoughts still moved slowly.

Jim frowned. "Fort Mims? The massacre? That was more than a year ago."

"Please, sir. Captain Thatcher thought Pierre Lafitte would be able to discover where he is now. His name is Will, and he's nine years old."

"And you're certain he came to New Orleans?" Jim looked toward the curtain, reminding them he had another obligation.

Charlotte shook her head, a rush of panic making her heart skip. He couldn't leave yet. "No. But I overheard the men talking about it. It was their intention to bring their captives to the city."

"I can get word to Lafitte," Jim said, looking back at her. This time his gaze took in her worn clothing. "But his network typically requires payment for their inquiries."

Charlotte pulled the pouch from her pocket, but Marchand put a hand over it, stepping in front of her to block Jim's sight. "Charlie, you cannot give him all your money." He spoke in a soft voice. "You must still pay for food and accommodations while you search for your brother."

She nodded, seeing the wisdom in his advice. She put the pouch away and fished out the ring. She refused to look at it, knowing she'd start to weep as she gave away the last tangible reminder of her parents. She held it in the palm of her hand and offered it to Jim, swallowing hard against her emotions as she did. "Will this do?"

Jim lifted the ring between two fingers and brought it close to inspect it with one eye. He glanced at her, studying her again. "It should be sufficient. Boy's name's Will? Can you give me a description?"

Marchand and Charlotte left the warehouse after shaking hands with Jim Stewart. He'd told them such an inquiry would likely take at least a week but to have faith in Lafitte's network. If the boy was or had been in New Orleans, they would discover it.

The pair decided to wait for Captain Thatcher in the marketplace, thinking he'd likely return to where he'd left them. Charlotte was surprised to discover the rough-looking men outside the warehouse were actually friends of Marchand. He introduced her, and she responded in the right places, but her emotions were raw and she felt too miserable for conversation. After a little while, they gave up on including her and reverted to speaking in French.

Perhaps Captain Thatcher wouldn't return. He hadn't given any indication he would. He was very likely becoming reacquainted with Marguerite LaFontaine. Perhaps the two were laughing over the misunderstanding or confronting René de la Croix about his deception. Even if he did return, it would only be to bid her and Marchand farewell as he returned to the happy life he'd thought was lost forever. She should be pleased that his broken heart was mended. That is how a true friend would feel—grateful for his turn of fortune. But try as she might, Charlotte could not.

The crowd began to move back toward the Vieux Carré, and Marchand's friends acted as if they'd go as well. After a moment of discussion, he turned to her. "Come, Charlie. There is to be a parade in the Place d'Armes."

They followed the crowd toward the main square, but soon the crush of people grew so thick Charlie grabbed on to Marchand's arm to keep from losing him. Music, drums, and cheering sounded around her, but Charlotte's small size prevented her from seeing anything aside from the people around her.

Noticing her dilemma, Marchand found a spot on a shopkeeper's step where she could stand and look over the crowd. He helped her climb up between the other spectators and remained close so they wouldn't be separated.

Charlotte watched the different companies march into the square, but she did not join in the cheering. She felt empty inside. The military companies looked distinguished and proud, even those without uniforms. Charlotte thought General Jackson's speech inspiring, but it worried her. New Orleans expected to be attacked, and she wondered what the result would be. Would fighting in the city keep her from finding Will? Would her shipmates be injured by the English? What about the *Belladonna*? If the English took the city, they would surely seize the ship. But Andrew Jackson's words were convincing. He thought the Americans could hold off the English army, even claimed they would be victorious. Were those words merely an act to keep spirits high? Or did he believe them?

The speech ended, and the crowd began to disperse.

Charlotte searched through the throngs for Captain Thatcher, but when she didn't see him she assumed he had probably watched the procession with Marguerite and returned home with her. She let out a sigh, feeling the tears that had threatened all day pricking at the backs of her eyes as she stepped down from the porch and joined Marchand.

"Come along, Charlie." Marchand's voice was gentle. "You will feel better once you eat." They started back in the direction of the marketplace. "In Farbourg Marigny is an inn which serves real Cajun jambalaya—not a fancy Creole imitation." He watched her, perhaps expecting an answer, but Charlotte's throat was tight, so she only nodded.

"I will help you find lodging, and you've at least a week to wait for news of your brother, so you will need employment as well." He continued to speak, even though she didn't answer.

He was right; her small pouch of coins would run out quickly. Tomorrow she would find work, and that should keep her mind distracted.

Charlotte wiped her eyes, gave herself a shake, and forced a smile through her melancholy. "*Merci*, Marchand. If not for you, I would be quite lost."

They entered a wooden building and sat at a table lit by a wrought-iron candelabrum. The room was crowded and noisy, with aromas of onions and roasting spiced meat coming from the kitchen and music from a band playing on the other side of the dining room.

Marchand ordered their meals in French from a young woman, and a few moments later she returned with two heaping bowls of sausage, shrimp, spiced rice, and vegetables, along with thick slices of crusty bread.

The smell from the jambalaya was strong, and Charlotte wondered what spices were used. The combination was unfamiliar, but it wasn't unpleasant.

Marchand took a bite and closed his eyes, savoring as he chewed. "*Exquis.*"

Charlotte took a bite as well, and a combination of tastes exploded in her mouth. She raised her brows. So much time had passed since she'd eaten anything so flavorful that it took her by surprise.

"*C'est délicieux, non?*" Marchand asked.

"Very delicious," she answered. Taking another bite, she watched Marchand. His eyes were unfocused, and a smile played on his lips. He seemed to be thinking of something far away. Or perhaps long ago. Charlotte realized that aside from the few facts he'd told her this morning, she knew almost nothing about the Cajun man.

"Tell me about your village, Marchand. You said you grew up on the bayou? What was it like?"

His gaze focused and turned to hers. "I imagine it was much like growing up in the Mississippi Territory. My village was very small, with only a few houses, a dry goods store, a blacksmith's shop, and a little school. On Sundays we took a pirogue to mass in a different town." He took a drink and ripped off a piece of the bread. "My parents lived in a small cabin where we raised chickens and tended the garden. *Mon père* and I fished and trapped animals for their fur. It was a pleasant childhood." He smiled and bit into the bread.

Charlotte smiled back. She liked hearing Marchand speak so contentedly. Reminiscing softened the lines on his face, and his manner was much gentler than the serious shipmate she'd known aboard the *Belladonna*. "Did your mother make jambalaya like this?" she asked.

His smile turned tender and his eyes warm. "Oui. But of course nobody makes jambalaya as well as *ma mère* did."

"Of course," Charlotte said.

Marchand took another bite. "She died when I was fifteen," he said. "And mon père a year later."

"You have no brothers or sisters?"

He shook his head. "Like I told you earlier, there is no one there for me anymore."

Charlotte nodded, spooning a piece of sausage. She understood him perfectly. Sometimes she thought she'd return to her old home in Bay Minette, but other times she thought seeing the surroundings of her old life would just remind her of what she'd lost. She glanced at her companion, wondering if she dared ask the question that pressed the most urgently in her thoughts. He'd been forthcoming and open; perhaps he'd continue in that way. She hoped her probing wouldn't make him regret disclosing such personal things. But she had to know.

"Your . . . the woman you loved . . . once you left, after . . . did the pain . . . ?" Her voice caught, and her eyes blurred. She blinked away the tears. "Did your heart ever stop hurting?"

Marchand studied her for a moment before answering. "The pain lessened, yes. But the regret remains, and the sense of loss." He gave a cheerless grin. "I was young and proud and said things I wish I had not." He sighed. "But such is life, Charlie. And I do not think I want the pain to go away completely. Or I might forget that what I felt for Gabrielle was real."

She considered what he'd said as they finished the meal, feeling overwhelmed and discouraged. His words were wise, spoken from years of experience, but Charlotte's heartbreak was fresh, and she didn't think she could bear the pain continuing indefinitely.

Three soldiers approached, weaving between the other diners. They stopped at Marchand and Charlotte's table. The man who appeared to be the leader had a thick barrel-shaped chest. He cleared his throat and rapped his fingers on the tabletop.

"Thought we'd wait until you'd finished eating at least." He glanced at Marchand and nodded then looked closely at Charlotte. "What's your age, son?"

A nervous quiver moved up her spine. "I'm eighteen."

"Small, aren't you?" The man shrugged and looked at his companions then back at her. "Can you hold a gun?"

She glanced at Marchand and saw that his brow was furrowed and his gaze intense. He looked worried. Frightened even.

"I can," Charlotte said. "My father taught me to shoot a rifle."

The man motioned for them to stand. "If you'd come along with us, please."

Marchand remained seated, the worried expression still on his face as he looked first at Charlotte and then at the barrel-chested soldier. "General Jackson has declared martial law?" Marchand pronounced the word *zheneral*.

"Correct." The man gave a sharp nod.

"What does that mean?" Charlotte asked. Seeing Marchand's worry was more frightening than knowing the English planned to invade New Orleans.

"Men over eighteen capable of bearing arms are required to participate in the defense of the city," the soldier said.

"Charlie, joining the militia means fighting the English." Marchand looked at her closely, as if waiting for her to say something.

Charlotte knew right away she didn't have to go. It would be easy to explain that she was not a man over eighteen. But where would that leave her? If Marchand went away to the militia, she would be alone in a strange city. And not only alone but alone as a woman. The thought terrified her more than joining the militia.

Marchand held her gaze steadily.

Charlotte straightened her shoulders. She would not even consider leaving her friend to fight alone. And if Will was somewhere in the city, she must do everything in her power to keep the enemy from invading. She wiped her clammy hands on her trousers and gave Marchand a confident nod. Then she stood, bowing to the soldier. "Charlie Bower at your service, sir."

Chapter 18

ALDEN HEFTED THE CANVAS BAG filled with small iron balls into the muzzle of the twelve-pound gun, pushing it in as far as he could and then used a ramrod to shove it the remainder of the way to butt up against the powder.

He grabbed onto the thick rope, heaving with the others on the gun crew to run out the cannon. The gun captain adjusted the aim then pulled the gunlock to fire. The blast shook the deck of the *USS Louisiana* and sent a ringing in Alden's ears. But after nine days of constant firing, the noise was no longer unsettling. Strange what a man could get used to.

He swabbed out the gun to extinguish any embers, and then the crew sat back to wait. Per General Jackson's orders, the firing was deliberately irregular.

"Water, Captain?" Turley offered a leather flask.

"I'm not captain on this ship." Alden took a long drink and glanced at the man from the corner of his eye. "How many times do I have to tell you?"

"Sorry, Captain." Turley winced, his dark beard bunching on his cheeks. "Feels strange not to call you Captain, Captain," he muttered.

"You might try Your Majesty. I wouldn't mind that. Or Your Supreme Highness." Alden handed back the flask. The ship he'd been assigned to was a ninety-nine foot sloop, a merchant ship fitted with cannons. He was relieved the general, so far, had no use for the *Belladonna* and also glad so many of his shipmates had been brought onto the *Louisiana*. He felt a responsibility for the men, liked them close, where he could watch out for them. But he spent an inordinate amount of time worrying about those who were absent: Gardner, Stafford, Marchand, and, of course, Charlie.

Charlie. Just thinking her name made Alden's breathing come fast as the familiar worry twisted in his gut. He tightened his hands into fists, frustrated he had no idea where she had gone or what she was doing. Was she safe? Had Marchand remained with her?

Though it was terrifying to imagine her alone, he feared even more that Charlie had been conscripted. As he considered various scenarios, he came to the conclusion that she would maintain her disguise. She wouldn't reveal herself as a woman to be left behind in the city. Not after what she'd endured. And if Marchand had gone to fight, he believed she would remain with him. Which meant his beloved Charlie could be at this very moment at the front lines in the path of English bullets. His lungs constricted, and panic invaded his thoughts.

Why had he rushed off so impulsively? he demanded again and again. If it were physically possible to do so, Alden would kick himself in the head for being such a fool. If only he knew she was safe, knew where she was, he could get word to her, explain.

But how would he even begin?

> *My Dearest Charlie,*
> *I apologize for deserting you in a filthy pirate's den to rush off in search of my previously thought-to-be-dead beloved. Curiously enough, I've come to the realization that while you were swabbing the deck of my ship disguised as a boy, I was falling in love with you, and . . .*

He rolled his eyes. Such a confession would need to be made in person. If he could even think of the words to convince her he'd not gone completely mad.

The boom of another cannon sounded from farther down the river as the *USS Carolina*, a schooner, fired. The two ships were anchored on the far side of the Mississippi, downriver from the American lines and directly across from the enemy's position. For the past week they'd acted as floating batteries, firing a steady barrage into the British camp. The intention behind the intermittent shots was psychological terror, harassing the English soldiers as the army gathered. Alden imagined the men in a constant state of fear, unable to sleep when the possibility existed of a cannonball or a burst of grapeshot falling on them.

Alden glanced up at the dark sky, wishing day would dawn and relieve him of the night duties. Rubbing his back, he grimaced and stretched his injured shoulder. Morning must be near.

He tipped back his head, remembering how Charlie had loved to find a quiet spot to gaze up at the stars. Was she looking at them now? He hoped she was doing so in a place of safety.

From their mooring on the far side of the river, the crews of the American ships had watched the English army grow day by day as more troops were brought on barges through the Bienvenue Bayou. Alden couldn't imagine how uncomfortable the enemy soldiers must be, cramped in a low boat with as many men as would fit, as well as ammunition, supplies, and weapons for a minimum of ten hours and then to finally arrive and not be permitted a decent amount of sleep. They must be exhausted, which is just what General Jackson wanted. Tired soldiers made mistakes.

The English army was camped in the field of one of the long plantations that stretched from the Mississippi River to the swamp. As plantation owners harvested their sugarcane at different times, the path toward New Orleans was an uneven mess of half-harvested fields, full patches of cane stalks, fences, irrigation ditches, and muddy farmland interspersed with the occasional deserted mansion. Between the river on one side and the swamp on the other, marching directly through the plantations was the only approach to the city. And Alden didn't think it would make for a pleasant walk.

Three days earlier, on Christmas morning, Alden and the crew had noticed a change in the mood of the English camp. The men cheered and moved about with new purpose, and he wondered if they'd all been visited by Father Christmas. But once the information from the other bank reached them, he learned the reality was much worse. General Edward Pakenham had arrived.

The man and his military strategies were famous on both sides of the Atlantic. A hero of the Peninsular War and brother-in-law to the Duke of Wellington, he was well-liked by his men and well-respected by his officers. Now that the general had arrived, Alden feared the invasion would begin.

The sky lightened, and for the first time in more than a week, the morning wasn't shrouded in fog. Alden and his gun crew started below for a well-deserved sleep.

Not bothering to wash the powder from his face and hands, Alden rolled into his hammock. He drifted to sleep immediately but was snatched from his slumber by a shout from the gun deck.

He and the others rushed up the companionway and to the rail. Across the river Alden recognized the glowing and smoke of a hot-shot furnace. Clumps of sticks and foliage were pulled away from the levee to reveal five cannons on hidden platforms, large naval artillery that was made specifically to broadside a vessel. The English must have constructed the secret battery during the night. General Pakenham had been busy after all.

A blast sounded, this time from the enemy's side of the river, the guns aimed directly at the *Carolina*.

All thoughts of sleep scattered. Seeing their sister ship was threatened, Alden and the other gun crews sprang into action, taking their battle stations and preparing their own cannons.

Alden loaded a cannonball, ramming it home. Then, in a practiced movement, he and the crew ran her out as he'd done hundreds of times since coming aboard this ship. But this time, instead of firing random shots against unseen enemies, the targets were clear, and hitting them vital. They aimed at the naval crews and their guns and, at Commodore Patterson's command, fired.

Downriver he saw the *Carolina* had only one gun capable of firing over the long distance. The crew fired with their twelve-pounder, and the *Louisiana* gave support, but it was apparent the English had the upper hand. Their weapons were superior, their aim expert, and the hotshot lethal to a wooden ship. None of the English cannons were disabled, but within five minutes the *Carolina* had been hit.

Smoke rose from the ship, directly in the center. Alden knew the position below the cables was not only difficult to reach to extinguish a fire but perilously close to the powder magazines.

Though he could not hear the shout, he could tell by the movement onboard that the order had come to abandon ship. Boats were lowered over the side as the smoke grew thicker. Within moments the ship was vacated. The *Carolina*'s crew rowed for shore just as the ship exploded.

The blast sent debris and ash into the air with incredible force, some flying so high as to land on the other side of the river. Glowing bits rained down through the smoke, and Alden's chest was heavy as he imagined Captain Henley watching what remained of his vessel sink into the water.

The English cheer could be heard across the water.

Alden scowled, thinking of names to call the enemy that would certainly have given his mother cause to wash his mouth with soap. But his anger turned to a cold wash of fear as the guns were swiveled on their platforms. This time they were directed at the *Louisiana*.

The first blasts missed completely, overshooting the ship and landing somewhere on the bank beyond, but the naval gunners were experts. They would adjust their aim, and it was only a matter of time before the burning shot hit the *Louisiana* as well.

"Furl the sails!" Commodore Patterson yelled from his position on the quarterdeck. "Weigh anchor! She's the only armed vessel on the river. Protect this ship at all costs!"

Men scampered up the rigging and across the yards, dropping the sails.

Alden joined the crew heaving the heavy anchor line. The moment the anchor came loose the ship shifted, but it was moved by the current, not the wind. There existed not a wisp of a breeze.

"Get her out of range!" the commodore yelled.

As another blast sounded, the boats were lowered, and men clambered overboard to take up oars. Towlines were run from the ship to the small boats.

Alden jumped over the side, motioning his crew to follow. They waded through the water until it was shallow enough to maintain their footing, and then a cable was tossed toward them as well.

The English cannons continued to fire, filling the air with smoke.

Alden set his crew along the rope, putting the larger men such as Turley on the end and spreading the remainder out along the line.

Commodore Patterson gave the order to pull, and as one the crew on the shore, as well as those in the boats, heaved. But the river pulled in the other direction, and the *Louisiana* didn't budge.

"Pull!" Alden yelled through clenched teeth. He pushed downward with his legs, leaning back and tugging on the cable with all his might. His muscles strained, and the coarse rope rubbed his hands raw. The bullet wound in his shoulder erupted in pain, but he didn't stop.

The men on the boats drew their oars through the water as quickly and with as much force as they possessed.

A shell smashed into the ship's deck, jarring it. The impact gave the crew a surge of strength as the possibility of the ship exploding like her sister became all the more real. Bolstered by fear and determination, they strained against the current, and the *Louisiana* budged. Inch by inch the crew pulled her upriver, towing the ship out of firing range.

Once the commodore gave the order to halt and drop the anchor, it was the Americans' turn to cheer. They were joined by General Jackson's army on the front line.

Exhausted, Alden dropped the rope into shallow water, rubbing his shoulder. Every bit of his body ached, and the burst of fear had ebbed, leaving him wrung out.

But the sounds of cheering and the knowledge that his men and the ship were safe gave him the strength to cheer with the others.

England may have superior weaponry, but they underestimated just how scrappy Americans could be.

Chapter 19

CHARLOTTE SCOOTED CLOSE TO THE camp's fire. She pulled the military blanket tighter around her shoulders, glad that at least for now the cold rains had stopped. Even though she'd been given new clothing, including a wool coat, she still had not been warm once in the seventeen days since she and Marchand were conscripted into the Louisiana Militia.

She leaned back her head, gazing up at the stars. Morning approached, but in the west the sky was still dark. The bugle would sound within a quarter hour, mustering the men for another day of training and ditch-digging.

General Jackson's defensive strategy was simple and consisted of widening and deepening an existing drainage canal that ran between two plantations. The trench extended from the Mississippi River on one end to the thick cypress swamp on the other. Without a ladder or bridge, crossing it was virtually impossible, especially with the high embankment braced with fence posts and strengthened with cotton barrels the soldiers had constructed on the American side.

The English army was encamped a few miles to the south, and Charlotte had seen their red coats on a few occasions as they tested the defensive line. Their only approach to New Orleans was along this stretch of land, and Andrew Jackson was going to make it difficult, if not impossible, for the enemy to get through.

When she'd been brought to the militia, Charlotte had been issued a musket, which she'd been told was similar to the Brown Bess muskets the English infantry carried. Quick loading, the weapon's aim wasn't terribly accurate, but when firing at a line of soldiers, the ball was sure to find a target. She'd learned that with the European method of combat—two armies facing one another in columns and lines across a battlefield—quick loading was preferable to aim. But for a man living in the hills of Kentucky or Tennessee, every shot counted and needed to be dead accurate. Feeding himself and his family depended on it. The frontiersmen used long rifles, and according to the men in her company, their aim was so precise they could "shoot out a squirrel's eye a mile away." Charlotte had committed the phrase to memory, thinking if she ever saw Mr. Allred again, he would love to hear about the Kentucky and Tennessee riflemen with their long hair and fur hats.

An occasional shot fired in the darkness. Though one ship had been sunk and the other moved out of firing range of the English camp, General Jackson had seen to it that the psychological warfare had not ceased. Tennessee and Kentucky sharpshooters filled the swamps on the enemy's right flank. Their deerskins kept them dry and warm as they stood camouflaged in knee-deep water all day and slept on floating logs bound together at night. If any of the enemy soldiers came near the no-man's land between the two armies, they risked a frontiersman's bullet or a sneak attack by the Choctaw Indians who blended into the swamps as well.

Digging ditches was fatiguing, and the men of Charlotte's company fell into their bedrolls each night, exhausted.

Charlotte, however found the quiet hours anything but restful, as she had nothing but time to ponder. Her thoughts returned again and again to Captain Thatcher. And when they did, her chest squeezed so hard she could scarcely breathe. She loved him, considered him her closest friend, but he was gone.

When Charlotte had lost her family, the pain had been intense, nearly paralyzing, but the captain hadn't been torn from her arms. Her insides felt crushed, and she felt foolish. Deep in the most secret part of her heart, she'd hoped . . . But of course that was impossible.

Even if he didn't love Marguerite, even if he knew she was a woman, she would hardly turn the head of a man like him.

Hearing a noise, she looked back and saw Marchand approach. He eased down beside her. "You are cold again?"

"Finally it's not raining," she said. "Maybe today we will see the sun."

"I doubt it." He handed her a hard biscuit then took a bite of his own. "I am grateful we had at least one real meal before ze provost marshals found us," he said, grimacing as he chewed.

The one exception had been two weeks earlier, on Christmas day, when the soldiers were served ham for supper and a dessert of bread pudding made by the ladies of the city. The holiday had pushed Charlotte further into her gloom as she remembered the last Christmas she'd spent with her family. Her parents had given her the special ring with its turquoise stone, and Will had been given a box of wooden soldiers. She remembered how peaceful it had felt sitting around the hearth with her family, drinking warm wassail and singing carols as a goose roasted over the fire and Will arranged his soldiers into rows on the rug. And now, two years later, she'd sold the ring to a smuggler for information about her brother's captors, her parents were dead, and she was building battlements in the freezing rain while the most powerful army in the world prepared to attack.

"You did not sleep." Marchand studied her face by the firelight. "Do not worry, Charlie, we will find your brother."

She forced herself to smile, knowing her friend was unaware of the full cause of her gloom and sought to reassure her.

The sky grew lighter, and the bugle sounded the signal for the camp to wake.

Marchand groaned as he rose, rubbing his back. He held out a hand to help Charlotte to stand. "Are you ready for another delightful day of digging, Charlie?"

She shrugged. "I almost think I'd rather be scraping the *Belladonna*'s decks."

"Oui," he said. "As would I."

In truth, Charlotte didn't mind the work. Her weeks of swabbing had strengthened the muscles in her back, arms, and legs, making the manual labor bearable. And she enjoyed the community. As she worked she heard soldiers speaking in French, English, Spanish, Indian languages, and backwoods slang. The men around her came from every imaginable background, from the wealthiest Creole to the poorest slave, but they worked together as brothers. The feeling of all the different groups coming together for one goal was inspiring, and she was happy to be part of it.

And she especially enjoyed when General Jackson rode along the line. The general would dismount and give direction and sometimes share a joke with the soldiers as they worked. He often spoke through translators, but the commander knew the names of many of the men, and Charlotte could see he was well-liked and even more well-respected.

As she and Marchand joined the other soldiers walking toward the mess tent for breakfast, another bugle sounded. The noise was distant, and the tune wasn't familiar. She cocked her head, uncertain if she'd truly heard it. It sounded again, and Charlotte realized it came from the direction of the English army's camp. But it was much too close.

A drumbeat started in the distance. A beat to arms.

"Battle stations!" David Sanders, a member of the Tennessee Militia, ran past with his rifle.

Energy spiked through Charlotte's limbs, and she felt dizzy.

Marchand grabbed on to her arm. "Stay close to me, Charlie."

They retrieved their weapons and took their assigned positions along the line. Looking over the battlement, Charlotte could see nothing but fog. But the drumbeat continued, and the disembodied sound sent a chill through her.

Charlotte loaded her musket with shaking hands, ramming the rod down and then pouring powder into the flashpan. The practiced movements helped calm her. She laid the muzzle over the top of the parapet, aimed toward the battlefield, and glanced to the sides.

General Jackson had assigned nearly three thousand men to the main line. They stood in position behind the breastworks, stretching from the Seventh Regular Infantry, Beale's Rifles, and the Regiment of Freemen on the right to the Kentucky and Tennessee Militias on the far left near the swamp. In the center, Charlotte stood shoulder to shoulder with the seven hundred Louisiana militiamen.

Cannons were embedded into the earthworks at intervals, sitting on specially designed platforms. They were manned by navy gunners, militiamen, and Baratarian pirates who stood at the ready, stirring hotshot with loggerheads in their furnaces.

Ahead of the line on the right side, a forward redoubt had been constructed as an artillery battery with two six-pounders that guarded both the levee road and the ditch in front of the breastworks.

Though their position offered the Americans a complete view of the battlefield, the fog still obscured any sight of the enemy. Blackened stones, the remains of the Chalmette Plantation house were the only blemishes in the thick gloom that covered the ground. Fearing the English might use the structure for cover, General Jackson had ordered the house be blasted.

Weapons loaded and artillery armed, the American line held their breath and waited, peering ahead into the fog. The only movement came from the whipping of the flag at the center of the line, flying the American colors. Charlotte's stomach turned hard as she wondered if it would still be flying this evening.

From the direction of the swamp a rocket fired, glaring red as it flew with a screech.

Charlotte ducked down, though it didn't come anywhere near.

"It is just a signal," Marchand said. "To begin zeir advance."

At his words, the red of British uniforms appeared as soldiers stepped from the fog. They marched in close ranks in a column of sixty across. Over their heads the sky was alight with rockets.

General Jackson rode the line. "They are only toys!" he yelled. "Don't fear the rockets. They can do no real damage."

On the American side the drummer boy played a marching beat. Charlotte looked up and smiled at Jordan Noble, a fourteen-year-old black boy whom she had grown quite fond of. He gave only a small smile in return, his expression serious as he performed his duty.

More rockets fired. The English column continued their advance, and on the right, close to the levee, another, larger force emerged.

Led by officers on horseback and wearing full uniforms, the advancing line appeared more like a parade. The soldiers marched in rhythm, and a proud company of Highlanders strode along in the rear.

"The soldiers don't look frightened at all," Charlotte said to Marchand.

"Zey expect us to run," Marchand answered. "Like ze Americans did in Washington City." He scowled toward the advancing enemy. "But today zey do not challenge inexperienced New England shopkeepers."

In a few moments the entire plain filled with redcoats.

Charlotte's pulse pounded in her ears, and she gasped.

"Steady, Charlie," Marchand muttered.

General Jackson took up position on the right side of the line. "Give it to them, boys; let us finish the business today." He held high his sword and brought it down. "Fire!"

The line erupted. The noise was utterly deafening. Charlotte held on to her musket, though she wanted to hide behind the battlement, squeeze her eyes closed, and cover her ears. The largest American cannon, a thirty-two pounder, shot musket balls into the advancing column, flattening a swath through the center. Men were flung through the air like dolls as hundreds were struck with one blast. Musket balls and rifle bullets hit their marks, and more Englishmen fell.

Charlotte's ears were ringing as she reloaded her musket, placing it onto the bulwarks and firing again. The well-trained British soldiers continued on, marching past their fallen comrades, and were met with the same fate.

On the left flank the frontiersmen were arranged in lines. One line would shoot and then move to the rear to reload their weapons. Their deadly aim dealt a fierce blow to the column carrying ladders and bundles of cane stalks intended to be used as fascines. The English plan to scale the battlements on that side were foiled, and their company ran for cover in the swamp.

The military band struck up the tune of "Yankee Doodle," playing along with the constant beat of Noble's drum.

From the west bank the battery lent support, firing across the Mississippi and into the English lines. Smoke filled the air with screams from rockets and men. Charlotte kept her eyes averted from the battlefield as she concentrated on loading and firing her weapon.

A cannonball from the English artillery struck the battlement in front of her, but the thick earth, strengthened with bales of cotton, repelled it as easily as a horse tail swatted a fly.

She looked over the breastwork and saw the battlefield had turned into chaos as men tried to reform columns. The officers attempted to regain some semblance of order but were shot from their horses, leaving the soldiers without direction.

An English officer rode on a white horse through the lines, calling out frantic orders to broken ranks. From his decorated uniform Charlotte assumed him to be General Pakenham, the commander the men had spoken of. As she watched, the general's arm was struck by a bullet and the horse shot from beneath him. His men assisted him onto a fresh horse, but a blast of grapeshot struck nearby, killing him and the men surrounding him.

A shout sounded from the right, and Charlotte watched, horrified, as a company of enemy soldiers scaled the battlement and seized the redoubt on the right flank. Taken by surprise, the Americans rushed away, across the plank that served as a bridge, to take cover behind the embankment.

The English soldiers swiveled the cannons toward the American line, but before they could load, the wealthy Creole group, Beale's Rifles, opened fire, picking off the enemy with their accurate shooting and expensive rifles. The near-tragedy was averted, and the men on either side of the shopkeepers and lawyers—freed blacks, Choctaws, and pirates—congratulated Beale's Rifles with cheers and pats on the back.

Exclamations came from around her, and Charlotte turned back, just as an Englishman rose over the summit of the American breastwork directly in front of her. Bullets hit him from all sides, and he tumbled over the embankment and into the enemy lines.

"Hold your fire!" Marchand yelled. He motioned to Charlotte, and with the help of two other men, they bore the injured Englishman from the line to a shady spot beneath a tree and laid him down gently.

Charlotte knelt beside him and took the dying officer's hand. Her throat ached as she watched the color drain from his face.

"What is your name, Major?" Marchand asked. Charlotte glanced at her friend. Though his voice was calm, she heard a tightness most would not recognize. He looked at the man's wounds but didn't bother to tend them. There were far too many.

"Wilkinson." The man moved as if he'd sit up.

"Rest easy, now. You are a brave man," Marchand said.

Charlotte swallowed hard, following Marchand's lead and keeping a composed countenance. Major Wilkinson laid back but pulled on Charlotte's hand, drawing her closer. "Communicate to my commander that I fell on your parapet and died like a soldier and a true Englishman."

"I will, sir," Charlotte said, tears choking her throat.

Major Wilkinson relaxed his grip, and, conscience clear, he died.

Charlotte looked up at Marchand and saw his eyes were teary as well. He helped her stand, and they returned to their positions.

When they reached the battlement, Charlie realized all had gone quiet. Even the music and the drumbeat had stopped.

She followed the gazes of the others on the line and saw a man approaching through the smoke, waving a white handkerchief on the end of a long stick.

At General Jackson's orders one of his officers approached, accepting the Englishman's surrender and his sword.

The American line erupted again, this time in celebration. The band played "Hail Columbia," as the defenders of New Orleans cheered and applauded their victory.

Charlotte felt a wave of relief. It was over, and they had won. But she couldn't quite find it in her to give a joyful yell when thousands of men like Major Wilkinson lay scattered over the Chalmette sugarcane field. She was pleased and humbled and dismayed all at the same time. The battle had lasted less than half an hour, and so much devastation had been wrought.

Marchand put an arm across her shoulders.

She leaned against him, feeling utterly wrung out. "It was so much worse than I thought it would be," she whispered.

"Oui." Marchand rubbed her arm. "But it is finished, and you are safe. For zis, I am grateful."

She glanced at her friend, realizing his worry hadn't been for his own life or for the city's protection, but for her. A warmth bloomed in her heart. Though he was typically gruff in his responses, Marchand cared for her as a father would, and Charlotte closed her eyes, letting the feeling wash away the fear and horror of the battlefield.

Chapter 20

ALDEN RUBBED HIS SHOULDER AS the next shift's gun crew arrived to relieve him, Dobson, Turley, Nye, Allred, and Nogales of their duties. They turned over the cannon and headed out of Fort St. Phillips. The artillery battery was set up on a higher level with drainage to keep the guns dry, but the same couldn't be said for the rest of the masonry fort; steady rains had turned the lower level into a pool of dirty water. Alden led the men along a ledge, skirting around the pool. Then, saluting the sentries, they left the fort and marched along the riverbank to the company's tents for supper and sleep.

He and his men shed their soaked clothes as soon as they entered the tent, removing from the clothesline the garments they'd hung to dry after their last shift and replacing them. The rotation of their clothing had become routine, as had gathering together beneath canvas coverings around the camp's fire as they ate their meals.

Alden sank down onto a dry patch of ground with a groan, and he rubbed his eyes. The constant blasting for the past weeks had left a ringing in his ears and a steady headache.

Turley distributed bowls of soup and a hunk of bread and cheese.

"How much longer can they keep this up, Captain?" Nogales asked.

"He's not the captain here," Turley reminded him.

"Major Overton is. Right, Captain?" Nye said.

Alden sighed, tired of correcting the men on titles and the chain of command. "I've no way of knowing, Nogales. The English ships have to run out of ammunition eventually." Luckily the American supply of balls and powder was steadily maintained by regular shipments from New Orleans.

Alden and Major Overton had discussed this very question at length. The fort's commander believed the assault was simply a distraction to keep the American army's attention while the English troops were ferried back through the bayou to their ships.

Alden agreed with him. The attack was merely a constant battering of cannon fire from a number of ships with no real attempt to take the fort or to sail farther upriver toward New Orleans.

He rubbed his eyes again, glanced up at the drips coming off the edge of the canvas, and moved farther beneath the cover.

After the disaster on the west bank, Alden and his men had been sent downriver to fend off a naval attack by Admiral Cochrane's flotilla.

Alden took a bite of stew, chewing a chunk of potato. The hot gravy warmed his insides. "This is good, Turley."

"Thank you, Captain."

"He's not the captain," Alden, Nogales, and Nye said in unison.

Eight days earlier, the English offensive had attacked General Jackson's main line. Alden and his crew, under the command of General Patterson, had kept up a steady crossfire from the west bank of the river over the English advance.

While the American line on the Chalmette Plantation had been victorious, the battery and defenses across the river were not so fortunate.

The night before the battle, General Patterson had received word that the English were digging through the levee. Just before dawn the enemy had launched barges armed with carronades and filled with soldiers across the Mississippi toward the west bank, but as Alden and the defenders watched, the boats were swept downstream. Apparently the commanders had failed to calculate the current, which was deceptively strong, and they'd landed much farther down the river than they'd intended.

The invaders had compensated by marching double time upriver, with their boats providing additional support on their right flank in a combined land and naval attack, charging through the smoke of the guns in an aggressive assault.

The American defenders had been pushed back, but rather than surrender the cannons to the enemy, Alden and the other gunners had spiked the cannons, leaving them unusable to the enemy.

If General Pakenham's plan had worked and the English force had landed in time, they'd have taken control of the battery, turning the cannons against the American line as the offense was launched, and the outcome of that day would have been quite different.

As it was, once word of the English surrender came from the other side of the river, the invaders were ordered back to camp, and the Americans claimed a victory that was by no means a result of the fight on the west bank.

Alden was sick when he thought of how close they'd come to losing the city. He shook his head, pulling his thoughts from the battle and listened to the men around him.

"Will you continue the story, Allred?" Nye asked.

Allred took a long drink and brushed crumbs from his shirtfront and trousers. He cleared his throat. "Well then, where was I?"

"Odysseus and his crew were preparing to sail past the island of the sirens," Dobson said in a bored voice. The quartermaster acted as if he was uninterested in the story, yet he was always the first to remember the details.

"Ah yes . . . the sirens." Allred shifted into a more comfortable position, leaning back on one elbow.

The others settled in as well, moving closer to hear over the sound of the rain.

"The sirens, you remember, were half-bird, half-woman creatures who sang an enchanted song that led any man who heard it to his destruction. The music was so sweet men fell under its spell and wrecked their ships upon the rocky cliffs of the island. You remember Circe warned Odysseus about the siren's song. He instructed his crew to stuff their ears with beeswax so they couldn't hear it."

A splash came from the water, and when Alden listened closer he thought he heard voices.

"Did the sirens have beaks?" Nye asked, his bushy brows pulling together. "Or mouths?"

"Listen," Alden interjected.

The group fell silent.

Another splash, and this one sounded as if it came from the river in front of the fort. Alden jumped to his feet and motioned to his men to follow.

Silently they made their way back along the path in the darkness and crept along the outside of the fort's walls to where they could get a better view of the water.

That his men didn't hesitate was a testament to how they trusted their leader. At least six gunships were firing constantly toward the fort, and they were walking right in the path of the cannonballs.

"A reconnoitering crew," Dobson muttered, pointing toward the shadow of boats moving on the water.

Alden could definitely hear voices now, and one in particular caught his attention. He recognized it the croaky-sounding man from the *HMS Falcon*.

Alden pushed back the wet hair that dripped water into his eyes. He motioned the group into a close huddle next to the fort's wall, speaking in a hushed tone. "Turley, Nye, and Nogales, move downriver. Don't let them see you, and watch where they go. I think the *Falcon* has joined the flotilla, but it must be out of sight, behind the bend."

"They may be delivering provisions and ammunition to the other ships," Dobson said. "Maybe messages."

"I believe you're right," Alden responded. He tapped his finger against his lip. "Dobson. You, Allred, and I will speak with Major Overton. If he'll grant permission, the use of a boat, and weapons, and once we know their position"—he grinned—"we'll plan a rescue mission."

The others nodded. "Aye, aye, Captain." Alden knew the men were tired of working a gun crew and looked forward to a bit of action, especially when it involved both punishing an enemy and getting their crewmates back.

The groups dispersed, moving through the mud. The rain was pouring heavily now, but instead of being bothered by it, Alden was glad. If the *Falcon* were truly around the river bend, it would be anchored at a fair distance from the other ships in the flotilla to give a decent swing radius, and if it was a supply ship, it would be out of range of the fort's cannons. The darkness and rain would help conceal the approach of Alden and his men, and they would have the element of surprise. If he could get onto the ship, find Stafford and Gardner, and escape without the *Falcon* calling for aid . . . He grinned, liking the idea of catching Captain Sir Percival Alfred Harrington unawares.

***

An hour later Alden and Dobson peered through the trees at the *HMS Falcon*. She was anchored around the river bend and not taking part in the assault. If he hadn't heard the marine's voice, Alden wouldn't have known she was there at all. Dobson was right—the ship must be delivering messages and provisions from the gulf.

Major Overton hadn't liked the idea of risking the gun crew and the possible loss of a boat, but when Alden had told him two of his own men had been impressed onto the ship and mentioned his previous experience smuggling boats and men past the English blockades in the Chesapeake, the fort's commander relented.

"Between thirty and forty on the crew, I'd guess," Dobson muttered. "Don't know how many are on the ship now. A quarter will be marines. We can't take all of them."

"A direct attack is too much of a risk." Alden squinted through the darkness. He thought he could make out two sentries moving on the ship's deck. "We'll need to get on and off that ship without being seen or recognized. The rain will help. And with boats coming and going throughout the night, there's a chance they'll just assume we're returning from a delivery."

Dobson shook his head. "The delivery crews are led by marines or officers. They'll notice if we board unaccompanied."

Alden considered. Dobson was right. Regular sailors wouldn't be sent off alone. With so many members impressed against their wills into the English crews, the sailors would be looking for opportunities to escape.

"A surveillance team could learn the routines, observe the watches, and determine when their defenses are down," Dobson said.

Alden nodded. "That would be the most prudent strategy. But we've no idea how long the *Falcon* will remain. If she's simply delivering supplies, she could easily weigh anchor at first light. We must act tonight, or we may not have another chance." He glanced at his quartermaster, knowing the man's mind was turning with scenarios. "We need a distraction."

***

Two hours later Alden, Dobson, Turley, and Nogales set out through the darkness, rowing toward the ship with wrapped oars to muffle the noise.

Alden was glad the cannon fire was on the other side of the bend, or their approach might have been revealed by the glare of the rockets. He kept an eye on the rail, but no heads or weapons appeared as they drew up alongside the ship. The small boats that had been going back and forth the entire night still floated in the river instead of being stowed on the deck. Apparently the errands were not finished.

Alden looked back and forth between the river bend and the ship's rail, his hands tight on the oars. This part of the plan had caused him the most anxiety, since it would leave them so vulnerable. If they were discovered before they even boarded, there was no chance of success.

"Where are you?" he muttered between clenched teeth.

A flicker shone between the trees, and Alden let out a relieved breath. Allred and Nye had come through.

A raft floated around the bend, alight with fire. Finding dry kindling in the wet swampland had been nothing short of a miracle, and with some lamp oil for accelerant, the craft shone in the dark, rainy night like a beacon—a beacon that would last for only a few moments before the rains put it out.

From above, Alden could hear the sentries hurrying to the starboard side of the ship to investigate.

"That's our signal." Alden led his men up the boarding nets, which, to Alden's relief, the English had not yet stowed, and peeked over the rail. Two sentries stood at the opposite side of the deck, watching the flaming craft float downriver.

"Should we wake the captain?" one of the men said.

"It's not a threat to us."

"I don't like it, Sergeant." The first man sounded worried. "Might be voodoo. New Orleans is filled with dark magic."

Alden's crew climbed silently over the gunwale and spread out on the wet deck. Dobson and Alden started below to find Stafford and Gardner, and the others went after the sentries. The plan was to take them by surprise, overpower them quickly, and then gag and bind them. Alden was reasonably certain his men wouldn't kill the sentries, but if asked to wager on his conviction, he'd decline, especially after the assault on the west bank battery.

Heart pounding, he led Dobson down the companionway, but below all was silent. The lower deck was lit only by a lantern, and the two moved instinctively to the shadows. Alden pointed toward the bow, where the crew's hammocks hung, and Dobson nodded, stealing away to find the two crewmembers.

Alden crept toward the stern in search of the weapons magazine. Aside from those the sentries carried, the other guns would be easily accessible but locked away, lest the crew use them to seize the ship. Alden couldn't imagine having to resort to armed guards to protect him from his crew. His men were more than just hired deckhands; he considered them friends, family even. A pity the English navy operated under such a different standard.

At the stern, a marine moved in the shadows. He had no doubt seen them come down the companionway, but the sight of men moving between decks was not enough to divert him from his guard duties, especially when nighttime missions were being carried out.

Alden moved slowly, remaining low and well away from the light. He located the weapons, set in an orderly row around the base of the main mast. A chain ran through the trigger guards, cinched with a lock. He crammed a wad of pine gum into the keyhole. He would have liked to disable the weapons completely, but the plan only required a few moments' delay should someone sound the alarm, and any other sabotage would either be too time-consuming or too noisy.

A hiss came from the companionway. Three figures stood there, backlit by the lantern. Alden grinned, recognizing the silhouettes of Stafford and Gardner with Dobson. He motioned them upward and turned to follow, but hesitated.

He glanced back at the stern to the closed door that led to the captain's quarters. An itching to go inside, to surprise Captain Harrington, to take revenge, was so strong Alden started forward. He could easily overpower one guard, and just thinking of the pompous captain sleeping helplessly twenty feet away was more than Alden could resist. In his imagination Captain Harrington wore a fancy pleated nightshirt and cap with a puffball at the tip. Alden reached for the handle, but stopped.

His motives were purely selfish. The hasty action could result in an alarm being sounded, and his crew could be spotted, captured, or even killed. And if he were discovered, what would become of Charlie? Above anything, he needed to return to her. Alden blew out a breath and let his hand drop, feeling a twist of regret that he wouldn't get his revenge. But he'd acted hastily before, rushing away without thinking, leaving Charlie behind in Lafitte's warehouse. And he'd regretted the impulsive action every moment for the past four weeks.

He crept back to the companionway and started to the upper deck. His men were no doubt already waiting in the small boat. Glancing to the starboard side, he saw the sentries in their red coats, bound hand and foot, gags tied around their mouths. Turning back in the direction of the boat, he nearly crashed into the marine with the scar.

"You." The man's eyes went wide, and he drew back, opening his mouth to yell, but Alden stopped him with a blow to the jaw.

The stocky marine staggered back, and Alden snatched away his gun, tossing it into the river, then rammed his fist into the man's gut for good measure. "Give my regards to your captain."

Having no time to climb down to the boat, he jumped overboard into the cold water of the Mississippi.

When he came up for air, he heard shouts and even some gunshots, but the night was dark, and he wouldn't be seen. He let the current carry him downriver, praying his men had gotten clear.

Still pulled by the current, Alden kicked his legs, making his way to the west bank, then crawled onto the muddy land and started back toward the fort. He estimated he had at least two miles to walk.

Twenty minutes later voices sent him taking cover behind a tree, but he recognized them when they drew near, and he stepped out to join his crew. "Did everyone make it out?"

Nogales jumped, startled by Alden's sudden appearance. "Captain!"

"I told you he could swim," Nye said.

Alden grinned, seeing the two restored crewmembers. He clapped Stafford and Garner on the shoulders. "Glad to have you back."

"Thank you, Captain," said Gardner. "For coming for us."

"You know I never leave a man behind," Alden said. He felt inexplicably happy to see the two men.

"Captain, where's Charlie?" Stafford asked, his voice soft.

"I don't know," Alden confessed. "We were separated in New Orleans. I believe she's with Marchand, but I'm not certain. Once this business is finished, I plan to go in search of her."

"She," Nye said. "Did you say *she*?"

"Yes, Mr. Nye," Dobson said as they started the hike back to their camp.

"Charlie's a girl?" Day said.

"No . . . ," Allred said. "Impossible."

"When we find Charlie, you can ask her," Alden said.

"You knew, Dobson?" Nye asked.

"I did."

"Why didn't you say anything? If I'd known . . ."

Alden marched ahead, the familiar impatience for the conflict to end making his jaw tight. They would find her. They had to.

He couldn't wait for her to see Tom Stafford. She'd be delighted her friend was safe. The familiar worry tugged at his thoughts. Would Charlie be happy to see Alden as well?

Chapter 21

CHARLOTTE DUCKED DOWN BENEATH A low-hanging swath of moss as she and Marchand rode through the bayou on a low barge. She heard trilling high in a tree and craned her neck, hoping for a glimpse of the bird that made the call.

General Jackson had released the volunteer militia troops four days earlier, and Charlotte and Marchand had gone directly to Lafitte's warehouse to speak to Jim Stewart. When he told them a woman from La Grand Pointe had taken Will, Marchand had gone very quiet. Charlotte suspected it was near the town where he'd lived as a boy, but she didn't ask him outright, sensing he didn't wish to talk about it.

Immediately after meeting with Jim, Marchand had arranged transportation with a fur trader who was headed in the direction of the village. The trip through the swampland was a quiet one. The fur trader spoke only French, and while he and Marchand spoke occasionally, he seemed used to spending time alone and not prone to long conversations. And Marchand was even more reserved than usual.

Charlotte felt selfish that her friend endured something that brought him such unease, but in truth, she couldn't do it without him. She didn't speak the language, she certainly couldn't find her way through the bayou, and when she finally reached Will . . . she didn't know what awaited her. Would those who had him be reasonable? Would they release him? Was he being treated cruelly? Would the curious boy she'd known still exist? Or had Fort Mims and the year after destroyed his carefree spirit? Having Marchand with her was a comfort, but it brought a bitter feeling of guilt.

They glided past alligators sunning themselves on logs and through narrow channels clogged with limbs, where they all three had to climb into the water and clear a path. When they'd returned to the boat, bits of duck grass covered their clothes.

In the evening they swatted insects and at night listened to the hooting of owls. Charlotte spotted turtles and egrets and herons, a pink spoonbill, and even a deer. She was watching a pair of ducks tipping forward in the water when Marchand called out, "*Arrêtez ici.*" He pointed to a bank between large cypress trees.

Charlotte looked closely but could see nothing to distinguish it from any other bank.

They drew near, and Marchand hopped onto the land then reached to help Charlotte. Bidding the fur trader farewell, they continued on foot.

"We are close to the village," Marchand said.

Charlotte's guilt wouldn't allow her to continue without clearing the air. "Marchand, I'm sorry. I know you don't wish to go to Le Grand Pointe. If you'd prefer, I could continue alone."

He glanced back at her. "You cannot trek through ze bayou alone."

"But I know the memories are difficult for you. I don't want—"

He held up a hand to stop her. "Charlie, whether it is ze hand of God or fate or simply luck, I believe zere is a reason people are brought together. And I know I am meant to do this, to bring you to Le Grand Pointe, to help you find Will." He gave a half smile. "Unfortunately destiny is not always comfortable—or convenient. And neither is friendship." At this last sentence his smile turned into a teasing smirk.

Charlotte warmed at his words. She knew Marchand was religious. And her own family had studied the Bible. But the horror of seeing her parents killed, losing her brother, and her subsequent captivity and treatment had made her feel God had abandoned her. Perhaps

He was never there at all. But as they walked through the bayou, the events of the past months and the people she'd encountered along the way took on a new light.

She thought of how she'd found a ship sailing to New Orleans, despite the English blockades, the American tariffs, and the city being under threat of invasion. The quartermaster had taken her on, even though she was inexperienced and small. She'd met a captain with ties to a pirate whose knowledge of the illegal practices in the city had located her brother. And she'd found a friend who not only spoke French but was from the very town where her brother was allegedly being kept.

Perhaps it was all a coincidence, but a stirring in her heart told her otherwise.

The route they took turned into a path, and soon, wooden structures were visible, spread out between the thick trees. Some were built back near the water, and others were closer to the path, with large gardens and animal pens behind.

Charlotte watched Marchand carefully, judging his reaction. He seemed calm, as usual, but beneath she could feel a tension. He pointed toward a building with a wide covered porch. "Ze dry goods store. We can inquire zere."

They climbed up the wooden steps and entered.

An older woman was behind the high counter, putting jars onto a shelf. The moment she saw Marchand her face lit in a wide smile. "Henri!" She rushed around the counter and grasped him by the shoulders, standing on her toes to kiss both of his cheeks.

Marchand's face reddened.

The woman spoke quickly in French, and though Charlotte couldn't understand the words, she could see the woman was overjoyed to see him.

Marchand visibly relaxed as they spoke, and a few times he even smiled. Once he could get a word in, he motioned to Charlie, introducing her.

The woman gave a nod. "*Bonjour*, Charlie."

"Charlie, this is Madame Guerin; she was a close friend of ma mère."

"Bonjour," Charlie said, self-conscious about her pronunciation of the French word. She held her hands behind her back to keep from wringing her fingers and appearing too anxious. They were so close to finding Will, and she knew she must be patient for just a few minutes more.

Marchand continued to speak, and Charlotte understood the word *frère* and Will's name among the jumble of French. She held her fists tighter.

Madame Guerin glanced at Charlie and nodded. "Oui." She pointed over her shoulder, speaking quickly.

At the name Villatte, Marchand's face darkened.

"Villatte," Charlotte said. "That is who has Will? Do you know them?"

"Oui." Marchand spoke in a clipped tone, making Charlotte wonder if Monsieur Villette was a particularly cruel person. Apprehension stole over her like a chilly wind.

Marchand bid Madame Guerin farewell and led Charlotte down the path without a word. He walked at a quick pace, and his movements were stiff. Charlotte didn't speak, though she was bursting with questions.

He stopped in front of a worn wooden fence and gestured to the house beyond. "This is ze Villette—"

At that moment a boy rounded the corner of the house, carrying a basket of eggs.

"Will?" Charlotte felt frozen. It couldn't be him.

The boy turned. He looked at the two curiously for a moment, and then his eyes rounded. "Charlie?" He dropped the basket.

"Will!" Charlotte screamed his name and rushed toward him, grabbing him in a tight embrace. Sobs tore from her throat as she held the brother she'd thought was lost forever. "Oh, Will, I found you." She pulled back, holding him at arm's length.

Will's face was scrunched as tears ran from his eyes. He buried his face against Charlotte, and she sank to the ground, holding him against her as they cried. She breathed in the smell of him, and memories crashed over her. "Will, Will, I'm here. It's all right now. Everything will be all right."

Will curled up in her lap like he used to when he was small. The sound of his cries made her both laugh and weep. She didn't think she'd ever felt such utter joy.

Charlotte brushed the curls from his forehead, looking down into his face. Will's cheeks were less round than she remembered, but he looked healthy. She'd been so afraid of finding him damaged by abuse and haunted by memories. She kissed his cheeks, and for the first time, he didn't push her away but snuggled close.

After a long moment, Will knelt facing her. He rubbed his sleeve over his eyes and tipped his head, studying her. He frowned and glanced behind her. "Who is this? And why do you look like a boy?"

Charlotte winced and looked up at Marchand. She'd wanted to find a gentler way to disclose the truth about her gender.

Her friend smiled down at her, and she was almost certain his eyes were wet. He held out a hand.

Charlotte took his offered hand and stood, pulling her brother up as well. "Will, this is my shipmate, my friend Marchand. He helped me to find you."

"Hello, Will."

Will bowed, just as mother had taught him. "How do you do?"

"Marchand," Charlotte began. "I didn't mean to deceive you. It's just—"

"Zat you are not a man does not come as a surprise to me, Charlie." He gave a teasing smile. "I have known for quite some time."

"Oh." She frowned, rather offended he'd so easily seen through her attempts at masculinity.

His smile widened as he looked between the two. "I admit, I did not anticipate such a happy ending to this story."

Now that Charlotte no longer needed to pretend to be a man, she embraced her friend, kissing his cheek. "Thank you, Marchand," she whispered.

"Your shipmate?" Will asked. "You were on a ship?"

Charlotte turned back to her brother and couldn't help but touch his curls again. "We sailed all the way from Georgia, and I even—"

"Will?" a woman's voice called from the house. "Will, *où es-tu?*" The woman stepped onto the porch.

Charlotte pulled Will behind her, wanting to protect her brother from his captor.

But the woman wasn't looking at them. Her gaze was locked on Marchand. "Henri?" She touched a hand to her mouth.

Marchand's face went pale. He gave a stiff bow. "Oui, Gabrielle. *C'est moi.*" His voice sounded choked.

Gabrielle? This was the woman who'd broken Marchand's heart?

Charlotte scowled, wanting to pull Marchand safely behind her as well.

Gabrielle looked between the three of them and then back to Marchand, speaking in French. He answered, and as they spoke Charlotte took the opportunity to study Gabrielle. She appeared to be in her early forties. She spoke with a soft voice and appeared by all accounts to be a mild-mannered person. Hardly the type one would imagine to purchase a child.

Marchand walked closer to the house as he and Gabrielle continued to talk. The woman folded her arms, keeping her head down and speaking quietly.

Charlotte kept an arm around her brother's shoulders. "Don't worry, Will. You are safe now. You don't have to stay here any longer. We've come to take you away."

Will frowned and pulled his brows together in a furrow. "Where are we going?"

"Anywhere you'd like, dearest," Charlotte said. "But no matter what, we'll be together, and you'll be safe."

He continued to frown. "But, Charlie, I don't want to go away. Can't we stay with Gabrielle?"

She stared at the boy. Of all the scenarios she'd envisioned, Charlotte had never imagined her brother would wish to remain with his captors.

"But she—"

"She is really nice," Will said. "And I help her. We work on the farm together."

Charlotte looked back at Gabrielle.

The woman glanced at Will, her forehead wrinkled in worry. She looked sad.

Marchand stepped down from the porch and motioned for Charlotte to join him. "Gabrielle has invited us to supper," he said. "And she would like to speak with you, Charlie."

Charlotte did not know how to respond. This woman had enslaved her brother and broken her friend's heart. She didn't wish to spend a moment with her. She opened her mouth to decline, but Will picked up the egg basket and brought it to Gabrielle. He spoke in French and seemed to be apologizing for the eggs that had broken when he'd dropped the basket.

Gabrielle smiled and waved her hand in the air as if it was no concern whatsoever. She took the basket and patted Will's cheek, looking at Charlotte's brother with such affection that Charlotte could only gawk.

"Things are not as they seem, Charlie," Marchand said. "Hear her out."

Charlie hesitated. She'd only felt anger toward the people who'd taken her brother, and now . . . she didn't know how to feel. The shift, along with the deluge of emotions, left her with the sensation much like she'd had that first day at sea, as if she was floating away, untethered.

She looked at Marchand, hoping he would provide some kind of anchor. "This is the same Gabrielle you knew before?"

He looked at her askance. "Oui."

Charlotte nodded. If Marchand could agree to supper, then she could as well. And she was curious about the woman's relationship with her brother. It seemed . . . loving.

The four sat down to a supper of turtle soup and cornbread.

Charlotte had watched her brother move comfortably through the kitchen, setting bowls onto the table and assisting Gabrielle with the meal. Her curiosity was tinged with a hint of jealousy that made her feel petty.

Will said grace in French, and Gabrielle nodded, giving him a warm smile.

Charlotte felt too wound up to eat. She was confused, overjoyed, and worried all at once. She took a polite spoonful, wishing Gabrielle would just explain how Will came to be at her house. And maybe while she was at it, why she'd chosen another man over Marchand.

Gabrielle stared at her soup, pushing the bits of turtle meat around in the broth.

"*C'est délicieux,*" Charlotte said, remembering Marchand's words when they'd eaten jambalaya. She hoped speaking would start the conversation.

"Merci, Charlie," Gabrielle said in a soft voice. She set down her spoon and looked across the table at Charlotte. She smiled at Will, took a breath, and spoke to Marchand.

Marchand listened and nodded. "Charlie, Gabrielle wishes you to know she is very happy you have come. Will speaks often of his sister, and discovering zat you are alive is a miracle. She does not intend to keep your brother from you." He paused. "However . . ."

"However what?" Charlie's defenses rose.

The Cajun woman spoke again, and this time, she wept, hardly able to speak some of the words through her tears.

Will sniffled, brushing his sleeve over his eyes again.

Marchand's expression was very serious. "Gabrielle has lived alone since her husband died eighteen years ago. She has no children and never remarried." When he said the last bit, Marchand's ears reddened. "She saw Will in New Orleans, his hands tied, as he was led to the slave auction. He was crying, he looked hungry and cold, his clothes were worn and dirty." Marchand glanced at Will and swallowed. "She paid ze captor and brought him home."

Gabrielle was sobbing now.

"Charlie," Marchand continued. "Gabrielle loves Will. She thinks of him as her son. She—"

Charlotte bolted from her chair. She circled the table and embraced Gabrielle. Even if she could have spoken, no words were sufficient to thank the woman who had saved her brother. She was ashamed for the anger she'd felt and for the jealousy. Gabrielle had been there when Charlotte could not be, and she could never repay her for what she'd done. The two women wept together for the boy they both loved.

"Merci, Gabrielle," Charlotte said once she had control of her emotions. She wiped her eyes. "Merci."

Gabrielle spoke to Marchand, motioning for him to hurry and translate.

"Oui, oui." Marchand nodded. "Charlie, she says she would never separate a family. If you choose to leave, she will not stand in your way. But if you would consider, Gabrielle would love for you both to stay."

"Can we stay, Charlie?" Will jumped up from his seat and joined the women, putting an arm around each of them. "Please? Will you live here with Gabrielle and me?"

Charlotte looked at her brother, and then lifted her gaze to Gabrielle, overcome with gratitude. "Yes. Oui."

Gabrielle gave a genuine smile, and Charlotte thought the expression must be one of the reasons Marchand had been smitten with the woman. Her smile was dazzling.

"And will you stay too, Marchand?" Charlotte asked. She wasn't ready to say farewell to her friend. And she thought perhaps Marchand might have unfinished business in La Grand Pointe after all. At the question it was not just Marchand's ears that turned red. His entire face looked like it had been painted with tomato. Charlotte had had no idea how easily her friend could blush.

He glanced toward Gabrielle and then looked back at his soup. "It has been a long time since I came home for a visit. Perhaps I will not hurry away too soon."

Marchand stood and joined them, placing a hand on Charlie's shoulder, and she was reminded of the warm feeling she'd had earlier as she'd contemplated the people God had placed in her path. She smiled to herself, wondering if she'd been placed in Marchand's path as well. She glanced at her friend, seeing him steal a glance at Gabrielle, and wondered if he considered destiny a bit more convenient now.

Chapter 22

ALDEN SWATTED AN ENORMOUS MOSQUITO, leaving a stain on his sleeve. He dug in his oar and grimaced as a gator slid into the water right beside their pirogue. The bayou was not for the faint of heart. He heard the sounds of Tom, Nye, and Allred slapping away mosquitos as well, often accompanied by a grunt or a curse. Stafford especially seemed to be a favorite of the insects. But none of the men complained about the journey. They were too pleased about being chosen to accompany Alden while the rest of the crew prepared for their voyage to India, and they were even more pleased to be going in search of Charlie.

Alden touched his breast pocket, feeling the metal of Charlie's ring. By the time Alden and the others were released from martial duty and returned to New Orleans, Jim Stewart had told him Charlie and Marchand had come and gone a full three weeks earlier. Hearing she was alive, that she was safe, had been such a relief Alden had nearly embraced the pirate. He could not stop the grin that pulled at his mouth. Jim had given Alden the name of the Cajun village, and when he requested payment for the information, Alden had learned Charlie had paid with the ring. Jim hadn't minded when Alden asked to buy it; in fact, he was certain the man had charged him much more than the jewelry was worth, but to a young lady who'd lost everything, it must be invaluable.

He smiled, imagining how pleased she would be when he gave it to her, but soon enough his familiar worry returned. What had happened when Charlie and Marchand had reached the village? Had they found Will? Or had they continued on to search elsewhere? It didn't matter. Alden would scour the earth for her if he had to. But he'd be thrilled if today was the day he found her at last. After more than two months of wondering, worrying, hoping . . . he ached to have Charlie back. Just to see her smile, to know she was safe. He'd never longed for anything so completely.

Another mosquito landed on his leg, and he slapped it, turning back to the member of Lafitte's crew they'd hired to take them to La Grand Pointe. "How much farther, Dubois?"

The man pointed with his chin. "Another mile or so, and then we walk."

They reached the village two hours later, and Alden realized immediately that locating Charlie—or anyone in this place—wouldn't be easy. The settlement was spread out over a large area, with houses built haphazardly along the water or near the central path that served as the main street. But the biggest challenge would be the people. Residents peered at them from behind shuttered windows. Cajuns were notoriously private and suspicious of outsiders. Alden glanced around, looking for a tavern or somewhere he could ask for information.

"Spread out," he said to the others. "See if you can find anyone willing to talk to us or at least to Dubois." He doubted anyone in the village spoke English.

"This might be a store, Captain." Allred pointed to a building with a wide porch.

Alden nodded, and Allred and Dubois entered. Tom and Nye started toward a side path, and Alden continued along the main road. He passed a house with a wooden fence and retraced his steps when he glimpsed someone in the garden behind. A woman wearing a wide-brimmed hat was pulling weeds.

"*Excusez moi, mademoiselle,*" he called out as he approached, not wishing to frighten her.

Her spine stiffened, and she whirled, standing and coming toward him in one swift move. "Captain Thatcher!"

"Charlie?" He blinked, seeing her dressed as a young lady for the first time. He couldn't believe her gender was ever in question. Charlie was lovely. The dark dress fit snugly in the bodice, revealing that she did indeed have feminine curves, and was pulled tight at the waist with a white apron.

Seeing him looking, she glanced down, and her cheeks turned pink. She held out the skirt with both hands and gave a sheepish curtsy.

The nervous action was charming. Alden's heart flopped over. "You look very pretty in a dress."

She scrunched her nose. "They are terribly impractical." She glanced to the side, looking uneasy. "Captain, I'm sorry I deceived you. I needed to get to New Orleans, and had no money for a fare, and I figured as a boy—"

"Charlie, I knew."

She pulled back, folding her arms, and gave an insulted huff. "You did?"

Alden couldn't help but smile. "Of course I did. Just look at you. How could anyone not realize? I was certain the moment you fell from the rigging."

She shrugged, frowning. "Well, I suppose I wasn't as convincing as I thought. Marchand knew as well."

"I believe most of the crew did."

"And they played along? Was it just a joke to everyone?"

"No. They—we—kept your secret. It was important to you, and you are a respected member of the crew. We knew you had your reasons."

"Oh." She held his gaze for a long moment, her lips parting and her cheeks coloring in the most enchanting blush.

Alden stepped toward her, but something behind him caught her eye, and her face broke into an enormous grin. "Tom!" She rushed to the large man, throwing her arms around him. "You escaped."

Alden scowled, wishing he'd gotten such a reception, and wishing Stafford could have waited five measly minutes before joining him.

"Not escaped." Tom patted her back, looking as if he didn't quite know what to do now that his friend was not only a woman but hugging him. "The crew rescued me."

Charlie gave an appreciative nod. "I'm so glad they did and you do not have to be on that horrible Captain Harrington's ship a moment longer. Mr. Gardner is safe too?"

"He is," Tom said.

"Hello, Charlie." Nye pulled on the brim of his hat.

"Mr. Nye." She curtsied.

Nye shook his head. "You really are a girl."

Charlie shrugged, grinning. "Charlotte."

"I'd have acted much more gentlemanly if I'd known . . ." He looked down at his feet.

"Do not apologize," Charlie said. "I'm so pleased at least one person believed my charade." She looked past him as Allred approached. "Mr. Allred, you're here too. All of my messmates are together again. I heard something very funny I hoped to be able to tell you, but first, you all must meet my brother."

"Will?" Alden said. He'd completely forgotten about her brother. "You found him?"

"Yes." She gave a mysterious smile. "And we've more news, but I shall let Marchand tell it."

***

Alden sat back in his chair, his belly filled with delicious Cajun cooking and his thoughts completely confounded by all that had befallen Charlie and Marchand since they'd parted ways at Lafitte's warehouse.

Not only had Charlie found Will safe and happy, but Marchand had found his long-lost love, and the two were married. Alden couldn't have been more surprised if a purple seagull had landed on his plate and sung "God Save the King."

Once supper was finished, the group gathered in front of the hearth. The men spread out around the room. Marchand sat on the sofa beside Gabrielle, holding her hand and occasionally sharing an intimate glance or a whisper. Alden hardly recognized the gruff man.

Charlie sat on the floor beside her brother. Will was exactly as Charlie had described. He'd asked the crew and Dubois question after question during supper, from which of them had seen a real shark to whether or not they had made an enemy walk the plank. The boy was curious and bright and happy, which was an immense relief. Alden didn't know if Charlie could have endured losing another family member.

Alden watched Charlie—Charlotte—throughout the evening. Seeing her again had only reinforced what he knew. He adored her. The way she scrunched her nose when she teased or tipped her head when she had a question . . . her jokes, her worries, her strength, her determination—all of her. Alden couldn't get enough. He'd missed her more than he'd realized and drank in every moment in her presence like a man at a desert oasis.

As they listened to Allred describe the rescue, Charlie laid her head on her brother's curls, just for a moment. Alden's throat felt tight watching her. Seeing Charlie happy made his heart swell like a sponge. But would she ever leave this? Marchand and Gabrielle had given Charlie and her brother a home. She had a family again. Would she give it up . . . for him?

Allred finished his story, and the group clapped.

Alden stood. "Charlie, if you don't mind, I wondered if I might speak to you privately for a moment."

She rose. "Of course, Captain."

He led her onto the porch and took her hand, placing it into the bend of his elbow as they walked down to the path.

He handed her the ring.

Once she realized what it was, she clasped it, tightly holding it against her chest. "Oh, Captain, thank you. This . . . my father gave it to me." Her voice caught. "I thought it was gone for good." She let go of his arm and slipped it onto her finger.

"I missed you, Charlie," he said.

"I missed you as well, sir," she said. She looked up at him then back at the ring. Her voice went very quiet. "I never heard . . . Did you find Mademoiselle LaFontaine?"

"I did."

"And was she pleased to see you?"

Alden nodded. "Yes. She hoped to begin again where we left off." He glanced at her, but Charlie's hair had grown just long enough that if she kept her face turned down, it hung forward and covered her eyes. He stopped. "Marguerite was every bit as beautiful and as gracious as I remembered, and the moment I saw her, I knew . . ."

Charlie stiffened, but she didn't look up, so Alden lifted her chin, brushing back her hair to tuck behind her ear.

"I knew I didn't love her."

Charlie's gaze rose to his, the line appearing between her brows. "You didn't?"

He shook his head. "I thought I did. I was convinced of it, but as it turns out, I'd fallen in love with someone else and didn't even realize it." He stepped closer, her skirts brushing his legs. "It's you, Charlie."

She gasped. "Captain . . ."

"Alden," he corrected. "Charlie, I knew when you yelled at the English Captain. I knew when you practiced and practiced to learn to climb the rigging. I knew when you tended my wounds and stayed by my side day and night. I knew all along, but for some reason I couldn't let go of the past. I couldn't see what was right in front of me."

"You don't really . . ."

Alden slipped his hand beneath her ear, cupping the back of her head. "When you jumped into the ocean to rescue Stafford, I was more frightened than I'd ever been in my entire life. Thinking of losing you . . ." He closed his eyes and rested his forehead on hers. "Please, Charlie, I can't lose you."

He touched his lips to hers and slipped his arms around her waist. Charlie was small and soft, and she melted against him, her arms moving hesitantly to his chest and then to clasp around his neck.

Her touch was tender, and Alden's heart pounded until he thought it would break free from his ribs. Kissing Charlie felt like the very thing he needed to be complete, and he wondered how he'd not noticed the Charlie-shaped part of himself missing before now. Charlie pulled away, and he immediately reached for her, feeling that the inches between them were too many.

"Captain." Her voice shook.

"Alden."

"You must be mistaken. I can't . . . I can't be with you." She took another step back.

A panicky feeling made breathing difficult, and he fought the impulse to pull her back to him. "You told me 'A person often meets his destiny on the road he took to avoid it.' Do you remember? That was me . . . Charlie, I found you. We are meant to be together." He felt dizzy.

"I'm sorry, Captain. I can't." Her chin trembled, and she folded her arms.

She couldn't be serious. Not when he had not one doubt in his mind or in his heart. He glanced back at the house, knowing her reasons. She'd just found Will. She had a family. And she didn't need him. Though he'd feared it, the truth was such a blow that he staggered. "But . . ."

"Excuse me." Her voice was a whisper. She started for the house.

Alden spun and walked back toward the boat, not looking back. He didn't care if the bayou was growing dark or if he stepped on a poisonous snake or became a meal for a gator. Inside, in the very same spot where his heart had been so full moments earlier, he was empty.

Chapter 23

CHARLOTTE HURT TOO BADLY TO weep. Captain Thatcher had been gone for a week, and she thought she'd never feel like smiling again. Even the spring colors on the bayou looked dull. She performed her chores automatically, feeling heavy and sluggish.

In spite of her melancholy, she knew she'd done the right thing. She couldn't leave Will behind. She couldn't hurt him and Marchand and Gabrielle. But the sadness wouldn't go away.

The night was cool, and Charlotte sat on the porch steps, arms around her knees, watching the stars. She wondered if the *Belladonna* had already set sail. Was Alden looking up at the stars? Or had he retired for the night? Was he still angry? She knew she'd hurt him; the look in his eyes when she'd rejected him pierced like a blade into the deepest part of her. Would he ever forgive her? Or would his hurt turn to anger and then to contempt?

She couldn't bear the thought that he may be on his ship right this moment despising her. She pressed her forehead against her knees, wishing she could make the pain go away.

At the sound of the door behind her, she looked up.

Marchand and Gabrielle came outside and joined her on the steps.

"*Bonsoir*, Charlie," Gabrielle said.

Charlotte tried to force a smile, but one wouldn't come. "Bonsoir."

"Charlie." Marchand shook his head, speaking in a quiet voice. "This cannot go on. You do not eat; you do not sleep. I know you miss Captain Thatcher." He leaned forward to catch her gaze. "I know you love him."

She didn't even have the energy to blush or act demure. "I do," she said miserably.

Marchand scooted down a step to sit next to her. "Charlie, you cannot only do for others. You must think of yourself too." He nudged her with his shoulder. "You give away your food and go hungry, you settle arguments and take on more work, you help everyone around you . . ." He sighed. "But you must think of yourself too. If you give and give, you will have nothing left."

Charlotte knew his advice came from concern. "I can't leave Will, Marchand. He lost everything; I can't—"

"Will is not alone."

"Charlie?"

At the sound of Will's voice, the others turned.

"Oh, dearest. What are you doing awake?" Charlotte held out her arm, and her brother came to sit on the step, cuddling up against her.

Gabrielle scooted down to sit on the other side of Marchand. She slipped her arm through his and rested her head on his shoulder.

"Are you going to marry the captain, Charlie?" Will asked.

Charlie's stomach sank. "I don't think so."

"If you do, can I visit you on the ship?"

She held him closer, and the four sat in silence, listening to the sounds of the swamp. The night was peaceful, and Charlotte felt love surrounding her like a warm embrace. But still, she was unsettled. Alden hovered at the edge of her thoughts, and . . . she *ached* for him.

After a long moment, Will lay heavily against her, asleep, and she moved his head to rest on her lap.

"I'm afraid, Marchand," Charlotte whispered. "I may have ruined everything."

"Ze captain is in love, Charlie. Such a strong emotion does not fade overnight." He glanced at Gabrielle and smiled warmly. "Whatever happens, your family is here for you." He put an arm around Charlotte and kissed her forehead.

A flame lit inside her, a flicker of hope, but it terrified her. "But I am a girl now. New Orleans is two days away; what if the *Belladonna* has already sailed for India?" Her hands were shaking.

"The Charlie Bower I know wouldn't let any of those things stop her." Marchand smiled.

"Will you—"

"*Bien sûr*, Charlie. You are not alone." He glanced at Gabrielle, who nodded. "We will all go."

***

Two days later Charlotte held Will's hand, leaning back to gaze up at the *Belladonna*. She remembered her apprehension the first time she'd seen the ship and hoped to join the crew. That worry was nothing compared to the misgiving she felt now.

Seeing Alden walk out of one of the dock offices, she gathered her courage, left Will with Gabrielle and Marchand, and stepped forward.

Alden folded a paper and slipped it into his breast pocket. He started toward the ship but paused when his gaze lit on her. His brows rose in question, but his expression did not soften as he met her at the bottom of the gangplank.

Charlotte curtsied. "Captain Thatcher."

"Charlie, what are you doing here?"

She winced at the lack of warmth in his tone. "I . . ." She shook her head. She'd thought of so many things to say when she saw him again, but they all felt wrong now. "I'm sorry."

He watched her, his expression not changing.

Charlotte took a breath. "I didn't mean to hurt you; I was afraid. Afraid to leave Will and afraid . . ." She shook her head again. "This is not at all what I wanted to say."

He continued to watch her, and she wished she knew what he was thinking. She could read nothing in his expression.

She steeled her nerves and blurted, "I love you." Once she started, the words tumbled out like she'd broken a hole in a levee. "I want to be with you, Captain—Alden." Her face burst with heat, but she didn't stop. "I'm in love with you, and I have been for so long I didn't dare let myself hope you might feel the same. All this time I thought you thought I was a boy, and it all feels so complicated . . ." She stared at her hands, not daring to see his reaction to her jumbled outburst. "I love being with Will and Marchand and Gabrielle, but without you . . ." She glanced up beneath the rim of her hat, grimacing at the fool she was making of herself. "What I want to say is, I was running away too, Alden, and I found you."

He held her gaze, stepping closer. A light glimmered in his eyes that hadn't been there a moment earlier, and a hint of a smile played on his lips. "A week ago I planned to leave New Orleans behind for good. This city had brought me nothing but heartache." He put an arm around her waist, pulling her closer. "But I shall have to change that assessment." He flicked the brim of her hat, sending it falling behind, cupped her face with one hand, and kissed her.

Alden's lips were hot and his whiskers scratchy. This kiss was different than the first. Instead of a hesitant, questioning touch, it was a promise of love, of hope, and forever. Charlotte's heart beat faster and faster, as joy threatened to lift her off her feet. She clung around his neck, returning the kiss with every last bit of her heart.

From the *Belladonna*'s deck, the crew broke out into a cheer.

Alden drew back, but he didn't release her. He grinned. "What do you think, Dobson?" he called. "Could this voyage use an arbitrator?"

"Aye, Captain!" Mr. Dobson yelled from the rail.

The crew cheered louder, and this time Marchand, Gabrielle, and Will joined in. Charlotte blushed, but she didn't pull away when Alden kissed her again, snuggling into his embrace.

Will ran forward and threw his arms around both of them. His young face shone with a smile. "I knew you would marry the captain, Charlie!"

Charlotte bent and kissed her brother's cheek.

Alden rubbed the boy's head.

Marchand and Gabrielle came forward and embraced each of them.

"Can we go on the ship now?" Will asked. "Captain Thatcher, do you have a spy glass? Can I shoot a cannon?"

Alden smiled at the boy and gave a curt nod. "I think you will fit right in with the crew."

Will's eyes went round. "Am I going on the voyage too?"

Giving Will a wink, Alden turned to Marchand. "How much preparation will you need to leave for Annapolis?"

Charlotte looked between the men, not understanding. Did Alden believe Marchand was returning to the crew?

Marchand lifted the bag of clothes and provisions they'd brought for the trip. "We can leave now."

"Alden," Charlotte said. "What . . . ?"

He slid an arm around her and started toward the gangplank. "I would not expect them to miss the wedding, Charlie."

Not bothering to be a lady, she kissed him again.

The ship set sail, and much to Will's delight, he helped raise the anchor. Charlotte changed into her trousers and put her shoes and dress in her cupboard, glad to be rid of them.

Alden showed Will how to hold the ship's wheel, explained the workings of the compass in the binnacle box, and pulled him at least five times from the rigging, complaining with a roll of his eyes that the boy was exactly like his sister.

Gabrielle found the galley and set to work straightaway, and Turley was delighted to have a new assistant.

In the evening, once the chaos had calmed, Will was safely asleep in his berth, and everyone was settled into their duties, Alden found Charlotte at the portside rail. He drew her to him, kissing her soundly. He brushed kisses over her cheek and pushed aside her hair to kiss her temple.

"Charlie, I think we shall have to establish some rules concerning displays of affection between the captain and swabbie on the ship."

She grimaced, and her skin heated. "Of course, I understand. It is hardly appropriate for . . . Yes. There should be no kissing on the deck."

He smirked, tightening his arms around her. "I was thinking exactly the opposite. If anything, I think there should be *more* kissing on the deck."

Before she could argue, he set his decree in place, and Charlotte thought the captain had made a very good rule indeed. She settled against him, feeling like the space between his arms was made just for her. He held her tight, and she sighed.

In Alden's arms she was no longer a frightened girl searching for her family. She was safe and whole and loved and exactly where she belonged.

Epilogue

Six weeks later

SPRING WAS BEAUTIFUL IN ANNAPOLIS. The days were warm but not too hot, and the evenings were pleasant. But on this particular spring day, Charlotte didn't care one fig about the weather.

She sat still on the dressing table chair while Lydia's maid, Francine, wove flowers into her hair. The smell of roses wafted through the guest room window beside her and mingled with the aromas coming from the kitchen below. In just under an hour, she and Alden were to be married, and Charlotte's cheeks ached from smiling.

The door opened, and a group of women entered, led by the mistress of the house, Lydia Steele.

Lydia was a beautiful southern belle with blonde curls and the largest blue eyes Charlotte had ever seen. She was married to Alden's adopted brother, Jacob, and the couple lived in this stately brick house. When Charlotte and Alden had arrived and declared their intention to be married, Lydia had immediately taken over the wedding preparations and had done an expert job, as she was used to throwing elaborate parties.

"Oh." Lydia touched her fingers to her breastbone. "You are just the loveliest bride, Charlotte." She inspected the hairstyle. "Francine, this is perfect." Up close, Charlotte could see the hint of a scar on Lydia's cheek, and at times she noticed that her smile bunched strangely on one side. Alden had told her Lydia had been injured in an English raid on her father's plantation.

Elnora Hathaway, Alden's adopted mother, came up beside them. Elnora moved slowly, and Charlotte suspected was recovering from an illness. She was slender and tall, with sleek white hair, and her movements were very elegant. "Your gown is pressed and ready, dear."

"Thank you," Charlotte said. Her heart started to flutter nervously. She wondered what Alden would think of the dress. It was much fancier than anything she'd ever seen in Bay Minette. But Lydia had insisted it was just the thing, and Elnora, Gabrielle, and Abigail had agreed.

Abigail Prescott was married to Lydia's brother Emmett. She was much more reserved than her sister-in-law and very intelligent. Charlotte noticed she always wore a necklace with a fascinating gemstone. When she'd asked about it, Abigail told her it was an opal.

Abigail's husband, a major in the American army, had been stationed in Canada, and apparently Abigail had worked as a surgeon with the battalion. Charlotte had thought it strange for a woman to have such a job but then remembered she herself worked as a deckhand on a merchant crew.

Once her hair was finished Charlotte turned her head from side to side, examining the arrangement in the mirror. "I love it." She blushed and fidgeted with her ring.

"And your heart is still set on wearing that bird charm?" Lydia rolled her eyes, teasing. She had been horrified at the thought of Charlotte wearing the leather string and tooth pendant with her gown, but Charlotte couldn't bear not to have Tom's gift with her. They had finally reached a compromise, with the leather string tied around Charlotte's wrist instead of her neck.

Gabrielle and Francine slid the gown over Charlotte's head, and Francine started on the buttons in the back. Charlotte swished the skirts, delighted with the rose-colored chiffon. The gown was embroidered at the waist with an ivy pattern and trimmed at the sleeves and neck with delicate lace.

"Ah, *ma chérie*." Gabrielle handed Charlotte a bouquet of roses and dabbed her eyes.

"Hair, gown, bouquet." Lydia counted the items off on her fingers. "Yes, it is all in order. Excuse me. I must see to the dinner." Lydia kissed Charlotte's cheek and swept from the room.

"Charlotte." Abigail handed her a small box. "Emmett and I thought you might . . ." She gave a shy shrug and motioned to the box.

Charlotte opened the box and took out a delicate silver chain from which hung a single pearl. She gasped. "It is beautiful."

"You don't have to wear it today if you don't wish to. I just thought, since you met Alden at sea . . ."

Charlotte stared at the pearl, enchanted by the lustrous white color and unable to believe a woman she had just met a few days earlier would give her such a treasure. She pulled Abigail into an embrace, making Gabrielle, Elnora, and Francine all suck in a breath, likely worried she might wrinkle her gown.

"Thank you, Abigail. It is so very beautiful." She turned. "Will you attach the clasp?"

Abigail attached the necklace and then left to find her husband.

"I should leave as well," Elnora said. "It is nearly time. My dear, I have never seen Alden so happy. I worry about that boy—that man—you know. He is so impulsive and brash and puts on a show of overconfidence. But inside he is still a boy who needs love." She kissed both of Charlotte's cheeks. "I am so delighted he found you."

Elnora left, leaning on Gabrielle's arm.

Charlotte thanked Francine again. She lifted the bouquet, inhaling the scent of the roses. When she stepped into the upstairs passageway, Marchand stood there waiting to escort her.

His eyes were shiny. "Are you ready, Charlie?"

Her throat clogged, and she could only nod.

Marchand cupped her cheek. "I know I am not your real father, Charlie, but thank you for allowing me to know what it is to love a daughter."

Charlotte wept, leaning against his shoulder as he held her. She loved this soft-spoken man. He had been a protector and a confidant and a friend, and if it weren't for him . . . She hugged him close, knowing no words could ever tell him what her heart felt.

"No more tears, Charlie." He used a red kerchief to wipe her cheeks. "Today is for celebration."

Charlotte kissed his cheek and took his arm. When they reached the top of the staircase, she caught her breath. Ribbons and bouquets and tulle were strung down the banisters, and vases of hothouse flowers adorned the entire foyer. In the dining room beyond, she could see tables set for a feast, but while all of those things were lovely, the decorations paled to the sight of the upturned faces smiling at her.

Her crewmates gathered on one side of the aisle. The men wore their finest clothing and had combed their hair and shaved. Alden's family, Elnora, the Prescotts, and the Steeles were on the other side with Gabrielle.

Will waved, and her heart melted at how adorable he looked in his neckcloth and jacket.

But it was the man standing beside the minister whose gaze made her heart turn over in a slow roll and her knees go weak. Alden's smile was soft, and the tender look in his eyes made her heart fill until she thought it would burst in a wave of tears.

They descended the stairs and walked through the aisle to where Alden waited. He accepted her hand from Marchand, and the minister began the ceremony.

Looking at Charlotte's face, Alden's brow furrowed, and he must have realized his bride was nearly overcome with emotion. He glanced at the minister then back to her and gave a wink. Leaning close to her ear, he whispered, "Did you arrange all of this just to get out of swabbing the deck?"

Charlotte squeezed his fingers, pretending to be offended, but she couldn't prevent a smirk. "Perhaps," she whispered back.

He gave an exaggerated sigh. "I should have known."

Charlie glanced up at him. She widened her eyes and looked pointedly at the minister, telling Alden silently to pay attention.

Alden leaned close again. "You have made me so happy, Swabbie," he whispered. The tease was gone from his voice.

Charlotte held his hand tightly, and her heart overflowed. "I love you, Captain."

Author's Notes

I INCLUDED MENTION OF DAVID Sanders on page 172 because he's my fifth great-grandfather. He was a Tennessee rifleman who fought and died at New Orleans.

One of the most consistent criticisms I hear about the Battle of New Orleans is that it was fought unnecessarily since a peace treaty was signed before the battle began and news just hadn't reached the troops in Louisiana. This is not entirely true. A treaty was drawn up between American and English representatives on December 24, fifteen days before General Pakenham's troops marched against Andrew Jackson's defensive line. But the treaty specifically stated that it did not go into effect until fully "ratified," which meant it needed to be signed by both the King of England and the President of the United States and approved by the U.S. Senate, which would take weeks.

And why was the battle even important? What was at stake? New Orleans was more than a swampy town at the mouth of the Mississippi that was perpetually flooded by hurricanes or burning with a city-wide fire. The city was the gateway to and from the heart of America. The Ohio, Missouri, and numerous other rivers emptied into the Mississippi, providing livelihood for lumbermen, farmers, trappers, and manufacturers from Pennsylvania, the Ohio Valley, the Cumberland Gap, and the Great Smoky Mountains. The goods were sent from New Orleans to ports around the world.

If the English had taken New Orleans, they'd have controlled the Mississippi, and with Canada on the North, Spanish Florida on the

South, and the Atlantic to the East, America would have been cut off. There would have been no westward expansion, and the country would very likely have returned to English possession.

The battle was an unbelievable upset—a miracle or a slaughter, depending on which side you were on. The English army was the most powerful force in the world, and the American hardly more than a volunteer militia and some guys with guns. Mistakes, a harsh terrain, and differences in battlefield protocol were the reasons for such an unfathomable upset. For one thing, Europeans had an unspoken rule that officers weren't targets in a battle. But the Americans killed officers first, leaving soldiers with nobody to command. Though sources differ, the final casualty count is estimated at more than 2,300 English soldiers lost and less than twenty Americans.

But what makes this battle truly important is the unity General Jackson was able to create in a divided city. The cultural, racial, and class prejudices in New Orleans ran deep, spanning generations. But Andrew Jackson knew division would be their downfall. If the various factions couldn't learn to work together, they would turn against one another. He took the different groups and turned them into an army. Wealthy Creoles fought side by side with Native Americans, slaves, pirates, and frontiersmen. They had a common enemy and a common goal that overrode their prejudices as they put into action Thomas Jefferson's truth, penned nearly forty years earlier in the *Declaration of Independence*, "that all men are created equal." They were all Americans.

Acknowledgments

FIRST I NEED TO SAY a huge thank-you to my family, friends, the jr. high carpool, my hairdresser, and random strangers who politely listened to me for the past two years going on and on about the War of 1812, the River Raisin Massacre, the *USS Constitution*, the burning of Washington, the attack on Fort McHenry, and the Battle of New Orleans. I love this period of American history, and you are all very understanding when I get nerdy.

Thank you to my husband and kids, who spent their spring break in New Orleans visiting museums and swamps and battlefields. You guys are the loves of my life.

Thanks to my critique partners and besties, Josi Kilpack and Nancy Allen. Your brainstorming and plot advice and friendship mean the world to me. And to the marvelous Margot Hovley, thanks for keeping me accountable on my goals.

Melanie Jacobson, thank you for sharing your knowledge of Louisiana, telling me where to eat and what to see, and for being such a gracious friend. And Mara Harvey, thanks for meeting me in NOLA. You are such an avid reader; I am in awe!

Thanks to Vickie and Butch Guchereau at Cajun Country Swamp Tours for a fantastic adventure on the Bayou.

Thanks, Carla Kelly and Laurie Lewis, for being such good history resources.

Thank you, Christina Marcano, for another beautiful cover.

And as always, thank you to Kami Hancock for your edits and deadline extensions and your listening ear. What would I do without you, matey?

About the Author

JENNIFER MOORE IS A PASSIONATE reader and writer of all things romance due to the need to balance the rest of her world, which includes a perpetually traveling husband and four active sons who create heaps of laundry that are anything but romantic. Jennifer has a BA in linguistics from the University of Utah and is a Guitar Hero champion. She lives in northern Utah with her family. You can learn more about her at authorjmoore.com.